Lady Disdain

The Unconventionals Book Three

Michelle Morrison

Copyright © 2018 Michelle Morrison

All rights reserved

The characters and events portrayed in this book are fictitious. Any similarity to real persons, living or dead, is coincidental and not intended by the author.

No part of this book may be reproduced, or stored in a retrieval system, or transmitted in any form or by any means, electronic, mechanical, photocopying, recording, or otherwise, without express written permission of the publisher.

ASIN : B07G9PKY76

Printed in the United States of America

Contents

Title Page
Copyright
Chapter One — 1
Chapter Two — 14
Chapter Three — 27
Chapter Four — 44
Chapter Five — 64
Chapter Six — 84
Chapter Seven — 96
Chapter Eight — 112
Chapter Nine — 131
Chapter Ten — 142
Chapter Eleven — 157
Chapter Twelve — 171
Chapter Thirteen — 182
Chapter Fourteen — 203
Chapter Fifteen — 215
Epilogue — 228
About The Author — 235
Books By This Author — 237

Chapter One

If ever there was a fish out of water, Sarah Draper reflected, it was she. Dressed in borrowed finery, her hair properly styled for the first time in years, and surrounded by a society she'd long since given up, Sarah clung to the wall and watched as her cousin's engagement was announced.

She couldn't be happier for Eleanor. Her cousin was the sweetest, most caring person Sarah had ever met in spite of, or perhaps because of the heartbreak she had suffered. Though Eleanor had been born into nobility, she treated everyone with compassion and genuine interest. And while Sarah rejoiced for her cousin, she recognized that her own life would soon be growing lonelier. Surely once Eleanor was wed, her new husband wouldn't approve of her working with Sarah in their charitable aid organization in one of London's most notorious slums. In fact, she realized with a frown, Eleanor's time was sure to be taken up immediately with wedding plans, for it wasn't every day that an earl's daughter married a bastard-turned-legitimate-heir-to-another-earldom.

With a sigh, Sarah resigned herself to the solitary life she'd lived before her stunning cousin had hurtled into her life two years ago. She'd managed to run her aid kitchen by herself before Eleanor had joined her; surely she could do so again. The only problem was that now she knew what it was like to have someone to share the load, someone with whom to share frustrations and victories alike. She had not realized how lonely she'd been before Eleanor had joined her, but she certainly would recognize it now.

Sarah's morose thoughts were distracted by the boisterous laugh of a man standing a few feet away. She blinked several times, her ruminations dispersing. Glancing over, she saw a tall, broad-shouldered man still grinning with mirth. His hair was a riotous mass of gold and honey and champagne, worn loose and uncontained by pomade as was the fashion. His face was stunning, with eyes so intensely blue Sarah could discern their color from several feet away. The strong lines of his face and sun-kissed complexion distinguished him from the fashionably pale faces of the other men standing next to him and when he spoke —more loudly than was seemly, the nasal tone of his accent gave him away as an American, bold as brass and confident as they came. He was exactly the sort of man who would glance at her dark hair and eyes and drab gown and see right through her to the dazzling debutante behind her.

Sara glanced down and fingered the rich dark blue satin of her borrowed gown. Well, perhaps not everything was so drab about her this evening. Eleanor's friend Juliette had loaned her this gown and it had taken very little alteration to make it fit like a glove. The regal swish of the heavy fabric made her walk more slowly and the nearly off-the-shoulder cut of the neckline caused her to stand up straight lest the gown slip. While she wasn't completely comfortable out of the familiar coarse broadcloth of the gowns she normally wore, it felt rather nice to know she could still appear presentable when the occasion called. Tonight, she felt like a different person than the woman who arose before dawn every day to feed and tend to hundreds of people.

She allowed herself one more glance at the golden Adonis when he laughed aloud again. He was too handsome by half. Or perhaps handsome wasn't exactly the right word when one compared him to the well-groomed men of the ton surrounding him, but there was something undeniably attractive about him nonetheless. He was exactly the sort of man she scorned if for no other reason than he was clearly the type given to frivolity and excess. One who lived only for pleasure. She had no idea why she was so certain about the American's character, but she knew it as absolutely as she could see that he was as at ease in his skin as she was uncomfortable.

As if feeling her gaze upon him, the Adonis looked over at her and she quickly turned her head, affecting interest in the crowd of people who were still congratulating her cousin and her new fiancée.

Eleanor appeared a bit dazed, and glancing at Eleanor's future husband, Lord Reading, Sarah realized he had the same bemused expression. Sarah wondered if either had known of the Earl of Southampton's plan to announce their betrothal less than twenty minutes before.

"I'm glad to see I'm not the only one you scowl at," a deep voice to her left said.

Startled, she turned to find the Adonis smiling at her. Crinkle lines around his eyes suggested he smiled a great deal. Or squinted from near-sightedness, she thought uncharitably.

"I'm not scowling," she replied sourly, but as she felt the muscles of her forehead relax, she realized she had indeed been frowning. "You're American," she said, trying to change the subject.

He held up both hands and said, "Guilty as charged. But what did she do to you?" he nodded in Eleanor's direction. "She seems as English as they come. Did she steal your fellow?"

"What?" Sarah asked, suddenly flustered. "No! She's my cousin. If she's happy, I'm happy."

"Uh huh," he said, clearly unconvinced, and Sarah realized her eyebrows had drawn together again. She reached up to smooth them with a gloved finger.

"It's just—I shall miss her, is all. We have grown very close in the last few years and I suspect I will not see her as much once she is wed." Or at all, Sarah thought, but she forced herself not to frown at the idea. She wondered why she felt the need to explain herself to this man. She certainly was unaccustomed to sharing any such personal feeling with people.

She was surprised when he simply nodded in understanding, a shuttered look in his eyes. "A feeling I can well relate to," he murmured. Then, in a quicksilver change of mood, he said, "What is it about you English and food?"

"I beg your pardon?" she asked, trying to figure out how that related to their conversation.

He lifted up his glass in demonstration. "You do spirits very well, I'll grant you, but would it kill you to put out some finger sandwiches?"

"There will be a large dinner later," Sarah explained.

"Yes, at midnight. Who wants to eat at midnight?"

Though she said nothing, Sarah agreed with him. She knew the answer was, "people who don't arise early to work," and wondered if this American worked. If so, she wondered that he found himself at a duke's party. Perhaps he was as much a fish out of water as she was. Except he didn't seem the least bit bothered by the notion, she thought sourly. He exuded the confidence of one who felt at home anywhere.

"And who are you to be here at the Duke of Andover's ball?" she asked sharply, turning her discontent against him.

He executed a slightly mocking bow. "Forgive me. I forgot I'm not supposed to be speaking to a lady without a proper introduction."

She almost told him she was no lady, but realized in time just how that would sound and bit her tongue and said instead, "That is only at public events, not at private ones such as this."

He nodded. "In that case, I am Samuel James. American, as you so astutely pointed out."

She narrowed her eyes at this, but he didn't appear to be mocking her.

"Though I suppose if I looked hard enough I could find a distant relative here in England. My great grandfather was from Surrey. Say, you don't suppose I might be related to royalty, do you? That would be awfully useful now, wouldn't it?"

"Er, I'm sure if your great-grandfather was related to the royal family, he would not have emigrated to America."

"Hmmm. Good point," he conceded. "Still, if there was even an off chance of my having a drop of royal blood, it would mean my sister's future mother-in-law would have to welcome, me, wouldn't it?"

Sarah frowned, trying to follow his rapid-fire dialogue. It had been so long since a man had simply conversed with her, she felt a bit out of her element. Then there was the way he was looking at her, as if she was, well, beautiful—something she had not felt in many years. Finally unraveling his last statement, she said, "Your sister is to be married, then?"

"Oh yes, that's the reason I am here in jolly old England and why I was invited to this foodless soiree. She's to be married to Lord Treason."

"Lord Treason?" Sarah was not familiar with the London social scene, but the name struck her as distinctly odd.

"That's just what I call him. Trowbridge is his name, but I rib him that he's a traitor to his country for marrying a Colonial."

"Oh," Sarah said, a bit overwhelmed at his overall volume and strength of personality, even as his invigorating dialogue awoke a part of her brain that had been long dormant.

"Of course, marrying a dollar princess to fill the family coffers may be considered a noble sacrifice to his kin, but who am I to judge."

"I beg your pardon. A what?"

"Dollar princess. No blue blood to speak of, what with all of our American-ness, but plenty of money in the bank to ensure we're tolerable. I'm given to understand dowries are the easiest way to save failing estates these days."

Though his tone was still humorous, Sarah saw a hardness in the bright blue eyes when she hazarded a glance at them.

"But who are you to judge?" she asked slyly.

He stared at her for a moment before bursting into that boisterous laugh that had first drawn her attention. She noticed people glancing in their direction and felt herself physically shrinking, trying not to draw attention to herself. Realizing what she was doing, she deliberately straightened her shoulders and refused to meet the wondering glances. She looked back at Mr. James and found him looking at her in a manner that made her feel positively fascinating.

"Disdain fairly drips from your tongue," he said, making it sound like the highest compliment. "You're a sharp one, my lady."

"I'm not—" she'd started to say again she wasn't a lady. "You do not address me as 'my lady.'"

"Why not?"

"I am not the daughter or wife of a nobleman."

"I thought everyone at these parties was a lord or lady. Except for we wealthy Americans, of course," he added.

She overlooked that acerbic comment and continued, "My parents are members of the gentility and so I am only addressed as 'Miss.'"

"Not 'Mrs.,' then?"

He seemed surprised and Sarah felt her chin raise defensively. She was old enough that were she active in the London scene, she would be considered a spinster, the most piteous position in society.

"As I am unwed, no." she said tersely. She pretended to study the crowd and noticed that her cousin and Lord Reading were nowhere to be seen.

"What is under gentility?"

"I beg your pardon?" she asked, turning back to him.

"If you have nobility and then gentility, what comes next?"

"Royalty," she replied.

He grinned. "Royalty is beneath gentility?"

"No!" she exclaimed, unaccountably flustered. "You forgot royalty. Royalty, nobility, gentility."

"And then what?"

"Well, I suppose you would simply say 'everyone else.'"

"We commoners, eh?" he said with a grin. "Unless, of course, I turn out to be related to the Prince."

In spite of herself she felt her lips quirk at his irreverent humor and strove to suppress the smile, forcing herself to think of the struggles of the people she tried to help every day through her aid society. She supposed they were common enough problems—trying to find food, shelter, security.

At his expectant look, she realized she hadn't responded. She also realized that for one evening she didn't want to think of her work. She wanted to enjoy herself, enjoy a spirited conversation with an outrageous and handsome man.

"Oh I can assure you, you do not have a drop of noble blood."

His tawny brows rose in surprise even as a smile tugged at his mouth. "Do tell. Is there some secret test? Shouldn't you need a sample of my blood to verify your assertion?"

"Not at all. It is simply evident in your carriage, your mannerisms, and the way you hold your liquor."

He looked a little taken aback and she wondered if she had overplayed her jest.

"I thought the Prince Regent was considered to be an abysmal drunk."

"Indeed," she said primly.

A sly smile curved his lush lips. *Lush?* She asked herself. Why on earth should she notice such a—

"And as I can stand erect without the aid of a corset, don't spend myself into the poorhouse and do not engage in public drunkenness, I clearly have not a drop of royal blood?"

She gave him a brief single nod, tilting her head a bit to the side so she could watch him beneath her lashes.

"And here I thought you English considered it perfidious to criticize your royal house."

"Perfidious?" she asked with a smile.

"Treasonable," he clarified.

She shook her head sadly. "Yet further proof you are not English and therefore cannot be related to the prince."

He grinned and his gaze roamed over her face with a look that made her feel as if she'd drunk an entire bottle of champagne. "Please explain."

"We consider it a point of honor to malign the Prince Regent. After all, we've received little other recompense for the hundreds of thousands of pounds we've provided to redeem his profligate debts."

"So you verbally abuse him amongst yourselves in return?"

She bit the inside of her cheek to keep from laughing. She could not remember the last time she'd had this much fun.

He cocked one eyebrow and stroked his chin thoughtfully. He looked nothing less than piratical. A golden, bronzed Adonis-like pirate.

She took a breath to deliver a further witty set down on the chances of him being related to royalty when a petite blonde strolled by in the company of an elegant redhead and Mr. James' appreciative gaze followed them.

Instantly Sarah felt her skin go cold and she drew back, wrapping her arms protectively around her waist. Ire replaced any charitable thoughts she had been developing for Mr. James. Ire and no small amount of hurt. Very well, a large amount of hurt. They'd been having such a lively conversation, and the way he'd looked at her made her feel interesting, almost...desirable. She should have known he was fickle, should have known she was poor company for one such as him. Ignoring her hurt feelings, she focused on anger as it was a far less debilitating emotion. This American was no different than any privileged nobleman. She pressed her lips into a disgusted line. He was a typical man, she thought scornfully, and reminded herself this was only one of many reasons why she didn't attend society functions. She turned to leave but felt a hand on her arm.

"You didn't tell me your name. Miss...?"

"I didn't, did I?" she replied before turning again and weaving her way through the crowd.

"Lady Disdain!" she heard him call out. "That's what I'll call you."

Her shoulders hunched as people turned at his loudness and she barreled out of the room as quickly as possible, only stopping when she found a quiet hallway.

Leaning against the wall, she willed her heart to slow from its furious pace. The horrid man! He was exactly as she'd known he would be, crass and overly confident. The only unanswered question was why he'd even approached her in the first place. Her mind's eye replayed Mr. James' gaze as it found more appealing women to ogle. Drat the man! And she'd been feeling rather lovely tonight. It was the first time in more than five years that she'd worn anything beautiful. She looked up and was startled to find a reflection of herself in a mirror across the hall. The deep blue satin of her borrowed gown draped in elegant folds. Her exposed shoulders and décolletage allowed more skin than she'd ever shown, having been but a shy debutant in Aylesbury Vale years ago.

The most daring outfit she'd owned back then had been an off-the-shoulder pink gown, but a heavy lace fichu has covered her to the neck. This gown, with its extravagant display of skin, was worth more than her entire wardrobe. And the meager furniture in her flat. Perhaps even the very building in which she lived. She took a breath and closed her eyes.

For five years, Sarah had been running a charitable foundation in one of London's poorest slums, an area in Southwark called The Mint, so named for the currency mint that had operated in the time of Henry VIII. Two years previously, her cousin Eleanor had joined her, giving up a life of noble luxury to help Sarah feed and clothe Southwark's poor and provide what medical aid they could.

Sarah had long suspected Eleanor's arrival did not stem from a heartfelt calling to help her fellow man, but she had never pushed Eleanor to explain her arrival, fearing her cousin might then wonder at her own reasons for leaving her family and working in a charity. Sarah had only recently learned of Eleanor's heartbreak and resultant scandal, which had prompted her to seek a new life. Her cousin's story, though not as dire as Sarah's past, had struck similar chords to her own. However, she herself would not be receiving the same absolution and happy ending as Eleanor, hence her awkwardness in conversing with Mr. James—or anyone, really. She was acutely aware that most in society would look down their nose at her, though if they knew what had preceded her move to Southwark, she would have been shunned altogether.

Sarah stared at her reflection, willing her eyes not to water. The urge quickly passed as she knew it would. She never cried anymore, for what good would it do? Her thoughts returned to her rumination. The three years before Eleanor had arrived had been ones of arduous work, toiling from dawn until long after dark, desperately trying to win the trust of the people she was trying to help. While rewarding work, it had been incredibly isolating and lonely. The residents of The Mint initially saw her as another privileged socialite looking down upon them. It had taken her months to gain their trust and even as they took the food and medicine she offered, it had taken over a year before she felt like a part of the community, when she was finally invited to one family's humble home for an even more humble meal. Despite that acceptance, however, Sarah felt separate from the residents of Southwark. It was not because of their poverty or social class—she knew it was some inherent flaw in herself that prevented her from connecting to other people.

Then Eleanor had arrived, and for the first time since she'd left her own family, Sarah felt a kinship with another person.

They had never spoken about their individual circumstances that had prompted their radical life changes, instead focusing only on their work and the immediate future. Still, Sarah felt closer to her cousin than anyone she'd ever known. It was going to be difficult to return to her solitary life, for despite Eleanor's deep commitment to their organization, she was an earl's daughter, soon-to-be-wife to an earl's son. Even if she wished to continue working with Sarah there would be no way her influential family would allow it, now that they knew where she'd been.

Deciding to try and salvage some enjoyment out of the evening, Sarah pushed away from the wall. She would seek out the pastry table and gorge herself. Despite Mr. James' claims to the contrary, there was plenty of food before the midnight dinner if one knew where to look. She would then beg Eleanor's mother to be allowed to return to their home. Lady Chalcroft had insisted Sarah remain with them in their Mayfair house rather than returning to Southwark tonight and Sarah intended to make the most of the evening by poring through Lord Chalcroft's library

She took a deep breath and re-entered the great drawing room, making her way along the walls to the tables where she had seen vast quantities of desserts spread out earlier.

"Drat!" she hissed under her breath. All that was left now were crumbs and a smear of chocolate on a crystal platter. She should have grabbed one earlier, she chastised herself. Well there was no sense in remaining here any longer. Eleanor's reputation and supposedly their charity's funding had been saved by tonight's events. She stood on tiptoe to try and find Lady Chalcroft and scanned the room, noting Eleanor had returned on the arm of the Earl of Southampton—her new fiancée's father. The two seemed to be thick as thieves, and Sarah lifted her eyebrows. Only this morning, her cousin had considered the man to be a cold-hearted evil reprobate.

Sarah let her gaze continue to roam until it landed on an older version of Eleanor's face. Keeping Lady Chalcroft in her line of sight, Sarah wove her way unobtrusively through the room. Her light touch on Lady Chalcroft's arm drew the woman's attention.

"I should like to return home." Sarah explained. "That is, to your home, if I might? This is all a bit…much for me."

Lady Chalcroft's brows drew together briefly as she studied Sarah's face, but she patted her hand and said, "Of course it is. Let me call for the carriage."

Sarah felt the tension drain from her shoulders. She was always unsure around Eleanor's mother, wondering if the lady disapproved of her personally or simply her chosen vocation.

"Please do not trouble yourself, my lady. I can see to it. You will wish to remain here with Eleanor."

"Very well, dear," Lady Chalcroft said, her expression softening. Sarah turned to leave, but Lady Chalcroft's hand on her shoulder stopped her.

"Sarah," she began hesitantly. "I never thanked you properly."

Sarah opened her mouth to ask why, but the countess continued. "For taking care of Eleanor these past two years. I'm very glad she had you."

Sarah felt tears sting her eyes for the second time that evening. What a fusspot she'd suddenly become.

"I was lucky to have her, my lady."

Lady Chalcroft dabbed at her own damp eyes and scowled briefly. "Sarah, do call me Cousin Elizabeth. We are related, after all."

Sarah couldn't have been more surprised than if the woman had declared her intention to come work herself in Southwark.

"I—" she began, then cleared her throat. "I shall see you at home, Cousin Elizabeth."

The older woman briefly touched Sarah's cheek, then turned as an acquaintance called out to her.

Sarah was grateful that she was largely invisible to the other guests as she made her way back to the entrance hall, for no one stopped her to talk. But when she reached the wide doorway, she felt a prickle along the back of her neck that she'd only ever experienced when she'd been in dangerous situations in The Mint. Frowning, she turned to see what danger there might be amongst London's *haute ton*. Her gaze was drawn immediately to Samuel James who, while tall, certainly shouldn't have seemed to tower above everyone around him, pulling her attention like iron filings to a magnet. He was staring at her with an inexplicable expression on his face, half smile, half challenge.

As her frown deepened, he raised his glass to her and gave her a droll grin, displaying white teeth and a dimple that truly did not belong in a drawing room. Feeling her cheeks go hot, she whirled around and left the room.

What on earth was the man up to, she wondered. It was

not as if a man like him would consider a woman like her—well, the idea was preposterous, but even more absurd was that she should even allow such a thought to form. She had no interest in a man like Mr. James. She had no interest in any man, she corrected herself. She was entirely too consumed with her work. Besides, those thoughts only led to heartache. Clearly Mr. James took a perverse pleasure in tormenting all women, but plain spinsters most of all. And with that sour thought, Sarah felt her normal equanimity return and she took herself off to find food and the Chalcroft library.

Chapter Two

Samuel James was stabbed awake by a shaft of light that slid between the heavy brocade drapes of his bedroom at the Cavendish Hotel. Though he squinted blurry eyes and sought refuge beneath his pillow, he in fact was responsible for the gap in the draperies that otherwise would have sealed the room in tomb-like darkness.

He could generally awake fresh and alert after even only a few hours of sleep if he could awake to the sun. However, if the room remained dark, or during the shortest days of winter, it was all he could do to drag himself out of bed. Now, even as he sought shelter beneath his pillow, Samuel's mind was awake and planning his day.

His sister was to be married in two weeks to Lord Trowbridge and he would have to escort her on any shopping errands she needed to finish as Caroline had not yet made any close friends with whom she could wander the many shops of Bond Street.

With a groan, he tossed back the covers and got out of bed to dress and ring for coffee. He would address the pile of correspondence that arrived every two days from the States from his publishing company, then spend an hour dictating his responses to the secretary he had hired while in London. His father had started as a small map publisher in Philadelphia shortly after the Revolutionary War, and in a country that was ever expanding west, new maps were constantly needed. But when Samuel had taken over the reins, he had expanded the materials published to include two periodicals and, more recently, a series of travel books. Most Americans had not had the opportunity to travel the world, busy as they were building a country and recovering from two wars, and his inexpensive, pithy journals had been well received.

Eschewing a valet as an English affectation, he quickly bathed and dressed and was already halfway through his stack of correspondence when his secretary arrived to begin taking dictation. When word arrived from his sister that she was ready for their expedition, Samuel immediately dropped what he was doing and dismissed his secretary until the next day.

Samuel loved his younger sister dearly; she was all that was left of his family and he would do anything to make her happy, including spending hours on Bond Street and at Burlington Arcade, helping her acquire the finishing touches to her trousseau. He would then escort her to whatever society event her fiancée's mother determined was best to cement her future daughter-in-law's place in the *haute ton* of London, that rarefied society of wealth and privilege that absolutely thrived on rules, strictures, and hierarchy.

He and Caroline were in a bit of a nebulous position. On the one hand, Caroline was engaged to Lord Trowbridge, the future Marquess of Huntley, whom she had met two years previously when she and Samuel had travelled to Italy. Sam had been in the process of compiling a travel book for his publishing house when Caroline and Trowbridge had clapped eyes on one another and immediately fallen in love. They had spent every available moment together while in Italy. Though Sam had extended their stay by nearly two weeks, Caroline was devastated when he could no longer delay their return to the States.

In the intervening year, letters between Caroline and Trowbridge had flown across the Atlantic to the point that Samuel declared it was fortunate he owned a publishing company and could buy paper at a discount.

Lord Trowbridge, it appeared, was having a difficult time gaining his parent's approval for an American nobody as his wife, which made Samuel inclined to doubt his devotion to Caroline. What grown man would allow his parents to tell him whom he could or could not marry? Caroline had passionately defended Trowbridge when Samuel remarked as much and he was subjected to an hours-long explanation of the English nobility's complicated hereditary lineage traditions.

"Oh, very well," Samuel finally said, throwing up his hands. "He's not strangled by his mother' apron strings. Don't see what good it does you, though." At which point Caroline had burst into tears, leaving Samuel feeling like a complete ass. He'd done his best to reassures his sister that everything would work out, but she grew morose as weeks passed without a letter from Trowbridge.

The reason for his silence became clear when Lord Trowbridge presented himself at Samuel's Philadelphia manor.

Lord Trowbridge's father had died, and with his death had come the family's realization that he had poorly managed the hereditary estates and the coffers were drained. Suddenly, the idea of a wealthy American daughter-in-law was not so appalling to the dowager Marchioness of Huntley, and Lord Trowbridge, now the Marquess, had pushed his advantage and without even a letter of warning, had hopped a ship to the States to ask for Caroline's hand. Valuing his own life, for he knew the insanity of denying his sister that which she most wanted, Samuel had not hesitated to grant his permission.

The only request the dowager marchioness had made was that the wedding take place in England so that she could ensure Caroline was accepted into the *ton*.

Now, nearly a year later, Caroline was days away from becoming the next Marchioness of Huntley, and Samuel's life seemed to revolve around the acquisition of satin gloves, embroidered slippers, and beaded reticules. It was a far cry from his daily routine of ink, paper weight, and letter dies. It was also, he realized, a damn site easier to acquire such fripperies than it was to find decent writers for his periodicals and travel books.

However, despite Caroline's soon-to-be elevated status, the Jameses were still Americans, decidedly lacking in either lineage or prestige. Or manners and refinement, apparently, though Samuel had not once propped his feet on a table or slurped his soup. Well, he considered, perhaps he was lacking in the finer qualities. For her part, Caroline seemed to have picked up things like which spoon to use for blancmange and when to say, "my lady," or "your grace," as if she were born to the life. Samuel suspected she had ransacked the back rooms of his publishing house's book collection and dug out any book on English etiquette she could find. Were it not for her accent and vivacious disposition, she could easily pass for an English debutante of good family. And considering her determination to fit in, he suspected her American accent would disappear soon, though he hoped her open disposition would not be so easily dampened. There was a freshness to the way Caroline greeted each new person and experience that made those around her feel they were seeing things for the first time as well.

Straightening his cravat and running a comb through his recalcitrant hair, Samuel grinned at his reflection in the looking glass. What a sentimental old sot he was becoming, he chided himself.

Once back in the receiving rooms of their suite, he found his sister adjusting a hat pin in her bonnet.

"Lady Trowbridge said I accounted myself well last night and that she thought I should make an adequate marchioness," Caroline reported, forgoing any morning greeting.

"And good morning to you as well," Samuel said wryly. He was about to offer an opinion on the old biddy when Caroline continued.

"I declare her effusive compliments nearly bowled me over. Imagine if she'd said I would make an *acceptable* wife for George? I fear such flattery would go to my head and I should turn into an unbearable bore."

Samuel opened the door and offered his arm. "And what makes you think you're bearable now?" he asked.

Caroline stuck her tongue out at him. "Lucky for me, I care not what either you or the marchioness think. George is the only person whose opinion matters to me and he thinks I am quite perfect."

"Well you'd best hurry up and marry him before he discovers the truth."

His sister raised a haughty eyebrow. "Such an ungentlemanly remark is going to cost you a new bonnet."

"I've no need of a new bonnet, thank you."

"Good, because you shan't be wearing it," she said as she led the way to the modiste.

Two hours later over ices, Caroline informed him of their evening plans. Samuel was content to let her words flow over him, confident that she'd tell him three more times what to wear before tonight.

"Samuel!" Caroline exclaimed in a tone that implied it was not the first time she'd called his name. "Who was that dark-haired lady with whom you were speaking last night?"

"I'm sorry, sister dear. I was envisioning what a beautiful bride you are going to be.

"Of course you were. Now answer my question."

"I spoke with many ladies last night, dark haired and otherwise. Trying to ingratiate myself with your *ton*, you know."

"Yes, but only one caused you to have That Look."

"What on earth are you talking about? I don't have A Look."

"No, you have eighty-seven. But the look I'm talking about is the one that says you've met someone who peaks more than your usual interest in women."

"And what do you know about my usual interest in women?" he asked with as much haughty older brother-ness as he could muster. Not surprisingly, it had no effect on her.

"Plenty," she scoffed, her American accent sharpening. "You are interested in all women. You don't have a preference in shape, form, or hair color. Debutante and widow appeal to you equally."

"One might think you were implying I had no standards," he said sardonically.

"Not at all. You simply appreciate all women. But I digress…"

"You don't say," he said, motioning for the cheque.

"You only get That Look when someone challenges you. When she attracts your wit and brain as well as your…well," she flushed and Samuel raised his eyebrows at her.

"Well, the rest of you. You know what I mean," she finished, flustered.

Samuel took pity on her and laughed softly. "I do indeed."

Grasping at her composure, she stood as he held out her chair. "The point being, you had That Look last night when you were talking to a dark haired lady in blue."

"She was not a lady," he said, smiling as he recalled his lesson in who was called lady and who was not.

"Samuel!" Caroline said, clearly appalled.

"Smooth your feathers, goose." He proceeded to explain what the mystery woman had told him.

"And so who was she?"

"I've no idea. She wouldn't tell me."

"How very vexing for you," Caroline mused in a near-perfect English accent.

"Not at all. She did, as you say, appeal to my wit and she certainly challenged me, but I assure you, it was a momentary attraction. The lady showed no interest in me and if you are so astute as to note the fine points of my preferences, you will have also noticed that I do not rise to an unnecessary challenge. If a woman does not return an interest in me, I move on. I'm not going to tread where I'm not welcome."

"Yes, but perhaps you are missing out on a true gem of a woman because you do not first seek to get to know her. Not all women are drawn only to your stunning good looks, you know."

"Stunning good looks, eh?" he said with a smile as he guided her out of the ice shop and across the street to her final shopping stop.

"Yes, well, I find your face only passable, but I *do* seem to be in the minority. The point being, I think you should try getting to know what's in a woman's mind before you dismiss her. You might be pleasantly surprised."

"Fell in love with Trowbridge's mind first, did you?" he asked mischievously. "As I recall, you declared that he was the man for you after just one dance."

"Yes but you and I are quite different," was her response, delivered as haughtily as only a younger sister could.

"And what is this sudden interest in my love life? You're not generally such a nag. I should warn Trowbridge that you've the makings of a fishwife. He may want to reconsider the marriage."

"He won't change his mind," she said with a sly little confident smile that made Samuel wonder how much he didn't know about her and her betrothed's relationship.

"But to answer your question, the reason for my nagging, as you call it, is that I'm worried for you. You shall be all alone when you return to Philadelphia."

"I'd scarcely call a house full of servants being alone."

"You know what I mean, Samuel. It's been just the two of us for so long now. I fear you shall be lonely. I should like nothing more than for you to find the kind of love Trowbridge and I have."

"I hate to burst your romantic little soap bubble, but I don't see myself leg shackled to one of these proper English roses. They just don't appeal to me."

"Except the lady in blue," Caroline persisted.

"Let it go, Caro," he snapped, at the end of his patience. "I appreciate your concern, but I shall be fine. Unlike your English lord, I've no need of an heir or a dowry to carry on the family estate and should I require companionship, I assure you I shall not be found lacking it." With this statement, he delivered her into the care of the seamstress and announced he would return in an hour.

Striding through the streets of the fashionable shopping district at an unfashionably brisk pace, he felt his spurt of annoyance at his sister dissipate. He knew she truly did love him and despite being six years younger, she'd always sought to mother him, making sure he ate regularly and worrying over how little he slept.

Caroline was correct in that he had no preferences when it came to women: he truly adored them all. Although, there was something about Lady Disdain's shiny mahogany hair and smoldering dark eyes that stood out from all other women. There was also that haughty tilt to her head that he suspected was more defensive than arrogant. As she'd stood there on the fringes of the ball last night, his attention had been drawn to her like a magnet to a lodestone. Her tawny complexion and dark slashes of brows didn't conform to the current standards of feminine beauty, but somehow that made her even more attractive to him. Her lips, though compressed in displeasure or disappointment, were full and lush, and the slender column of her neck positively begged to be kissed, as did the curve of gently rounded shoulder exposed by her gown. The understated midnight blue gown fit his impression of her: subtle beauty and sophistication that camouflaged hidden depths.

Alright, he would concede that Caroline was right, he'd been intrigued.

But it was also true he rarely bothered pursuing a woman if he didn't sense an answering and active interest from her immediately. He knew such a trait would probably be considered unmanly, especially by his friends who thought the challenge of winning over a woman was proof of their masculine vigor. But Samuel had always considered such behavior to be egotistical in the least and downright offensive in the worst cases. To convince a woman to care for you just to prove you could seemed the height of disrespect for the fairer sex. And so he had become an excellent judge of determining if a lady was receptive to his attentions—be they mild flirtations or more salacious pursuits—and quickly abandoned any woman who did not promptly return his interest. Who could fault him for such a code of conduct? he thought, firmly dismissing his sister's words.

Yet, as he turned left on Oxford Street intending to take a

circuitous route back to the seamstress's shop, Caroline's suggestion that he had been missing out kept niggling at the back of his mind.

His flirtations and love affairs had satisfied his cursory desires. He was not, after all, looking for a wife. Perhaps he'd not spent time with women who wished to discuss more than the latest party or newest fashion, but he had plenty of mates to discuss weightier issues with over a pint.

Unbidden, an image of Lady Disdain again rose in his mind's eye. Their interaction had been brief, but talking with her had invigorated his brain in a way he could not remember experiencing before with a woman. He could perfectly recall that lush dark hair piled high, those judgmental dark brows over almond-shaped eyes and the graceful stillness with which she held herself, as if she'd never coyly fluttered a fan or swished her skirts coquettishly. But he'd met plenty of beautiful, graceful women over the years. Not many had remained so coolly aloof when he turned on his charming smile and engaged in teasing flirtation. None had verbally baited him or made him scramble for a response as she had. He liked that he'd had to stay on his toes with her. He'd had to reach beyond the glib small talk that usually won ladies to his side within a few minutes.

What would happen if he approached her again? Could he interest her enough to learn why she had seemed so removed from the crowd last night?

With a start, Sam realized he'd already made his way back to the seamstress shop. Shaking his head at his own distraction, he decided to leave Lady Disdain to the great mysteries of life. He had no idea who she was and—he paused midstep. He did have one clue, he realized. He knew that she was related to the girl who'd got herself betrothed at the duke's party. Pulling open the door, he stepped into the dim interior, sunblind after his walk. Perhaps he would allow himself to rise to his sister's taunt and actually learn more about the woman in blue. Then again, he thought, as a petite blonde emerged from the back of the shop and dimpled prettily at him, perhaps he would leave Lady

Disdain to fate. The shop girl brushed his hand lightly as she took his hat and gloves. The sway of her hips became exaggerated as she showed him back to the large fitting area where his sister was finishing her selections. There were plenty of women in London who did not find him a bit thick in the head and why should he deny them—or himself—the pleasure of their welcoming company?

Fate did not deliver Lady Disdain to him in the next week, but it did see fit to provide him with her name and an intriguing bit of her history. It was two days before Caroline's wedding and they were attending the final congratulatory party in honor of she and her fiancée. Caroline was in her element on Trowbridge's arm and the crowd at the private event was in the palm of her hand, hanging on her every word and laughing at what he knew were her terrible little jokes.

He propped an elbow on the fireplace mantle of Lord and Lady Wycliff's large drawing room and smiled at his younger sister. For the first time in a year, he allowed himself to admit how very much he would miss her. Aside from her unnecessary mothering of him, she had been his confidante and friend, using her sisterly status and wry wit to poke fun at him and keep him humble in the most loving way. He would no doubt become an unbearable boor without her to keep him in his place.

"These events get to be a bit much when you haven't spent your entire life trained to attend them, don't they?"

Jolted out of his reverie, Samuel turned to see Lord Reading holding up the other end of the mantle. Though the two men had not met, Samuel knew his name from the party at which he'd met Lady Disdain. Lord Reading had become betrothed to Lady Disdain's cousin amidst some kerfuffle.

Kerfuffle? he thought with a mental chuckle. He'd clearly been in England too long.

"I've found them bearable when I discover the host's secret stash of whiskey," Sam said, raising his glass of said libation.

"It seems reports of American ingenuity are not unfounded," Reading replied with a grin. "Alex Fitzhugh," the man said, extending his hand in what was a decidedly informal gesture.

"Samuel James," he said, grasping the outstretched hand. "Forgive my American-ness, but aren't you an earl or something? Don't you normally introduce yourself by some long title?"

Fitzhugh laughed. "Yes, I suppose you're right. It's only that I just, er...came into the title recently and I can't say that it sits comfortably on my head. It's my father who's the earl, by the way."

Sam frowned. "Again, I invoke my citizenship as an excuse for my ignorance, but aren't you usually saddled with that title at birth?"

Fitzhugh's mouth twisted wryly. "Yes, well, there was a bit of estrangement between my father and I since before I was born."

"Forgive me," Sam said quickly. "Even for an American, I know that was rude to ask."

"Think nothing of it," Fitzhugh said with a wave of his glass.

"So you find these events a bit much too, I take it?" Before Fitzhugh could answer, Sam rushed on. "Don't mistake me—I enjoy a good rout as much as anyone, it's just normally I don't have to second guess everything I want to say, wondering if it's considered 'inappropriate' for the company. You English have rules for absolutely everything, you know."

Fitzhugh laughed again. "This level of society does, at any rate," he said with a nod at the assemblage of elite guests. "Trust me, you needn't second guess your words at your common English party either."

"Well that's a damned relief," Sam said, eliciting a laugh from the other man. "Oh, I suppose at this point I'm supposed to offer my congratulations."

Fitzhugh inclined his head, a genuine grin lighting his face. "Thank you. I am most fortunate."

" A love match then? Not one of those, 'Your land adjoins

my land so let's join forces and bank accounts' arrangements?"

"Well our lands do adjoin," Fitzhugh said with a frown.

Sam felt his neck flush. He liked Fitzhugh and hadn't meant to be insulting. His irreverent sense of humor tended to run roughshod over any sense of decency. "I'm sorry," he said, abashed. "I didn't mean to imply—"

Fitzhugh burst out laughing. "I've no idea where her family's lands are, to be truthful. I've no idea where my father's estates are either. It is a love match, for which I'm damned grateful."

Sam laughed, both in relief and at being neatly ensnared in Fitzhugh's joke.

"And is your fiancée here this evening?"

Sam didn't consider himself terribly perceptive at reading other men's emotions, but he sensed a bit of wistfulness in the other man's voice.

"No, she runs an aid society in Southwark with her cousin who had need of her tonight."

Sam's ears perked up. Surely the cousin Fitzhugh referred to was Lady Disdain.

"I believe I met your lady's cousin the night your betrothal was announced."

"You met Miss Draper? You were one of few, then. She kept to herself that night. I suppose she feels even more uncomfortable at these high born events than we do."

"Why is that?" Sam asked, refusing to consider just how much he wanted to know.

"She's been running her organization for close to five years, I believe. Removed herself entirely from Society to help feed and care for London's poorest. Not many in her position would do so."

Sam mulled that over for a moment as he nursed the last of his whiskey. Lady Disdain—Miss Draper—grew more intriguing. What would cause a lady to undertake such a lifestyle? Clearly Miss Draper bore a bit more investigating. His sister would be delighted. He stared into his empty glass, wondering how he might run into her again.

"Ah, my father signals he's ready to leave," Fitzhugh said. "I suppose I shall see you in a few days at your sister's wedding."

"Oh?" Sam said. He had no idea who was on the guest list as his main contribution to the event was footing the bill.

Fitzhugh grinned in understanding. "Don't worry, it will all be over soon."

Sam laughed and extended his hand. "I look forward to seeing you then. I'll supply the secret stash of whiskey.

"I shall hold you to that," Fitzhugh said before departing.

Sam mulled over what he'd learned of Miss Draper and wondered if Reading might be persuaded to arrange a meeting. Otherwise he might be forced to wander the streets of Southwark in hopes of running into her, an idea he suspected would not meet with his sister's approval.

Chapter Three

Sarah ladled the last bit of soup into a bowl and handed it to a young boy with eyes too large for the gaunt angles of his face.

"Don't tell anyone I gave you seconds," she warned. "They'll think I'm playing favorites."

The boy nodded, his large eyes widening in fear.

"I'm teasing," she said with a laugh. "Eat up."

The boy returned to his table and Sarah dabbed the sweat from her brow with the hem of her voluminous apron. She wished there'd been one more bowl of soup as her stomach growled, but she would never deny a hungry child a second serving, or a third if she could swing it.

Fumbling beneath her apron, she pulled out the small pin watch she wore. It was the only piece of jewelry she still owned and the only reason she hadn't yet sold it was that she desperately needed it to help her keep track of her day. Otherwise she was wont to get immersed in a project and forget the three other appointments she'd arranged.

She had nearly an hour before her meeting with Dr. Kendall—the newest physician to take up residency in The Mint. Most doctors who treated the patients in Southwark did so either because they were freshly out of university and needed some experience, they had new and untested procedures they wanted to try, or their skills were so lacking that only the destitute would consent to treatment.

Dr. Kendall, however, was in a category of his own. An American by birth, he was trained at the University of Glasgow in Scotland and he was eminently qualified. He clearly had a strong desire to help his fellow man, but Sarah suspected that his residency here in The Mint had more to do with the color of his skin than his desire to treat the ague and set broken bones amongst London's poorest. Sarah had worked with enough doctors to recognize that Jeremiah Kendall was possessed of a brilliant scientific mind. He should be teaching other doctors and conducting groundbreaking research under the patronage of England's greatest academic institutes. Instead he was living in a drafty set of rooms, seeing patients in a makeshift surgery at the front of the house. He was the first black man she'd ever met and she'd felt an instant kinship to him as a fellow social outsider.

Sarah removed her apron and carried the empty soup pot to the back of the room where a woman was scrubbing dishes.

"I'll be back in time for the dinner service, Ida. I'm off to meet with Dr. Kendall and see what medicines he's lacking."

"Watch yerself, miss. His kind's been known to attack women sech as yerself."

Sarah pressed her lips together to keep from snapping at Ida. Hers was not an uncommon prejudice and Sarah had learned the hard way that she couldn't argue away such ridiculous thoughts. Instead, even though it galled her to do it, she employed a more subtle attack.

"Oh Ida! You know Dr. Kendall is a true gentleman. And didn't he save your daughter-in-law just a fortnight ago?"

Ida looked skeptical as she dried the large pot. "She might have recovered on her own."

Sarah forced herself to take a deep breath. "I've seen many people with her same ailment die just like that." She snapped her fingers in illustration. "Dr. Kendall saved her life. He's a great physician."

"You be careful nonetheless," Ida finished.

Forcing herself to take a deep breath, Sarah realized this was not a battle she could win in a day, but as she headed out, she vowed to change Ida's mind about the doctor if it was the last thing she did.

When she entered his office, Dr. Kendall was working

over the wailing and writhing form of a boy of eight or nine whose pregnant mother was trying to hold him still. Sarah rushed over to help and recognized the boy. A quick glance told her Dr. Kendall was trying to extract a shard of glass from the boy's bare foot.

"Now Thomas," she cajoled. "Let the good doctor finish. The more you hold still, the faster he'll be done."

"But it hurts, miss!"

"Of course it does, but no battle wound worth the retelling has come without a fair bit of pain."

The boy's thrashing ceased for a moment and his mother seized the opportunity to lay awkwardly across his legs, immobilizing them as the doctor cleaned out the wound.

"Battle wounds?"

"Yes, of course. An injury such as this is not without its discomfort to be sure, but imagine the glorious and bloody story you'll have to share with the lads about your bravery."

"That's true," the boy said, reaching a grubby hand to wipe his nose.

As the doctor began stitching the wound, Thomas sucked in a great breath preparatory to yelling. But a glance at Sarah who winked conspiratorially made him clench his jaws together and exhale loudly through his nose.

"Ah yes, stabbed by pirates, I believe," she said. "After being impaled by the horn of a mysterious sea monster."

Sarah kept up her ideas for the glorious feats that led to Seamus' injury until the doctor finished bandaging his foot.

"Keep it clean, keep it dry. Try to stay off of it a few days. Where are your shoes? You'll want to protect those stitches."

"I ain't got no shoes," Thomas said and his mother added, "It's summer, no need for shoes."

Dr. Kendall frowned, clearly at a loss. Sarah stepped in, speaking to Seamus' mother. "Get him home as best you can, then come by my place this evening. I'll find something for him to wear while he heals."

"Thank you, mum," Mrs. Sampson said, helping her son

hobble out of the room.

"Where are you going to find him shoes?" the doctor asked.

"I haven't the faintest idea," Sarah confessed with a laugh. "But I have a few hours. Perhaps I can call in a favor."

"Well if you're calling in favors, I could use more laudanum and several days' supply of linen bandages. I've never run through supplies like I do here! Southwark—and The Mint in particular—is not the safest place to live. If you're not starved, you're run down by a cart or tackled by a falling down building."

"And that is the reason for my visit," Sarah replied. "I believe I will be able to help with your supply shortage very soon. My cousin Miss Eleanor, whom I think you met only once, has been able to convince the Ladies' Compassion Society not only to continue our funding, but to increase it."

Dr. Kendall looked impressed. "How did she manage that? I thought those ladies were notoriously parsimonious."

Sarah grimaced. "You have no idea. But my cousin has surprised us all. She is quite resourceful and not a little bit ruthless when she needs to be."

"Has she worked with you long?" he asked, rinsing off his instruments before dropping them in a pot of water on his small stove.

"About two years, though I suspect that will change now." Trying to distract herself from that thought, she asked. "Why are you boiling your instruments?"

"I find a clean scalpel or suture reduces the chance of infection. There is a Hungarian doctor who advocates the use of chlorine to remove bits of illness that may remain on instruments, but as I have to ration bandages and basic medicine, purchasing chlorine is not an option. Boiling them is the closest I can come." He rinsed his hands and turned back to Sarah, wiping them on a cloth. "Why might Miss Eleanor not continue?"

"Miss Eleanor is actually Lady Eleanor. She is the daughter of the Earl of Chalcroft. Her parents…ah, weren't aware she was here in Southwark. Now that they know, I'm sure they'll not wish her to live here even if she does continue our work. And more importantly, she's recently become betrothed. I cannot imagine once she's wed her husband will allow her to continue working."

Dr. Kendall hung up the square of linen. "You might be surprised. There are some men who find an independent woman quite appealing."

Sarah laughed and then considered that Alex Fitzhugh—Eleanor's betrothed—had not grown up in the nobility and had forged his own way in business. If any man might be radical enough to accept a wife with her own vocation, it might be he. Still, she didn't hold out much hope.

"Well, only time will tell," she said prosaically. "In the meantime, if you could make up a list of supplies you need most, I will endeavor to acquire them as soon as our funds arrive."

Dr. Kendall laughed. "How very English you are, Miss Draper."

She frowned. "What did I say?"
He affected an English accent and imitated her. "I shall endeavor to acquire them."

"What should I have said?" Sarah asked, perplexed. She flattened her tone in an attempt at an American accent. "I'll do my best to get my hands on them?"

Dr. Kendall laughed again. "Touché."

As he saw Sarah out, he said, "One day Southwark will lose you too. You'll want to start a family of your own."

"The people of The Mint are my family," she said tightly.

Dr. Kendall started to say something else but Sarah nodded and quickly said, "Good day, Doctor."

She felt the rigidity in her body as she wove through the maze of Southwark streets to the plain building in which she had her set of rooms. Once inside, she removed her bonnet and threadbare gloves and shoved open a window to relieve the stuffiness. Her stomach reminded her she'd had nothing to eat since morning but instead of looking for a bit of bread, she stared out the window as dusk settled over the city, softening the broken edges of Southwark and hiding the ugliness of its poverty in the soft periwinkle light.

She didn't know why Dr. Kendall's parting words had upset her so much except that perhaps she was simply a bit emotional from her ruminations about Eleanor's imminent departure.

Marriage would never be in her future. A family was an unattainable dream.

Sarah pressed clenched fists to her midriff as she stared into the deepening gloom. The scent of fish frying from the floor below made her hungry stomach clench, but in her mind she could smell the dusky fragrance of Sweet William and stock in the meadows of her family home as she'd laid in the sun warmed grass staring at the early evening stars winking on and holding the hand of the man she'd thought she would marry.

Peter Greene was the only son of Sir Nathaniel Greene, the local baronet. Sarah had known him since she was a child, when she was a gangly gap-toothed girl and Peter a pimply faced boy. There had been a small band of children who had played together, exploring Aylesbury Vale until their parents had deemed it inappropriate for boys and girls to spend so much time together. Sarah and Peter had always gotten on particularly well but they'd not seen one another while Peter was away at university and then serving in the Army. In the years he was away, Sarah had lost her coltish clumsiness and her smile had filled in. She'd also stopped climbing trees and making mud pies, though she still took long walks through her childhood haunts.

The intervening years had matured Peter too. Physically he was broad shouldered and fit. The horrors of war had softened his caustic sense of humor and heightened his awareness of the feelings of others.

When they met again at a ball the baronet hosted in honor of his son's return, it was as if all the stars had aligned to create an ambiance tailor-made for the two childhood friends to fall in love.

Hundreds of candles illuminated the Greene's house,

casting a golden shimmer upon the guests. An orchestra hired out from Oxford filled the air with sweet melodies and enticed dancers to the hall cleared of furniture. Peter wore his dress uniform, scarlet red wool with silver embellishments across the chest and a high stiff collar. Though his beard was clipped close and his hair trimmed neatly, his eyes held a wildness that betrayed his discomfort with the loud celebration and constant congratulations…

The sound of men yelling at one another in the street below startled Sarah and she leaned out to close the window. She remembered exactly how Peter had looked that night. Remembered how confident she had felt in her gown straight from a London modiste. She'd smoothed her velvet gown and surreptitiously pinched her cheeks to pinken them as she followed her parents across the room to greet Sir Greene and his family. She wondered if Peter would remember her and what he would think of how she'd grown up.

She was watching him closely and so noticed the tense lines about his eyes ease slightly as her mother introduced her.

"Sarah Draper? But this can't be! There are no twigs in her hair and I can spy not a single rent in her gown."

Sarah's mother was mortified at this accurate description of her daughter as a girl, but Sarah laughed aloud.

"Peter Greene, how have you managed to grow a beard? Did you steal it off a French soldier?"

Peter's shout of laughter drew curious stares from around the room, but he ignored them, instead offering his arm to Sarah.

"Actually it was off a Maratha warrior in India. Perhaps I may share the harrowing tale with you while we fetch some lemonade?"

It was the most natural thing in the world to place her hand in the crook of his arm and allow him to lead her to the refreshment table. She stared at the lines of tension about his eyes and mouth, noticed when he handed her a glass that his hands shook. They chatted about little things like the temperature of the water in the Arabian Sea ("Like taking a bath! Not at all like trying to dip your toes in the Channel!") to the status of Mr. Pepper's ancient nag ("She'll still try to take a bite out of you even if she can't see, poor dear"). But throughout their easy conversation, Sarah felt that her old friend was strung as tightly as a violin string. When they'd run out of both small talk and lemonade, Sarah set her cup down and turned to him. She pondered how to gently draw him out but in the end decided on frankness.

"Now tell me how you really are Peter. Out with it."

Peter looked at her with a quizzical smile. "I don't know what you mean. I'm perfectly—"

"No you're not Peter. We may not have seen one another for many years, but I've known you since we were five. You are like blown glass, a jostle away from shattering. Talk to me."

He started to protest again, but as she stared at him in earnest, his expression crumbled, the smile melting into a grimace. He raised a trembling hand to cover his mouth but his anguish was evident in his tortured gaze. His breath came in rough bellows.

Shocked, Sarah acted instinctively, grabbing his arm and steering him out of the nearby French door onto the wide terrace. Several people milled about and Sarah urged him around the corner of the house where the only illumination was the sporadic light of the moon as it ducked in and out of clouds.

Peter walked to the balustrade and gripped it tightly. Sarah stood at his side, unsure if she should touch him, but wanting to help him if she could. He reminded her of a caged animal, desperate for escape. His breath came in short, rapid pants and a fine sheen of sweat covered his face. He scrubbed his hands through his hair, then pressed them into his eyes. After a few minutes, he inhaled deeply and spoke.

"It was awful. Brutal. The worst."

"But I thought you were in the supply—"

"I was at the front. I lied to my parents so they wouldn't worry."

Sarah gasped and reached a tentative hand out to touch

his. He pulled away, startled, then, as if realizing it was her, gripped her hand as if it were a lifeline.

"They laugh and comment how clever I was to obtain a safe position in the Army. They never wanted me to join, you know."

"I know," she whispered.

"And while they think I was filling out requisitions for sides of beef and crates of tea, I was holding my best friend's innards in my hands while he died in a dusty trench in India." He paused and when he spoke again, she could barely hear him. "That's not even the worst of what happened to me."

Sarah felt her eyes fill with tears. "And you've told no one?"

Even in the bleached white of moonlight, she could see the bleakness in his gaze.

"I can't believe I told you," he rasped.

"Of course you did. We shared everything when we were children." She bit her lower lip, trying to decide how best to help him. "Now, once you collect yourself, we'll go back inside and you'll ask me to dance. I promise I've learned not to step on my partner's feet."

"I can't—"

"Yes you can. Then I shall develop a terrible headache. My parents won't want to leave, so you'll offer to escort me home."

"But—"

"We'll take a maid with us as chaperone." She smiled. "Can you believe we now need a chaperone?"

He returned her smile with a shaky one of his own and she was pleased to see that the haunted expression had left his eyes.

"Then when you return, you can sneak upstairs and avoid the rest of the party."

"You've figured it all out, haven't you?"

"Almost," she replied. "Tomorrow we shall go for a nice long walk and you will tell me everything."

"No. I can't. There's too much—"

"I shall bring my dog Whiskers. You remember him, don't you? Anything that's too awful to tell me, you can tell him. Nothing bothers him."

"You don't understand. Talking makes it worse. It makes me want to—to—to do something drastic."

"We'll just be quiet then."

He laughed harshly. "That makes it even worse."

"Then try talking, Peter. I won't judge you. Whiskers certainly won't. But it can't be good to keep all that grief inside you."

He frowned, staring into the darkness. "A man should be able to contain his emotions. I should—"

"Pish tosh," she said impatiently. "Let's meet out in nature. You know how much you used to love being outside when you were a boy. We'll walk. Perhaps we'll talk. You won't be healed then, but you'll be better. I promise."

The shadows in his eyes seemed to recede a bit and he gave her a weak smile. "You're quite certain for a green girl of eighteen."

"How dare you, sir. I am nineteen as of last Tuesday."

"I know when you're birthday is, imp. I was just teasing you."

"Good," she said, because if he could still tease, there was hope for him.

The following months found them strolling hours and miles around the lush green hills of Buckinghamshire.

The locals gossiped that they were courting and Sarah would have agreed had they ever spoken about anything but the war. But their walks were spent with Peter talking about everything from how they managed laundry on the front to the Indian soldier he'd had to kill with his bare hands.

"He wasn't any older than my cousin Phillip," he'd whispered in agony. "But I knew if I didn't kill him, then he would kill me. He was that terrified."

Some things he would whisper to her dog Whiskers while she sat at a distance beneath a tree or walked slowly behind.

And then one day, he stopped talking.

They were sitting beside a burbling stream that ran along the back of her family's land and after he told her about having to eat a rat one dinner, he simply stopped talking.

"Enough for today?" she asked with a smile. Sometimes he could only bear to revisit his memories for a short time.

"No," he replied.

"No?" She smiled in confusion.

"That's enough. I'm done." Then a smile dawned over his face, one that showed the boyish and relaxed man he had once been. "I'm done with the war. I'm sure it's not done with me," he said, a shadow of the attack he suffered that first night flicking through his gaze. "But I no longer wish to talk about it. I think—I think I have to force myself to move on." He paused, studying her face as if seeing her for the first time. "Thank you," he said quietly.

"You're welcome," she said, equally quiet. They stared at one another for several moments. She saw the childhood friend he had once been, saw what looked like the promise of a future.

He moved slowly, lifting his arms to cradle her face in his hands as if she was fragile, might break at the slightest move. She slowly closed her eyes as he drew near and kissed her. Softly at first, but when she leaned into him, he deepened the kiss, nibbling and licking at her lips until they parted and then plundering her mouth with greater ardor.

From that day on, their walks always led to a secluded place where he would kiss her senseless, lavishing adoration on her mouth, neck, ears, breasts. Then one day, he made love to her in the sheltered green curtains of a weeping willow. Sarah never questioned their actions, never worried for the future. Of course they would marry. They'd known each other their whole lives. Even without the incredible bond of his sharing his war experiences with her they would have ended up together for they had never met another who understood them as well as they understood one another. Announcing a betrothal felt simply like a formality at this point. She knew they couldn't delay indefinitely, but it was just so delicious to sneak away and enjoy those stolen moments of decadent passion...

Sarah turned sharply from the window of her flat, a gasping sob escaping her. She pressed a fist to her mouth to prevent any more sounds escaping. She should eat something, she told herself firmly. She was growing maudlin and if she waited much longer, she would develop a headache that would not go away.

She tore a chunk of bread off the linen-wrapped loaf in her cabinet. She lifted the lid off the pot on the cold stove and found there was still a bit of pea soup left from last night's dinner. Not bothering to warm it, she simply dipped the dry bread in the soup and ate quickly. How Eleanor would ring a peal over her head for that. No matter how meager their meals, Eleanor always insisted they heat it properly and sit at the tiny, all-purpose table. It was one of the things she would miss most about her cousin—the way she forced Sarah to have a care for herself and find some enjoyment in each day. Without Eleanor's influence, Sarah knew she was at risk of running herself into the ground with work. Such had been the case before Eleanor had appeared on her doorstep.

Sara scraped up the last bit of soup with a bread crust. In honor of her cousin, she cleaned her teeth, washed her face, and brushed her hair the fifty strokes Eleanor insisted upon before climbing into bed and succumbing to a restless, dream-filled sleep.

"Wake up sleepyhead!" Eleanor's bright voice called.

Sarah cracked one eyelid and saw that the window showed a sun well up in the sky.

"Goodness, you're not ill are you?" Eleanor asked, coming to lay a soft hand on Sarah's forehead.

"No, no," she replied, swinging her legs off the bed. "I just didn't sleep very well."

"Were the Johannsen boys drunk again?" Eleanor asked, lighting a small fire and putting a kettle on to boil. "I vow, I've never heard two men sing so loudly and be so off key as they do."

Sarah smiled and scrubbed her hands over her face. "No. Just too much on my mind, I suppose."

"Shall we make a list?" Eleanor asked. She picked up one of the slim notebooks in which Sarah tracked every penny she spent. "That seems to help settle your mind. Or should I say, *you* make a list."

Sarah took the notebook from Eleanor with another smile. Though her cousin had never told her the details behind it, Sarah knew that Eleanor had difficulty reading. She could write if pressed, and her penmanship, while cramped and lacking in punctuation, was surprisingly neat with sharp straight lines of letters completely lacking in flourishes.

But as Sarah had a trunkful of her own secrets, she had never asked Eleanor about her difficulties and her cousin had not offered an explanation.

"What are you doing here so early?" she asked.

"It's hardly early. It must be near eight o'clock."

Sarah looked at her cousin askance. It was true, their day usually began before dawn. Still… "It's dreadfully early for a lady of the *ton*." From her one foray into society at eighteen, Sarah knew it was quite common for debutantes to sleep until noon after having been at a ball until the wee hours of the morning.

Eleanor waved her hand dismissively. "The past two years have ruined me for sleeping in, I fear. Besides, what use would I be to you, arriving after you've already served two meals?"

Sarah rose and splashed water on her face, washing away the puffy grogginess from her eyes. Stepping behind the dressing screen, she began to pull on one of her two gowns. The brown serge was a far cry from the rich blue satin she'd borrowed a few weeks past, but it hid the magnitude of stains she acquired as she ran the soup kitchen and visited families with her basket of medicines, treating those ailments she was able.

"You do know that I don't expect you to continue working with me now that you are betrothed," she called out as she buttoned up her bodice. "You're starting a new life and your husband will wish you to be at home." She emerged from behind the screen to see Eleanor looking at her tousled hair with horror.

"I told you I didn't sleep well. And yes, I did brush it last night."

"You didn't tell me you then wrestled a hedgehog. And lost, by the looks of it. Sit," Eleanor ordered. As she began to comb the tangles out of Sarah's long dark locks, she said, "I told Mr. Fitzhugh that I intended to keep working here."

"You did what?" Sarah said, turning in the chair. Eleanor whacked her lightly on the head with the brush. "Ow!"

"Well sit still, then." She resumed her ministrations. "Of course I did," she continued. "Our work here is too important to the people we help and to me."

"Yes, but—"

"Alex was quite understanding. He said his work was important to him and he could understand why it meant so much to me."

"How very forward thinking of him," Sarah murmured.

Eleanor pushed the final hairpin into Sarah's chignon. "Yes, well, he is a very forward thinking man." She sighed happily and Sarah turned to look at her cousin.

"Also, I am ridiculously in love with him," she said with a silly grin on her face.

Sarah felt a stab of something like jealousy in her breast, but she quickly smothered it and stood to hug Eleanor. "I'm so very happy for you. No one deserves it more."

"Except you," Eleanor replied, holding their embrace a few more moments.

Sarah felt tears prick her eyes and abruptly pulled away. "Don't be silly. I'm married to Southwark."

Eleanor shuddered. "What a great stinking husband you have."

"Demanding, too," Sarah said with a smile.

Eleanor's expression sobered. "I do fear I shan't have quite as much time as when I lived here full time, however."

"Of course not! And once you become pregnant, you must give up this vocation completely. It's perfectly natural for you to move on, Eleanor. I would never expect otherwise."

"Yes, well, that won't be happening for a while. In the meantime, we shall find someone else to join us and I will train them as my replacement."

Sarah smiled at her cousin. She'd worked nearly alone for three years before Eleanor had shown up on her doorstep. Volunteers she'd had come and go—many of them the poor helping to feed themselves and their families—but finding people with the desire to spend day in and day out working on her various projects to better the community was not easy. Nevertheless, she would not allow her doubts to dampen Eleanor's enthusiasm.

"Well I believe our new doctor will be of tremendous assistance. After he performed that surgery that saved Martin McCafferty's life two weeks ago, more people have been going to his clinic. With him seeing to the medical care here in The Mint, I will have much more time for our other endeavors."

With doctors a transient commodity in The Mint, regular medical care had fallen to Sarah and Eleanor. Eleanor had developed a natural skill for midwifery and Sarah had seen to things like the setting of broken bones and the stitching of gashes.

"Oh!" Eleanor exclaimed. "I nearly forgot! It's the reason I'm here! You must come into town this afternoon. I've arranged for the Ladies' Compassion Society to transfer their fundraising money directly into your account. You'll need to sign some papers."

"What? They've never given us the money directly. We've always had to apply to have each expense paid directly."

"Yes, well that is a terribly inefficient method as you've always said."

"I have. But how—"

"I convinced Lady Augustus that you have far greater buying power if you were able to pay for supplies directly instead of forcing vendors to wait weeks for their payment from the Ladies."

"Well yes, but I don't see why they've changed their minds now after five years."

Eleanor affected an interest in a hangnail. "Yes, well I might have allowed Lady Augustus to cajole me into joining her advisory board."

"You what?"

Eleanor looked flustered. "It's silly. Stupid, really. I can't read properly and I surely don't know the first thing about all of the administrative work. I suppose she just wants the connection to my father."

Sarah laughed. "Lady Augustus is no idiot and only an idiot would have watched your impassioned speech at that fundraising ball and not wanted you on her committee."

Eleanor flushed and absently tidied the tea things. "You weren't even there," she prevaricated.

"Juliette told me."

"What?"

"She said you were magnificent, which honestly, is no shock to me. Now, dispense with false modesty—"

"It's not false," Eleanor protested.

"Then dispense with the real modesty and recognize your talents. And also tell me where I'm supposed to go to sign these papers."

"I'll do you one better. I'll have our driver take you there."

"You brought a coach into The Mint?"

Eleanor flushed again and Sarah marveled that after two years of living together in Southwark, in their tiny flat no less, her cousin could still feel embarrassment about anything.

"My father insisted. But I had him hire a plain, modest one without his crest on it."

Sarah smiled and stood. She smoothed her plain dress and patted her hair. "Will I do for a bank visit, then?"

"Yes. You look quite official," Eleanor replied.

"I still can't believe you managed to get them to give us the money directly," Sarah said as they descended the narrow staircase and made for the community kitchen. Their conversation skipped from what they would be able to purchase for the organization to the rhapsodic qualities of Alex Fitzhugh (this from Eleanor) to who they could hire to spend more time helping them with the day-to-day operations. Three hours later a footman held open the door and Sarah climbed in, thankful she would not have to walk to the city today or pay for a hackney cab.

"What? Aren't you coming with me?" she asked when Eleanor did not follow.

"Good heavens, no. I've got to check on Mrs. Sampson. She's due any day now."

"But—"

"You'll be fine, Sarah!" Eleanor called as the coach pulled away.

"Easy for you to say," Sarah grumbled to herself. "Earl's daughter."

Chapter Four

Samuel James stood in the center of the Bank of England on Threadneedle Street and found himself at a bit of a loss. He had just finished setting up an account for his sister and it was his last act as her guardian. She was well and truly married; all her possessions had been moved into her new home and the newlyweds were preparing for a wedding trip to Paris in a few weeks. There was nothing left to keep him in England and while he was eager to get back to work, he also felt as if his life would never be the same again.

"Damned foolishness," he muttered, and with a last glance around the stately lobby, made to leave. He'd taken not two steps when he paused. Was that Lady Disdain coming out of a back office? He watched her shake hands with a short, rotund bank employee and turn to leave. He lengthened his stride so that he reached the front doors at the same time she did.

"Lady Disdain," he called out. "Can it be you?"

She turned, a slight frown marring her brow, but when she saw him, her face went expressionless, though two splashes of pink colored her cheekbones.

"Mr. James," she said coolly and he was absurdly pleased she remembered his name.

"How lucky that I should run into you one last time before I return home. To America, you know," he added, just to needle.

"Is it?" she asked, her tone as brisk as a winter's morning.

"Well of course it its. How else could I thank you for your invaluable advice?"

"What—" She was jostled by a large man entering the

bank and she stepped to the side of the doors. Samuel followed.

"I wasn't aware that I gave you any advice, Mr. James."

"Perhaps it was more instruction, then." Before she could voice her obvious frustration at his obliqueness, he continued. "You taught me the proper forms of address for this imperative-obsessed country."

She opened her mouth, clearly intending to take umbrage with his critique of England. When she clamped her jaws shut, he wondered if she was simply forgoing an argument or if something made her decide he was right. Intriguing, he thought, if it was the latter.

"I nearly referred to one of the footmen at my sister's wedding as 'my lord.' Thanks to you, I remembered that, much like me, he fell into the 'everyone else' category of commoners. So I simply said, 'Thank you Mr. Braxton,'" he lied.

"Footmen are referred to only by their last—" he saw the moment she realized he was teasing. A grudging smile tugged at the corner of her mouth. "I'm so glad I was able to be of assistance." She nodded and made to leave.

"There's something else I was hoping you could help me with."

She paused, her left eyebrow lifted in question. Samuel had always wanted to master that expression—it seemed the perfect complement to a rakish grin, after all.

"Yes?" she prodded as he stared at her eyebrow.

Coming out of his reverie, Samuel scrambled for a response. He hadn't had an actual request; he'd only been trying to keep her from leaving. Inspiration struck when he remembered her aid work.

"I've been, ah, looking to make a charitable donation before I return to America. I've been given to understand that you might be able to advise me."

He pasted a beatific smile on his face and tried to look sincere.

"I see," she said slowly. "And why would you want to do that?"

"To, ah…ensure my sister is happy in her new country."

"You think she might have need of an aid society here?"

"Of course not. It just seems like a, er, good will gesture to bring her continued good luck," he improvised.

"There are many reputable aid societies in London, and across the country, if you'd prefer."

"A London charity, I believe," he said quickly.

"I shall send you a list."

"But don't you run one?"

She pulled back slightly and Samuel wondered if he'd overplayed his hand. Ah well, he reflected, might as well go all in.

"I do."

"I should like to donate to your aid society."

"Why?" she asked suspiciously.

"I understand you have worked steadfastly for a number of years. Such dedication implies the money will be put to good use."

She appeared undecided. "Very well," she finally said, and then, although it clearly galled her to say it, "We should be very grateful for your contribution."

"Excellent! Are you returning there now? I would like to accompany you and tour the facilities."

"What? Why?" she asked, startled.

"So I can best determine what amount to donate."

"But…but donors don't visit Southwark."

"Why not?" he asked.

"It's not safe," she sputtered.

He smiled at her unease. "But my dear Miss Draper, if it is safe for you, how could it not be safe for me?"

"Because they know me. And how do you know my name?"

"You think I would know you run an aid society in Southwark but not learn your name?"

"Yes, of course," she stammered. "Very well. When would you like to visit?"

"How about now?"

"Now?" she all but squeaked.

For some reason the sound sent an erotic thrill through his body, as if he could hear her making just such a squeak as he nibbled at the tender skin of her inner thigh. Ah, he thought, so it's going to be like that. He'd found her beautiful and intriguing when he first met her. Only now did he realize just how attuned his body was to her every gesture and sound.

"Now," he said in a low voice. He pulled himself abruptly out of the sensuous spell he'd inadvertently lapsed into. Now was definitely not the time for *that*.

Clearing his throat, he gestured to the door. "I can get us a hansom cab."

"I—I have a carriage," she said, sounding a little embarrassed and surprised all at once.

"You do?"

"Well, it's Eleanor's, that is Miss—I mean, Lady Eleanor's. Well, her father's I suppose. Oh bother!" she finished, flustered. "Are you coming or not?"

"Lead on, my lady," he said with a grin.

She took a breath to correct or chastise him, he wasn't sure which, but he could tell when she realized he was teasing again. She let out her breath in a huff, but as she turned to exit the doors, he could have sworn he saw her lips twitch in a smile.

The carriage ride to Southwark was awkward. Well, not for Samuel, but she was clearly uncomfortable. He asked her questions about how she'd come to work in Southwark but she was evasive about exactly why she'd left whatever her past life was. Samuel sensed there was a story there, but he didn't press, moving on to safer topics. He asked her about the day-to-day activities of her organization. She initially answered in one or two word sentences, but as he probed and cajoled, she began to open up, telling him about the Southwark residents who helped her serve the two daily meals, cooked, cleaned, and stocked supplies.

"And do you pay them?"

"Yes, of course. The point of my organization is not to simply feed people, but to employ them and train them for future employment. Plus, I find it helps build a stronger sense of community when people are feeding their neighbors.

"That makes sense," he agreed. "And do you pay yourself?"

"Certainly not!" she snapped, two hot bursts of color cresting her cheeks. "Every penny that is donated goes directly to the people. To imply otherwise is to impugn—"

Sam held his hands up defensively. "Easy there. I didn't mean anything by it. I was just curious. You surely earn a salary."

She pressed her lips together and stared out the window. They were clattering over London Bridge and Sam could practically see the thoughts racing through her mind. He was struck by the strangest desire to know her so well he could tell what she was thinking. After a few minutes, she turned to him.

"I apologize, Mr. James. I overreacted."

"It's no prob—"

"No," she said firmly. "I behaved appallingly and I'm truly sorry. It's just that—" she paused to take a calming breath. "It's just that recently I almost lost all of my funding because the donors believed I was profiting from their donations."

"They were exceedingly wealthy, weren't they?"

"I beg your pardon?"

"The donors who accused you of profiting off your charity. They were wealthy, weren't they? Probably privileged, too. Am I right?"

"I don't see how that—"

"Were they?" he persisted.

"Yes," she answered.

"I thought so. Exceedingly wealthy people are often suspicious of other's money because they have done something worthy of suspicion themselves in the acquisition of their wealth."

She stared at him, a funny expression on her face.

"What?" he asked.

"Nothing, really. It's only that my cousin said very much the same thing."

"Miss Eleanor?"

"Lady Elea—" she began and then saw his teasing grin.

"Are you wealthy, Mr. James?"

"What an impertinent question," he said with a mock frown. "But to be brief, yes I am."

A breath of a laugh escaped her, no doubt at his boastful sounding statement.

"I'm not Duke of Andover wealthy, I'm sure, or even Stephen Girard wealthy if you want to look at Americans, but my father saw a vital need when he started his business and filled it. I've since expanded it a good deal from then."

"And have you earned any of that money by ways which would make you suspicious of others in turn?"

"I can honestly say no. And I know plenty of wealthy people who have come by their money justly as well."

"Then why your cynical comment?"

"Oh I've known even more wealthy people who would steal the shoes off a baby to make a profit."

She laughed and covered her mouth, as if shocked that she had done so. "Yes, well, I'd like to see them try in The Mint. Most children haven't a pair of shoes, much less the babies."

He smiled. "Then it sounds as if I am looking to the right place to donate."

In truth, his idea of donating to her cause had been born simply out of a spontaneous desire to spend more time with her. But seeing how passionate she was about her vocation, he was now genuinely intrigued.

"Ah, here we are," she said, reaching for the door and hopping down before the coachman or Sam could assist her.

Sam was left to follow and as he climbed down he heard Sarah dismissing the coachman.

"I don't feel right keeping him waiting all day," she told Sam. "When you are ready to leave, I will find you transport."

"I'm sure I can manage to get myself home," he said wryly. "It can't be that much harder than getting across the ocean, after all."

Sarah glanced at him out of the corner of her eyes, but said nothing. She struck out with long, purposeful strides, and Sam adjusted his own pace to match.

"So where are we off to first?" he asked as they wove their way around piles of stinking refuse and pools of fetid water. He choked back a gag as the breeze delivered a miasma of smells, all of them rotten.

"You get used to it," Sarah said, offering a sympathetic smile.

"No one should have to get used to that," he replied, resisting the urge to cover his nose with a handkerchief.

"There are worse things than the smells," she said, shrugging her shoulders.

Sam followed her through numerous twists and turns to a short street that was slightly less run down than every other one they had traversed.

"I have to pick up some supplies. I won't be a moment if you'd like to wait here."

Sam glanced at the wooden sign indicating the apothecary shop and nodded. While he waited, he marveled that Sarah Draper lived in such an environment. When he'd seen her that night at the Duke of Andover's party, she had seemed somehow removed from the other guests, as if she wasn't comfortable with them. He could certainly understand; the world of the *haute ton* was so removed from most people's reality, even he himself had felt a bit of a fish out of water when he first arrived.

But this? he thought, noticing a pair of rats scavenging in a pile of who-knew-what in an alley across the way. This was where she chose to live. With Eleanor Chalcroft as a cousin, she clearly had family connections that would have afforded her at least a meager living away from the abject poverty of Southwark. Sam wondered again what event in her past had led her here. The bell on the apothecary door rang and he turned to see Miss Draper, her arms full of packages and a strained look on her face.

"We must hurry," she said, brushing past him to race down the street. She dropped several of the cloth-wrapped bundles and stopped.

Sam gathered them up and took another few out of her arms. "What's wrong?" he asked as he followed close at her heels.

"I must help the doctor. He's gone to tend to Mrs. Thackery's broken arm."

"Is that such a dire emergency? I broke my arm when—"

She paused at an intersection to wait for a lorry pulled by a tired nag to pass.

"If Mrs. Thackery has a broken arm, it's because Mr. Thackery broke it. And he won't take kindly to a stranger—especially one like Dr. Kendall—interfering."

The lorry finally passed and Miss Draper dashed across the street. "I just hope he's not drunk."

"Hold up," Sam said, grabbing her arm to stop her. "It sounds like we should call for a constable."

"There are no constables here, Mr. James. Besides, that would only set him off more. I think I can talk him down, but we must hurry."

"You think?" he repeated as she pulled her arm free and continued her race.

"You need not come with me," she called over her shoulder.

He caught up with her as she opened a rickety door on an even more ramshackle building.

"What kind of man do you think I am that I would leave you to this?" he said, his brows lowered in outrage.

"I'm sure I have no idea, Mr. James. I've lived here without your august protection for five years now." And with that, she turned and ran up the stairs. Sam followed so closely he nearly trod on her skirts. He felt a bit foolish at his statement and her rejoinder but he could not quell the protective urges he had for her.

The sound of yelling grew louder as they raced down a dark hallway. Miss Draper stopped in front of a door so abruptly that it was all Sam could do not to run into her. The yelling was clearly coming from the other side of the door.

"What are you waiting for?" he asked.

She had her eyes closed and was taking deep breaths. She finally opened her eyes and reached for the doorknob, entering the room as if she lived there.

"I've brought that tonic you asked for, Mrs.—oh, hello Mr. Thackery. So nice to see you today."

Sam entered the room to see a woman in obvious distress sitting on the floor clutching her right arm. A black man in his shirtsleeves was seated on a chair a few feet from her, while Mr. Thackery stood in the center of the room, a knife in his hand and belligerence in his gaze. When Miss Draper spoke in her friendly, breezy tone, the man frowned and shook his head as if he wasn't sure she was real.

Miss Draper set her packages down on a table and turned to Mrs. Thackery, though Sam noticed she didn't turn her back to the husband.

"Here, let me assist you off the floor, Mrs. Thackery," Miss Draper said as if the woman had merely sat down to rest. "Mr. Thackery, will you bring the other chair over?" She smiled prettily at him.

Though every fiber of Sam's being was focused on the knife-wielding man, ready to tackle him if he so much as gestured toward Miss Draper, a part of his brain couldn't help but notice that he was seeing a side of Miss Draper he wouldn't have thought existed.

The way she smiled, her whole face brightening, the light, carefree way she spoke made Sam wonder if this was what she was like as a girl. Only his hyper focus on keeping her from harm allowed him to see the strain around her eyes as she kept her gaze on Mr. Thackery.

"'Er, geddaway from 'er," the man snarled as Miss Draper helped his wife to stand. He took a staggering step toward the women. Sam instantly moved to intercept him but Miss Draper cut a look at him and shook her head slightly. It was all Sam could do not to take the man down, but he willed himself to be calm and let Miss Draper handle the situation.

"Of course, Mr. Thackery. Would you like some tea? I have some in that packet there."

Mr. Thackery's head wobbled as he turned to look where Miss Draper was pointing.

"Tea?" he asked, as if he'd never heard of it before.

"Yes, of course. You look like you could use a strong cup." As he nodded, she continued, "Now tell me what happened today to upset you. I'm sure we can set it to rights."

Miss Draper set about finding a battered pot in which to boil water and collecting a chipped mug, all the while getting Mr. Thackery to tell her about his inability to find a job—though as he described it, "The bastards who can't appreciate a man's talents."

To Sam, the excuses told him Mr. Thackery was not a man inclined to exerting himself, but Miss Draper clucked sympathetically as she brewed the tea and handed him the mug. Quite without Mr. Thackery realizing it, she took the knife from him and led him to sit on the low cot in the corner of the room.

Amidst his rambling grievances against the world, Miss Draper urged Thackery to keep drinking his tea and as the man's eyes grew heavy and his speech even more slurred, Sam realized Miss Draper hadn't given the man tea at all. In the corner of the room, he noticed the doctor was splinting Mrs. Thackery's arm and binding it.

Miss Draper kept up her litany of understanding assurances and at long last, Mr. Thackery tumbled over on the cot. Miss Draper rescued the mug before it crashed to the ground and then turned to the man's wife.

"Will you now go to your sister's in Bath, Mrs. Thackery? The offer still stands of a train ticket."

"Wot, for this?" the woman asked, nodding at her bandaged arm. "I fell. Landed wrong is all."

Miss Draper crouched in front of her. "Mrs. Thackery, I am worried that one of these days when you fall, you won't get back up again. Please, you must go someplace safe."

Mrs. Thackery's lips compressed. "I won't. I won't leave me

husband. 'E needs me, 'e does."

The doctor was fashioning a sling while the women spoke. His face was expressionless, but Sam saw the man's eyes flash with disbelief or outrage at the woman's protestations.

Miss Draper tried several more arguments for convincing Mrs. Thackery, but in the end, she left a packet of herbs to help her bone knit and advised she hide Mr. Thackery's knife. They left Mrs. Thackery tucking a blanket around her snoring husband with her good arm.

"That wasn't tea," the doctor said.

Miss Draper shook her head. "Laudanum. It's not the safest thing to give an intoxicated person but with someone prone to violence, I choose expediency over caution."

"I agree," the doctor approved.

Sam wrinkled his nose. "How'd you get him to drink that? The stuff tastes awful."

"When he's that inebriated, Mr. Thackery would drink water from the Thames and not taste it," she said, leading the way out of the building.

Once outside, Sam took a deep breath, marveling that the fetid air now smelled fresh after the close smell of misery inside the building.

Miss Draper performed the introductions and as he shook Dr. Kendall's hand, Sam realized that even in Philadelphia, this man would be relegated to menial work instead of serving as a physician.

"Are you American?" Sam asked, as he heard the doctor's accent.

Dr. Kendall glanced at Miss Draper and then looked Sam directly in the eye. "I was born there, but I consider myself a Scot as that is where I received my medical training."

Sam nodded, realizing uncomfortably that, given how preoccupied he was with his business, he'd never thought to challenge the low status of black citizens in Philadelphia, nor given much thought to those enslaved in the southern states of his country. Feeling suddenly ashamed of himself, he extended his hand once again. "The people of Southwark are fortunate to have you."

Dr. Kendall nodded shortly and murmured a few words to Miss Draper as she explained the contents of her packages while handing them to him.

Once the doctor departed, Sarah indicated the direction they should take and Sam offered his arm. After a moment's hesitation, she took it and they set out.

"Why would that woman not leave her husband? Something tells me this is not her first injury."

They walked several paces in silence before Miss Draper replied. "No, it's not her first injury. Nor will it be her last. I've encountered many women who make every excuse possible for the men who beat them. But is it so surprising? The law says a wife is her husband's property, to do with as he sees fit. You'd be surprised how many women believe that."

Another half block passed in silence. "That was a pretty neat trick you did back there," he said.

"What?"

"Talking to Thackery. Distracting him from using that knife, getting him to take that tea. My inclination was to knock him down and see how he liked it."

She smiled sadly. "I've had a bit of practice at talking someone out of mayhem."

"With Thackery?"

"With any of a dozen men here in The Mint who take their frustrations at life out on their families."

"Nonetheless, it was well done," he said sincerely.

She smiled again. "Yes, well, sometimes I do want to knock their heads together, but seeing as how I haven't the strength, I've had to improvise."

They rounded a corner and ran smack into a broad-shouldered man in rough clothes. His heavy brow was lowered in anger and his lips were curled in a snarl.

"Oi!" the man snapped. "Watch where yer goin', aye?"

"Sorry, brother," Sam said, and moved to guide Miss

Draper around him.

"Oh, 'brother,' is it? Well, *brother*, hows about you spare your family here some coin. We'll call it a relations toll for running me down." With a twist of his wrist, a knife was in his hands and he advanced menacingly on them.

"Great. Another knife," Sam muttered. With a look at Sarah, he said, "Mind if I handle this one my way?"

"Be my guest," she said, gesturing calmly at the brute.

Sam reached into his pocket as if he were reaching for money. Their would-be robber held out his hand to receive it, whereby Sam grabbed his extended hand, twisted it, and spun the man so that his wrist was bent at a painful angle in the middle of his back.

"Awright, awright! Didn't mean ye no harm. Lemme go!"

Sam kneed the man in the side of his leg just above the kneecap. The man's leg collapsed and he howled in pain. Sam reached down to retrieve the knife. He held it beneath the writhing man's nose before flinging it into a dank alley.

"Have a good day, *brother*." And after running a hand through his mussed hair, he offered Miss Draper his arm again as if nothing had interrupted their stroll.

She said not a word and after a while, he asked, "Are you alright?"

She laughed shakily and glanced up at him. "It's been a rather...eventful day."

A grin tugged at one corner of his mouth. "Damn I could use a drink. And so, I think, could you."

Without a word, she tugged on his arm and he followed her across the street and into a pub. Crowds of people—mostly men, but a few women—filled the low-ceilinged room. Many were eating a post-work dinner, all were enjoying a pint of some brew.

Sam followed Miss Draper as she wove her way between people, some of them calling out a greeting to her, others tugging a forelock at her. The barkeep bestowed a nearly toothless grin on her as she shoved her way between two men at the bar.

"Evenin' Mistress! Might ye be wantin' supper or a pint?"

"Good evening Mr. Everly. I'm afraid today calls for something more serious, if you don't mind."

Mr. Everly winked broadly. "I know just what you mean, Mistress."

"Er…," Miss Draper hesitated. "For two, if you don't mind."

The barkeep's surprise was evident but he said nothing, only nodded.

"Is there a table in the back?" she asked.

"Oi!" Mr. Everly shouted over her head at the men at a table in an isolated corner. "Shove off! Ye've finished yer drinks. Head home, ye sluggards!"

The men grumbled good naturedly and left. Sarah indicated the empty bench and slid into the corner seat. Sam glanced at the bench across the table. He realized it put his back to the crowd and instead sat next to her.

Mr. Everly appeared with two reasonably clean glasses and a bottle of indeterminate brown liquid. He poured two generous servings and moved to leave when Sam raised a finger.

"You may leave the bottle, Mr. Everly."

Sarah lifted an eyebrow at him as she pulled off her gloves. "I trust you can foot the bill?"

Sam pulled out a handful of coins and handed them to the barkeep.

"Slàinte," she said, raising her glass and then neatly knocking it back. Sam followed suit and only just managed not to cough. "Scots whiskey," he gasped through paralyzed vocal chords.

"Mr. Everly's brother-in-law is from Scotland. Smuggles in cases of the stuff," she said, and poured them each another tot.

"You are one surprise after another, Miss Draper."

She shrugged. "Only if you are accustomed to typical English ladies."

"I assure you, I am not. You are surprising even compared to spirited American ladies."

"Spirited? Is that a compliment or critique?"

"A compliment, of course," he said.

She shrugged uncomfortably as she sipped her drink. "I only do what needs be done, Mr. James. And sometimes this work requires a strong drink to wash away the foul taste."

"Why do you do it then?" he asked, genuinely interested.

"Because there is such a great need and so few people are willing to help."

"Yes, but how did you start? Your speech and manners, not to mention your kinship to Lady Eleanor suggests you must have left a more privileged life."

Sarah buried her nose in her glass. Sam waited patiently, sensing she was trying to decide what to tell him. "The priest of the village near where I grew up suggested it."

"But why?" he asked, puzzled. "Surely your parents would not have wanted—"

"My parents did not know what to do with me. Father Gregory had me help him with those charitable deeds needed in our area to take me off their hands. I found it…soothed me to help others. He knew someone—a monk who was coming to Southwark. I agreed to come serve as an assistant. Unfortunately, the man died two months after arriving. Instead of returning home, I took over the aid society."

Sam poured her another drink as he mulled over what she'd told him, especially the part about her parents not knowing what to do with her. There was clearly much more to her story. He glanced at her face and saw that it was tense, despite the healthy dose of whiskey she'd imbibed, so he put aside his curiosity and set out to make her laugh.

"Did you know I can recite the alphabet backwards?"

"I'm sorry," she said, obviously taken aback at the abrupt change of topic. "What did you say?"

"The alphabet. I can say it backwards. Fast like. I don't have to think about each letter."

"How…unusual," she replied, clearly wondering if he was off his rocker.

"I can also say only every third letter in the alphabet."

"Why would you wish to do that?"

He shrugged. "I guess just because no one else can."

She took a small sip of her drink, a twinkle of mischief in her eye. "Can you recite every third letter backwards?"

"Huh?"

"Can you recite only every third letter, but going backwards?" she repeated.

"Why would I want to do that?" he asked with a grin.

She shrugged—something he'd learned recently from his sister that well-bred ladies did not do.

"It's just that I think I knew someone who could recite every third letter of the alphabet—or every fourth if one preferred, though I never requested it—but I've never known anyone else who could do that backwards."

"The devil, you say!"

She shrugged again and tried to look apologetic, but he could see that she was taking great delight in teasing him so he played up outrage at his supposed downfall.

"Who was this person?" he demanded.

"I believe she was, oh, six or seven years old. She came through the kitchen last spring. Why, how old were you when you discovered your...talent?"

"Ten," he replied grumpily, signaling for a pint of ale.

"Well I'm sure you were the only one in America who had mastered such a skill," she said, patting his hand in mock consolation.

Despite his delight in their verbal sparring, Sam couldn't help but notice the way his skin actually quivered where she touched him. It made him wonder what her hand would feel like on his neck, or his chest, or—

A barmaid plunked an overly-full pitcher of ale down in front of him and Sam had to swipe the resultant spill quickly from the table before it ran into his lap.

"This child prodigy," he said, and noticed Miss Draper start out of her contemplation of her fingers. "Could she whistle without pursing her lips?"

"I beg your pardon? How is that even possible?"

Sam let his lips go lax and pushed his tongue against the inside of his top teeth. He whistled a short tune.

"Your lips pursed," she retorted, staring at his mouth.

"They did not!" he argued. "They were perfectly still."

She shook her head slowly, still watching his mouth, and Sam had the strongest urge to lick his lips just to see if she would react.

"Try again," she said and he noticed her cheeks had pinkened.

He acquiesced and she shook her head no. "That not right. You're still doing this," she said and puckered her lips to demonstrate. The effect was a sensuous pout that made his toes clench in his boots.

Sam couldn't resist. She was so damn alluring with her sparkling eyes and flushed cheeks and deliciously pursed lips. He leaned forward slowly, his eyes locked on hers, giving her the chance to draw back, but when she didn't, he touched his lips to hers, softly at first, just noting their silken texture, feeling her short puffs of breath against his cheek. Then he began to kiss her in earnest, molding their mouths together, tracing the seam of her lips with the tip of his tongue.

After the briefest hesitation, she responded, parting her lips and matching the erotic play with her tongue.

He slid closer to her on the bench and cradled her face in one hand while his other slid around her back to hold her close to him.

Seconds passed…minutes, while he tasted the whiskey on her breath and discovered the underlying sweetness that was entirely her. He felt her hand come up to rest against his cheek and while it was the most tender of gestures, Sam's body reacted to it intensely. He deepened the kiss, his hand sliding from her cheek to cup the base of her head, holding it as if it were a fragile robin's egg.

A raucous chorus of laughter across the room brought both of them to their senses and they sprang apart at the same time. Sarah—there was no way he could think of her as Miss Draper now—covered her face in her hands and Sam craned his neck to see what the ruckus was about, briefly standing to see over the heads of the pub's patrons.

"It's ok," he said, turning back to her and gently pulling her hand from her face. "No one saw us."

"Then what were they— "

"Someone appears to have brought a chicken into the bar and they're feeding it ale."

"That's terrible!" she said with a frown, half rising as if she was going to go insist they stop. His hand on her arm stayed her.

"I quite agree. Everyone knows poultry prefer gin."

Her mouth twitched in a suppressed smile and she resumed her seat. He debated trying to kiss her again, but she was sitting stiffly, her hands clasped in her lap. She started to speak several times before she finally said, "I think it's time I went home."

"Of course," he said, quickly standing and offering his hand.

Once outside in the dusk, Sam offered her his arm. She pretended not to see it and he pretended not to notice her pretending. Even still, they walked in companionable silence back to her apartment.

"Oh!" She exclaimed as they drew closer. "Eleanor hasn't left yet. Perhaps she can give you a ride back into the city." She increased her pace and he lengthened his stride to keep up. They reached the apartment building and the carriage just as Lady Eleanor was coming out.

"Oh, Sarah!" Lady Eleanor exclaimed. "I'm so glad you returned before I had to leave. Mrs. Sampson shows no signs of being ready to—er," she glanced at Sam and he lifted his eyebrows, wondering what embarrassing thing Mrs. Sampson was not prepared to do.

"No sign of being ready," Lady Eleanor amended and Sam guessed that the woman in question was pregnant. "Will you check on her for me tomorrow? I'll be back the day after, but the poor dear's feet and hands and face are so swollen, I'm worried about her."

Sarah frowned and Sam had the feeling that she was suddenly uncomfortable.

"I will have Dr. Kendall look in on her."

"Oh no! Don't trouble him. I'm sure it's nothing. I'll just feel better if I know you've stopped in."

"Very well," Sarah acquiesced. "Oh, forgive me. Allow me to introduce Mr. Samuel James. Mr. James, this is Lady Eleanor Chalcroft."

"My lady," he said, bowing formally over her hand. "I believe best wishes are in order. I was at the party the night your betrothal was announced."

Lady Eleanor laughed, a bright, happy sound that brought a smile to Sarah's face as well.

"Yes, that was quite an evening. And your sister's wedding was beautiful. My betrothed and I were guests of his father who is related to your sister's husband's family. The connection is utterly convoluted! Forgive me for not offering my felicitations directly that day."

"Oh I had nothing to do with it, save paying the bill," he said. "Oh, I forgot, I'm not supposed to mention money in England, am I?"

He grinned at Sarah and she rolled her eyes, but Lady Eleanor responded, "In polite company, no, but Sarah and I have pinched pennies so many years here, it's quite normal for us."

"Eleanor, do you mind giving Mr. James a ride to his—I'm sorry," she said, turning to him. "I don't know where you're staying."

"The Cavendish Hotel."

"Of course," Lady Eleanor replied happily.

Sam paused before accepting. "Again, even though I'm American, my sister drilled into my head that unmarried ladies shouldn't—"

"Oh, yes, yes," Eleanor said, waving away his concerns. "Again, two years of living in Southwark has stripped me of my concern for many of society's rules. But fear not, Mr. James. Your reputation shall remain unblemished. As you see, my carriage is unmarked and my coachman shan't say a word. Will you Charlie?" she called over to the man holding the carriage door open.

"I try to forget everything about these trips, my lady," he said, his expression deadpan.

"You see? We shall drop you at your hotel and no one shall be the wiser. Shall we be off?"

"I thank you, my lady," Sam replied with a bow.

Lady Eleanor hugged her cousin tightly and then climbed up into the carriage.

Sam turned to Sarah, suddenly unsure of what to say. How could he arrange to meet her again?

"Shall we meet at the bank to arrange the transfer of my donation?"

Sarah licked her lips—an action that caused every muscle of his body to tighten with desire. He could still taste her on his lips and wished for nothing more than to kiss her again.

"May I send word on when I'll be in the city again? I've much to attend to here over the next few days. Oh! Unless you are departing before then?"

"I've no immediate plans to leave," he lied, for he did have a ticket booked. Suddenly, returning to Philadelphia did not feel so urgent.

"Very well," she said, her voice softening so that it lacked the firm, no-nonsense tone it normally held. She stuck out her hand tentatively. He took it, but instead of merely bowing over it, brought it to his mouth and kissed the back of it, letting his breath blow hotly over the bare skin at her wrist it for a mere second.

When he straightened, she clutched her hand to her breast as if it had been burned.

"Good evening, Miss Draper."

Chapter Five

Sarah woke with the sun the next morning feeling bright and refreshed, which was surprising considering her dreams had been full of struggles and fights and...sensuous embraces.

She washed her face with cold water, hoping it would cool the heat in her cheeks as she remembered how Mr. James had kissed her last night. And how she had returned it in full measure. She could still feel the faint rasp of his stubble on her upper lip, fancied she could smell the delicious healthy maleness of him, overlaid with the faintest hint of sandalwood shaving soap. Her hand curled, mimicking the shape of his face as she'd held it close to hers. Her tongue darted out to trace her lips as he had.

"I must be mad," she whispered aloud. It was only a kiss, no doubt brought on by two dangerous encounters and no small amount of alcohol.

Resolutely pushing thoughts of the kiss from her mind, she quickly dressed and arranged her hair in a simple plaited bun low on her neck. She gathered her basket with its collection of herbs and medicines and headed out to make several home visits before reaching the soup kitchen mid-morning.

Busy as she was, however, she found herself staring into space throughout the day, remembering the feel of his arm beneath her hand as they walked, or the handy way he had dispatched their would-be thief. And though she admonished herself every time it happened, she could not seem to prevent her brain from conjuring images of their kiss. What's worse, she found herself daydreaming about further kisses, longer embraces, and thoughts of other activities she had no business entertaining.

It was only when she burned an entire batch of rolls due to her distraction that she finally erupted in self-anger.

"Drat! Curse it to blazes!" She dropped the still-smoking rolls with their blackened bottoms on the battered worktable in the center of the kitchen.

Behind her, Ida laughed. "Why, it must be somethin' terrible wrong to make you say 'drat,' Miss Sarah."

Sarah felt the other woman peer over her shoulder.

"Eh, it's only a bit o' burned bread. I'll have the boys scrape the burnt off and we'll serve it for supper none the wiser."

Sarah smiled at Ida. "I'm just feeling a bit out of sorts today. I think I'll step outside for a bit of fresh air."

At this, Ida laughed louder. "Aye, well, let me know if you find any o' that in Southwark. I'll bottle it up and sell it, I will."

Sarah smiled again. "Yes, well, perhaps just a change of scenery."

"You do look peaked, miss. Take as much time as ye need—we've everything under control here."

In the narrow courtyard behind the kitchen, Sarah found a seat on a wooden crate and stared at the overcast sky. What she wouldn't give at this moment for a glimpse of Buckinghamshire blue sky, dotted with puffy white clouds, the smell of fresh-mown hay filling her nostrils instead of the rot of a rundown slum. She wondered what Mr. James would think of her home in Aylesbury Vale, and if Philadelphia routinely had blue skies or if it was usually gray.

"Oh for heaven's sake," she said aloud and realized she'd developed quite the propensity for talking to herself. Still, she could not afford to have her mind go wandering every five minutes. She knew what she must do to banish such fanciful thoughts. Closing her eyes, she carefully pulled out her last memory of Peter Greene after he had come home from India.

Their rendezvous beneath willow trees and beside hidden streams had been like lush stories from another land. So completely isolated were they in their hidden enclaves, it was as if they were the only two people in the world. At first, it was all they could do to wait until they'd reached their destination to pull each other's clothes off. They explored each other's bodies with wonder and delight, learning what brought the other pleasure.

After a few weeks, they began to enjoy more than just the initial passionate joining. They would take turns packing picnics or sneaking bottles of wine to share as they lay on an old quilt and watched the sun filter through the leaves overhead.

Sarah stood from her rickety seat on the crate. This was not the memory she had been seeking to quell her fanciful heart. It was the last one—that rain soaked Thursday in October.

"I can't marry you, Sarah. I can't. And even if I could, my father would never allow it. He hopes to marry me off to a woman with a title. Someone who will aid his social climbing aspirations." She remembered the crisp, distinct snap as her heart broke, the crushing weight on her chest, the months of anguish that followed.

Ahh, thought Sarah. *There it is. There's the coldness I was looking for.*

Like a late freeze after the spring flowers had bloomed, Sarah felt the distracting visions of Samuel James crystallize and harden. The flush that had warmed her cheeks all morning faded and though her hands shook, she knew she would think of nothing else this day but the work at hand.

Her prediction proved to be accurate as she finished up at the kitchen, then spent hours delivering clothing and food to various families. She checked on those patients Dr. Kendall couldn't get to, including the very pregnant Mrs. Sampson, whom Eleanor had asked her to watch over.

But when she arrived home at nearly nine o'clock, foot sore and exhausted, her single-minded focus was shattered by a note from Eleanor, whose neat but cramped and punctuationless missive instructed Sarah that she must attend a party with Eleanor the following night and that Eleanor herself would be in Southwark tomorrow to pick Sarah up.

Sarah wondered if Mr. James would be at the party and instantly dismissed the notion. The brash American did not move in the same circles as Eleanor, and besides, he was no doubt preparing to return to America any day now.

"I've borrowed another gown from Juliette for you," Eleanor said the next day as she bustled Sarah into the carriage. Juliette was one of Eleanor's closest friends and had loaned Sarah the blue satin gown on the night of Eleanor's betrothal.

"Why is it so imperative I attend the party?" Sarah asked once they were underway. "My presence has not been requested at an event in the five years I've run the aid society. Now I need attend two in as many weeks?"

"I need you there for moral support," Eleanor said blithely, taking an interest in the passing buildings. "I'm still not entirely comfortable being back in society, if you must know and you're such a calming influence on me."

Sarah studied the back of her cousin's head skeptically. "Oh, really?"

"Mmm hmm," Eleanor replied. "Also it will be good to have you visible as a face for our organization. So people are more inclined to donate, you see."

This gave Sarah pause as it did sound plausible, though Eleanor was certainly the best person to serve as the "face" of their charity. Still, something didn't quite ring true.

"Is that all, Eleanor?" she pressed.

Eleanor busied herself by digging in her reticule, ostensibly looking for something, though the tiny bag could hardly contain more than a handful of coins.

"Hmm? Oh, well, you might run into some interesting people as well. Say, perhaps, Mr. James?"

"What?" Sarah screeched. She cleared her throat and took a deep breath. She did *not* screech. "Why on earth would you think I wish to see him?" she asked in a carefully modulated voice.

At that, Eleanor finally looked at her, a mischievous smile on her face. "Really Sarah, how can you ask that. The sparks were practically shooting off the two of you yesterday. I know all too well the look of two people who are smitten with one another. If you two didn't kiss yesterday, you came very close."

Sarah blinked rapidly. Eleanor had difficulty reading the written word, but her skill at reading people was unparalleled. Still, she felt it necessary to protest.

"What are you talking about? What would give you such an absurd notion?"

Eleanor returned her question with an expression of utter disbelief. "Do you deny it?"

It was Sarah's turn to look out the window, affecting an interest in the passing scenery. "No," she finally said.

"Aha!" Eleanor exclaimed in a most unladylike shout. "I knew it! Which was it? A kiss or a near kiss?"

"A kiss," Sarah answered shortly.

"Oh how delicious! It was wonderful, wasn't it? I could tell by the stars in your eyes it was wonderful."

"I didn't have—how could you possibly—"

Eleanor laughed her musical laugh and Sarah couldn't help but smile in return.

Her cousin sobered and said, "I hope he proves to be as wonderful as that first kiss."

"Why? Nothing will come of that, Eleanor," Sara insisted. "It was a chance occurrence spurred by our being in two dangerous situations back to back. Furthermore—"

"Ah, we're here," Eleanor interrupted and hopped out of the carriage as soon as the footman opened the door. Sarah was left to sputter at an empty coach until the footman reached in to help her down.

Once inside, there was no further opportunity for private discussion with Eleanor as she was set upon by her cousin's lady's maid. Three hours later, fed, bathed, groomed, and primped, Sarah found herself downstairs in a receiving line welcoming guests to the Chalcroft home.

"You didn't tell me your parents were hosting the party," Sarah hissed out of the side of her mouth.

"I didn't?" Eleanor said blithely. "Well, you know I'm a terrible correspondent. I'm simply happy you understood there to be a party this evening. Ah, Lord Reading!" How lovely to see you this evening," Eleanor cooed to her betrothed.

Sarah watched with a smile as the two gazed at one another as if they were the only two people in the room. She felt her cheeks warm as their gaze continued over the proper clasp of their gloved hands—it seemed incredibly intimate to watch two people so in love, lost in each other's eyes. At long last, Lord Reading moved on, pausing to bow over Sarah's hand even while his gaze strayed back to Eleanor.

"Do you think anyone noticed?" Eleanor whispered in her ear.

Sarah smothered a laugh. "Only anyone with at least one eye. Don't worry," she reassured when Eleanor bit her lower lip. "It's also obvious you two are a splendid match."

"We are, aren't we?" Eleanor said with a happy sigh. "Oh, I can't bear it any longer. I'm going to find him. Be a dear and keep mother company, will you?"

"Eleanor!" Sarah exclaimed. "You can't leave me on my—" but her cousin was already across the room, linking her hand through Reading's arm and smiling brilliant up at him.

"Damn, she whispered under her breath.

She was startled by a familiar American accent behind her. "Why Miss Draper, you do show up in the most unusual places. Are you slumming tonight?"

She turned to see Samuel James, his golden blond hair decidedly *not* pomaded into place. It looked as though he'd ridden here without a hat as it was slightly rumpled. Or as if he'd run his hands through it. Or as if she had—she shook her head slightly and surveyed the rest of him. His jacket, though perfectly tailored and no doubt of the latest fashion (though truly, after five years of living in the same two dresses, Sarah had no idea what constituted current fashion), just did not fit him like an Englishman's jacket did. His shoulders seemed too broad, the swing of the coat too...casual, as if he were relaxing at home in a smoking jacket instead of dressed formally for a society event. Amazed at the fanciful turn of her thoughts, Sarah struggled to remember what he'd said.

"I beg your pardon, what is 'slumming?'"

The left corner of his mouth lifted in a half grin that made her pulse race. The man was ridiculously handsome, there was no denying it.

"Slumming. You know, like visiting the slums. Going somewhere low-brow, but for fun."

She frowned, trying not to be distracted by the dent in his cheek—was that a dimple?

"But I live in the slums, Mr. James. There's really no place 'lower' for me to go. I don't understand."

His grin turned sheepish. "I suppose it's more of an American turn of phrase. Lost in translation." He paused and glanced at the traffic jam of people in the receiving line behind him.

"Must you greet all these people?" he inquired.

"Cousin Elizabeth—Lady Chalcroft—asked me to."

"Do you know them?"

"Not a one," she admitted.

"Then you can show me where the refreshment table is. I'm famished and too American to figure it out myself."

She fought not to smile, she really did. But he was so absurd and so absurdly good looking, and so very…him, that she found herself taking his arm and guiding him out of the crush of people trying to enter the room.

"I know just where the refreshments are, Mr. James, and if we're lucky, there will still be lemon cream left. I've been given to understand it is a particular specialty of the Chalcroft's cook," she said as she navigated him through the growing crowd.

"Are you recovered from our, ah, adventures of the other day? That was an unusually eventful afternoon."

Sarah smiled at him over her shoulder. "Unusual, Mr. James? Perhaps for you. For me, it was simply another day in The Mint."

"Yes, and why is it called The Mint?" he asked.

"Because they used to mint money there back in Henry VIII's day."

"Hmm. Pity they don't still make money there."

She smiled.

They reached a table loaded with finger foods and desserts. A footman waited with silver tongs to fill delicate china plates for hungry guests.

"Oh we're in time. Here," she said, handing him a small bowl of lemon cream and a spoon.

"Is this to see if I like it?" he asked, scooping half of the bowl's contents into his mouth.

"I beg your pardon?" she said, taking a dainty nibble of the tart and sweet dessert. She closed her eyes briefly to savor the taste. Delicacies such as this were nonexistent in her daily life.

"Is this a taste to see if I'll like it and then you'll give me a real serving?"

She giggled—giggled! She couldn't remember the last time she had giggled.

"Ah, no," she said. "That's the serving."

"Pity that," he said, affecting an English accent as he looked at his empty bowl.

"Here," she said, handing him another.

"If the other day was typical of your work, how many times have you been held up at knife-point?"

She thought for a moment, watching him devour his second lemon cream with obvious relish. "Fourteen."

"Fourteen?" he asked with raised brows.

"Thirteen if you mean knife point specifically. One time a broken bottle was involved."

His surprise turned to a scowl. "Were you ever hurt?"

"Oh, no," she said breezily, though in truth every incident had left her shaken. "Sometimes my assailant or someone nearby would recognize me and I'd be left alone. There is some reward in serving a community for five years. Other times, I just let them take my basket. There's generally nothing of any value in it—a few herbs, some bandages, perhaps a small packet of food. I either find the basket dumped nearby or someone recognizes it as mine and returns it."

Mr. James' scowl had deepened.

"Twice I fought them off."

"You what?" he exclaimed so loudly that a few people turned to stare.

"Shh!" she said, and depositing their empty bowls on a servant's tray, took his arm and urged him to stroll about the room. She paused in front of a large portrait and pretended to be pointing out the artist's skill.

"One time there was a young man whose family I'd helped for years. I suppose he thought I'd be an easy mark because I would still wish to help him."

"He was wrong, I take it?" Mr. James' scowl had diminished and Sarah felt a warm glow at the admiration on his face.

"He was. I batted his knife away with my basket, grabbed him by the ear, and marched him back to his mother."

"Ah, a fate worse than prison, no doubt," he said with a smile.

"Indeed."

"And the other incident?" he prompted.

"Ah," she prevaricated. "That was the time a broken bottle was the weapon of choice, though for once I was the one so armed. I'd just returned from the city and my basket was full of some rather important medicines—things too costly for the local apothecary to carry.

"I was in a foul mood—I'd had to walk most of the way because the supplies had cost more than I'd anticipated and I had no money left for a hansom cab. I was hot and a bit frazzled and my arms hurt from carrying the basket."

She glanced at Mr. James and paused. There was an intense look on his face, one she was at a loss to describe. It seemed worried, caring, and even a bit outraged. She stared at him until he said, "Go on."

"Oh! Well, I decided I wasn't going to give up my hard-won supplies. He made a grab for my basket and knocked my bonnet askew." She smiled ruefully. "Something inside me snapped. I was so furious, I quite lost whatever self-possession I had. I dropped my basket, tore off my bonnet, and grabbed a full bottle of brandy out of the basket. I smashed it against the side of the building and advanced upon my would-be assailant with my own makeshift weapon." She laughed, still a bit surprised at herself, even a year later.

"What did he do?"

"He turned tail and ran. I still regret losing that bottle of brandy, however. Especially since I'd lugged it around all day!"

He smiled at her and she felt it like a caress on her face—on her entire body, really.

"I need to kiss you. Now."

"I beg your—what?"

"You heard me." He took a step toward her and she quickly backed up.

"Not here!" she hissed.

He smiled, a wolfish grin. "Then where?"

She glanced around and saw the open French doors that led to the gardens. He followed her gaze and said, "Go. Now."

Her every nerve was stretched taut by the time she made her way across the room. She felt a quiver of anticipation deep in her belly…and lower. She was convinced that everyone in the room knew where she was going and why, but a quick look around showed her that the party was in full swing with champagne and conversation flowing like water. No one spared so much as a glance at the misfit cousin of the Chalcrofts.

She hurried outside, unsure if Mr. James was right behind her or intending to follow at a distance. Her heartbeat was so loud in her own ears, she could scarcely hear anything else. She practically ran across the wide verandah and down the shallow steps into the torch lit gardens. Her borrowed slippers crunched on the gravel path as she raced between flower beds and sculpted hedges. At the end of one path, she paused, unsure of which way to turn. A sudden awareness ran up her spine and she spun around to see Samuel James stalking purposefully toward her.

She opened her mouth to say something—she knew not what—but in that instant, she was in his arms and his mouth was claiming hers.

As if they'd choreographed the movement, his arm slid around her waist as hers entwined around his neck. His mouth was hot against hers and there was no awkwardness as their heads found the perfect angle to seal their lips together.

She inhaled and recognized the familiar scent that was distinctly him. Champagne flavored his tongue tonight instead of brandy, but the hot wet slide of his tongue against hers was just as delicious as it had been before. Her fingers grazed along his neck to stroke his cheek; he'd clearly shaved just before coming tonight as there was no fine prickle of stubble beneath her fingertips.

He pulled her tighter to him and she willingly pressed her body against the length of his, absorbing the imprint of his long, muscular body separated from hers by only a few layers of fabric.

A rush of blood pounded in her ears, sent tingles to her extremities, awoke sensations in private areas she'd long ago banished: all proof of her body's excitement. And yet, despite, or in addition to, that excitement, Sarah felt the greatest sense of comfort, of ease. As if she'd finally found her place in the world.

The notion was disconcerting and she drew her head back to look at him. His intensely blue eyes, inky dark in the torchlight, glittered beneath passion-drowsy lids. His lips, as hers must be, were swollen and damp from their kisses. He slid a hand up to cup her face, his thumb playing across the sensitive skin of her lips. She let the weight of her head rest in his palm and he supported it easily, his gaze steady upon her.

After several long quiet moments, she lifted her head, tilting her chin up. He slowly bent down. This kiss began tentatively, slowly. A gentle exploration rather than a combustible passion. He nibbled gently at her lower lip and she delicately traced the corner of his mouth with her tongue. Her pulse, so frantic a few moments ago seemed to slow to a steady pounding rhythm, and as her fingers trailed to the pulse in his neck, she realized her heart was beating in time to his and the awareness made her body sink more completely against him. They were pressed together from knee to shoulder, her entire weight dependent on his support. The sweet perfume of a late summer garden was a subtle counterpoint to the intoxicating scent of Sam's skin. Sarah buried her face in his neck above his cravat, drawing in his scent like the bouquet of a fine wine. Her tongue darted out, sampling the taste of him and finding it just as delicious, she latched her mouth on to his neck, nibbling and kissing and sucking. His fingers clenched convulsively against her back, pulling her even more tightly against the hard length of his body. The evening air had held a slight chill when they had first come outside, but Sarah felt as though she were standing at the edge of a huge bonfire, for heat radiated off of Sam in delicious waves that enveloped her.

A delicate throat clearing registered in Sarah's ears, but lost as she was in Sam's kisses, her brain tried to believe he had made the sound. It was only when an "Ahem" followed that Sarah drew back. Sam's mouth followed her but she turned her head and saw Eleanor and Lord Reading standing a discreet dozen paces away, their gazes carefully averted. Sam's lips grazed over Sarah's jaw, nestling in the hollow beneath her ear.

She pushed against his chest and his attention immediately snapped to.

"What is it?" he whispered.

"We have company," she said, nodding in Eleanor's direction.

He moved to put Sarah behind him, attempting to shield her from further scrutiny. She smoothed a hand over her hair but had no way to know if she was presentable or a complete mess.

"Sarah, will you help me?" Eleanor called out. "I, er, seemed to have torn a flounce on my dress."

"Of course," Sarah murmured, stepping around Sam and crossing quickly to her cousin. They made their way back to the stairs and at the top, Sarah turned to see Eleanor's fiancée talking with Mr. James.

"I hope Lord Reading doesn't feel it necessary to, ah, defend my honor."

Eleanor glanced over her shoulder. "I imagine he is tearing into Mr. James quite deservedly."

"But—" Sarah began, but Eleanor continued.

"For usurping the best spot in which to steal a kiss. Do you know how difficult it was for the both of us to disappear unobtrusively? Really, Sarah, of all the thoughtless gestures."

They were near enough the windows that Sarah could see Eleanor's face and knew she was teasing. She laughed in relief.

"Yes, well, you might give me a bit of advance notice next time. Perhaps we should establish a schedule of illicit assignations to avoid mishaps like this in the future."

"Sarah Draper! Was that a joke? And a rather risqué one at that! I've never heard you tease before."

"What? That's not true! I have a sense of humor."

"Oh I know you do," Eleanor said, leading the way back into the brightly lit drawing room. "But you're always so serious. You're never the one doing the teasing. I must say, my estimation of Mr. James has increased."

"Why?" Sarah asked.

"If he was able to break through to your teasing nature, buried as it was under five years of a too-serious life, he is indeed a man of great fortitude."

Sarah felt she should argue some point, but her lips were still puffy from Sam's kisses and her fingertips well remembered the fortitude of his muscular arms and shoulders and back. Besides, she didn't want to argue. She wanted to relish the memory of their assignation. *Oh very well,* she thought. If she was honest with herself, what she most wanted was to return to that torch lit garden and resume what had been interrupted.

The drawing room seemed overly bright after the soft ambiance of the torch lit garden and the noise of conversation and music quite bombarded Sarah. She paused a moment to get her bearings, then slowly followed Eleanor to join the small group gathered around Lady Augustus—the head of the Ladies' Compassion Society who provided the majority of Sarah and Eleanor's funding.

Eleanor responded brightly to Lady Augustus' comments and answered the other ladies' questions about their life in Southwark, but Sarah was only able to nod and smile. She felt like this sparkling atmosphere was ethereal, like a dream, and her true reality was outside in the garden.

Or rather, entering the drawing room with Lord Reading. Sarah's heart thumped extra hard. He was making his way toward her.

"Ah, Lord Reading," Lady Augustus cooed as the two men approached and made their bows. "Your lovely fiancée was just telling us some fascinating stories of her work with the indigent. Are you quite sure you approve of such a vocation?"

"Not only do I approve, I support her completely. Lady Eleanor and Miss Draper's work is of vital compassionate importance."

"What a refreshing and...enlightened view," Lady Augustus said, clearly a bit surprised by his response. She was trying very hard to be ingratiating to Lord Reading. And no wonder, thought Sarah. A few weeks ago when Lord Reading was simply Alexander Fitzhugh, Lady Augustus would not have given him the time of day. Now, however, as he was the heir to an earldom, she was most effusive in her treatment of him.

Sarah's observations of Lady Augustus' and Lord Reading's interactions happened on the periphery of her awareness, however, as the skin on her neck, each breath she drew, even the fine hairs along her arms were intensely sensitive to the tall man who stood next to her, his jacket sleeve brushing against her in what she knew was no accident. She felt as if her entire body was vibrating with awareness of him.

With a start, she realized that Lord Reading was introducing Mr. James to Lady Augustus.

"And I believe you know my fiancée, Lady Eleanor Chalcroft, and her cousin, Miss Draper."

"I have been so honored, yes," Mr. James said, entirely too properly. He bowed over Eleanor's gloved hand, but when he took Sarah's, he squeezed it meaningfully and glanced up at her mischievously. She was sure her cheeks were scarlet, but she was unable to tear her gaze from his and when he finally released her hand and straightened, she felt a bit off kilter.

Conversation continued around her. At some point, a glass of champagne was pressed into her hand and she sipped automatically. It was the most disconcerting feeling for a woman so accustomed to being in control, not only of herself, but of her surroundings, to feel so utterly consumed with sensation. Mr. James—really, shouldn't she think of him by his given name after that garden encounter? —stayed at her side, to all appearances engaged in conversation with Lord Reading, Eleanor, and those partygoers who flowed through their conversation. If he stood a bit too close, his sleeve brushing her arm, his fingers occasionally stroking hers, it could be attributed to the closeness of the room, packed as it was with guests. If he had to bend his head close to speak in her ear, his breath tickling the fine hairs of her neck, his lips almost skimming her sensitive skin, it could easily be because the noise in the room made conversation a challenge. And if her complexion flushed when he murmured that he could still taste her on his lips, well, the stuffy heat of the room could surely be to blame.

At long last, Mr. James departed, though it was only at Eleanor's insistence.

"Much as my cousin and I enjoy your company, Mr. James," she said, her voice low, though she smiled and waved at an acquaintance. "In England it is unseemly for a gentleman to spend an entire evening in a lady's company. It might be best if you circulate a bit."

"Of course," he said immediately, and executed another round of proper bows before leaving.

"Goodness, the man is enamored," Eleanor exclaimed when it was just the three of them.

"Reminds me a bit of myself, actually," Lord Reading remarked, gazing at Eleanor with a grin. Eleanor responded in kind, her exquisite face somehow growing more beautiful as a smile that seemed to radiate from her soul lit her features.

Sarah suddenly felt like an intruder in their private moment and buried her nose in her champagne glass.

The rest of the evening passed rather uneventfully. Sarah shadowed her cousin as she moved about the room, visiting with everyone. Eleanor was one of those people who could talk to anyone. Young or old, male or female, she had the uncanny ability to draw a person into talking about himself. Combined with her radiant golden beauty and elegant carriage, it was no wonder she had the *ton* eating out of her hand. The people of Southwark loved her too, Sarah reflected, because Eleanor treated them the exact same way she treated dukes and countesses, with a sincere interest in every detail of their life.

Sarah admired her cousin's ability even as she recognized she could never emulate it. She was a private person by nature and her experiences with Peter Greene as a girl had only tightened the protective bubble she kept around herself. She knew she was well liked and respected by the residents of The Mint, but she also knew they respected her distance. She wondered what it would be like to be more like Eleanor, but quickly dismissed the notion. The thought of opening herself up like that made her palms go clammy It was simply how she was and nothing in her life would change that.

Until Samuel James had barreled into her life. She glanced across the room and found him watching her. He kept up an animated conversation with the crowd around him and glanced at them from time to time, but always his gaze came back to her.

Yes, she was a different person when she was with him. She was more talkative, more animated. In short, she felt more alive. And yet—

"Ridiculous," she muttered under her breath.

"What is?" Eleanor asked, causing Sarah to start in surprise. "Your attraction to Mr. James or the fact that you've pledged yourself to a life devoid of pleasures?"

Sarah stared at her cousin. "I quite enjoyed the lemon cream earlier and I shall relish the down mattress of the guest bedroom later. I wouldn't say my life is devoid of pleasure."

Eleanor gave her a skeptical look, her lips pressed flat as she waited Sarah out.

"Oh very, well. If you must know, both are ridiculous," Sarah said finally.

"I don't see why your attraction to Mr. James is ridiculous. He's handsome, clever, and successful. Not to mention his personality is as strong as yours. You could never enjoy a man who couldn't stand up to you, you know."

Sarah frowned but realized her cousin was right.

"So if your attraction is actually perfectly rational, and you've just admitted you have nothing against pleasure, what is the problem?"

"There is no future for us. He is returning to America soon and I need to focus on my work."

"He's not in America yet, is he? And his sister moved here. Perhaps he will as well."

Sarah felt her heart race at Eleanor's words and she grew irrationally angry at herself.

"He is a distraction I cannot afford," she said tersely. "I have plans for our charity now that you've secured our funding and it is going to take all of my time and attention." Sarah tried to ignore how officious she sounded.

Eleanor raised her eyebrows and said, "As to that, I have some ideas as well and they involve bringing more people into the day to day running of our services."

"What? There is no way we could pay for that—"

"I have induced a few additional wealthy patrons to sponsor my ideas," Eleanor replied archly.

Sarah felt poleaxed. She couldn't tell which emotion was stronger, her admiration for her cousin's inspiration or her resentment that she was initiating things without consulting Sarah. When she opened her mouth to speak, she realized which unfortunate emotion held sway. "You have no right to make such decisions without me!" Hot tears stung her eyes and she fought to keep her voice low.

Lord Reading glanced at her, then Eleanor, and with a small nod, moved to intercept the small group who were making their way over.

"That organization has been my life. My *life* for the past five years. I have devoted everything I have to building it and helping people." She swallowed hard, trying not to cry. The night had been filled with too many emotions. She was unaccustomed to feeling anything other than exhaustion and occasionally satisfaction at a job well done. This—Samuel James, and kisses, and lemon creams, and an Eleanor who was suddenly exerting authority—was too much.

She felt her cousin's arm slide along her back and turn her away from the crowded room. Eleanor led her to a settee where they sat. With everyone else standing, they were afforded a bit of privacy.

"Sarah, you know I would never do anything without your approval, don't you?"

Sarah sniffed and blinked rapidly, trying to keep the tears from falling. "Yes," she said.

"Our work—*your work*—is vitally important. Imagine the lives of the people you've helped over the last five years if you had not been there, helping them, feeding them, providing medical care, finding clothing, jobs, decent places to live.

"But life is so much more than work, regardless of how valuable that work is. You are entitled to more than grueling days of service, Sarah. You are allowed to be happy and enjoy life as well."

"I am happy," Sarah said petulantly, but she glanced at her cousin, whose beautiful face was filled with compassion and love and said, "Alright. Yes, I understand." She *had* been a trifle too fixated on the seriousness of life, she supposed. When she first arrived in Southwark, she'd had to eschew any distractions to simply survive and establish the charity. And then as word got out and more people sought her aid, she'd been so busy that there simply hadn't been time or energy for the enjoyable aspects of life. And then it had become habit, the constant working. It became second nature to her and she forgot what it was to sit with friends and simply chat. She forgot what it was to laugh at the silliness of life. She certainly forgot the pleasure of music and dancing. In short, she forgot that surviving and living were two very different things.

A tingling awareness lit across her skin and she glanced across the room. The ebb and flow of the guests had allowed a clear path to form between their settee and Mr. James who stared at her with a concerned frown.

Sarah dashed a gloved finger beneath her eye to make sure no tears had escaped and Mr. James immediately started toward her. She gave her head a tiny shake and he stopped, though the concern in his face said he did not wish to. Then the crowd shifted and he was lost to sight.

When Sarah crawled in bed that night, she tried to force herself to review the list of things she needed to do the next day, but her brain would not cooperate. It would have been easier for her to return to Southwark tonight, but Lady Chalcroft would not hear of it, so Sarah was ensconced in a huge comfortable bed with crisply pressed, lavender-scented sheets. But it was not the luxury of her current surroundings that distracted her from her mental recitation of the next day's duties. Try though she might to focus, her brain kept returning to those delicious stolen moments in the garden. Her skin prickled in memory of the almost preternatural awareness she seemed to have of Mr. James—Samuel she thought with a sleepy smile. As she began to drift into sleep, she replayed the moment he had seen her upset and had moved to come to her. For a careless, brash American—and a man no less—he'd proven remarkably sensitive to her emotions, she thought with a small smile. He really was not at all what she had first thought he would be. When consciousness faded into dreams, she was again in the ballroom, only this time, he crossed the room heedless of the people around him and gathered her in his arms to comfort her.

Chapter Six

Sam awoke the next morning feeling like a pubescent boy. He gingerly felt about the sheets, relieved he was not that far gone. Still, his dreams had been some of the most erotic he could remember. They had all started with that passionate kiss in the garden. He rubbed his mouth as if he might better remember Sarah's lips against his. She had felt so damn perfect in his arms, a little taller than most women so that he hadn't had to hunch over to kiss her properly. The way her body had molded to his had been exceptional as well. She had worn no stays beneath the rose-colored, high-waisted silk gown. He paused in his reflections to curse the weeks of accompanying his sister on her shopping trips for imbuing the awareness of the color referred to as "rose," as well as the knowledge that gown's waistlines were currently nowhere near a woman's natural waist, cinching in just below the breasts.

That notion brought him back to thoughts of Sarah in his arms. The thinness of her gown had allowed him to feel the lush fullness of her curves pressed against his shirtfront. He'd caressed her trim waist and back and had just grazed the side of one perfect breast when they'd been interrupted.

Sam punched his pillows into a more comfortable shape and lay back, his hands propped behind his head.

Yes, they'd been interrupted, though at least it had been by Lady Eleanor and Alex Fitzhugh—Lord Reading. (Things might have soured if some old gossipy biddy had caught them.) But in last night's dreams, he had tugged the small puffed sleeves from her shoulders until her perfect breasts had popped free. At this point, the dreams seemed to vary. He recalled one in which they'd ended up in the grass with her skirts bunched at her waist. In another, the garden morphed into a hotel room. He glanced around. Not this hotel room, but surely one he'd stayed in before. Other dreams he could only grasp an image of, or even just a feeling, an ambiance. He shook his head, unable to make the images coalesce. One thing was certain however. In all of his dreams, Sarah Draper had been the most perfect experience of his life. He wondered if she were as perfect in real life as she had been in his dreams.

He rolled out of bed and crossed the room to splash cold water on his face. Given the way she had affected him with a few kisses, he would stake his life on it.

An hour later, bathed, groomed, and in the midst of reviewing a contract with a new ink supplier he had found here in London, he found his attention wandering back to Sarah, wondering what she was doing. He hoped she wasn't having to talk another abusive husband into drinking her laudanum tea. He frowned as he remembered her stories of being robbed at knife point. For all that she was tall, she was not a big woman. If one of those ruffians had decided to take more than her coin, there would have been very little she could do to stop him.

With a shake of his head, he forced his mind back to his work. She had survived five years in Southwark. Surely she knew what she was about better than he did.

Not thirty minutes passed, during which time he was outlining his travel log about London (he grinned at his note *not* to include The Mint in his favorite places he'd visited) and he suddenly realized that the buildings in which Miss Draper worked—and no doubt lived—were dangerous. From what he'd seen, most were a stiff breeze away from toppling over, no doubt with Miss Draper in the middle of them.

He stood and began pacing. He wondered if he could convince her to operate her—what had she called it? —soup kitchen out of doors while he hired a structural architect to make sure the place was completely safe. Realizing the length of his receiving room was not long enough to properly stretch the worry out of his legs he grabbed a hat and left the hotel, determined to walk off his sudden obsession with Miss Drapers' safety beneath the leaden London sky.

He made his way down Piccadilly street, navigating his way around casual strollers and dodging running delivery boys.

Perhaps, he considered, his recollection of the few kisses he'd shared with Miss Draper were colored by the fact that he'd been without feminine companionship for nearly six months. Oh, he'd been in constant company with his sister, of course, but she certainly didn't signify.

It was entirely possible that in the six months since his last…flirtation, he'd forgotten how delightful the feminine form felt in his arms. It was conceivable he simply didn't remember how a pair of velvety lips and a silken tongue could set his very blood on fire and fuel his dreams with vividly erotic images.

But the worry over a woman—the gut-wrenching, heart-pounding fear at the thought of harm coming to her—that was new. He paused on the corner of St. James' street and waited for a break in the traffic. He thought of his sister and tried to recall if he had ever worried for her safety as much. True, Caroline had never lived in as dangerous a place as Southwark, but she'd also been a bit of a hellion growing up, climbing trees, sneaking out at night, and breaking an arm in an incident involving a ladder and a sheep that had never been completely explained.

He'd viewed such activities with an indulgent protectiveness. He loved his sister deeply but had never been terrified of the thought of something terrible happening to her. It occurred to him that if something were to happen to Sarah Draper, it would be as if he'd lost a limb. And this after only a handful of hours spent in her company!

"Oi! Look out, guv!" yelled a man carrying a huge barrel on his back. Sam realized he'd stopped in the middle of the street, blocking traffic. He hurried along, wiping his hand over a face that was suddenly clammy: not from his near-miss, but from the idea of a life without Miss Draper.

How on earth could she have come to mean so much to

him in such a short amount of time?

He quickened his pace, his strides eating up the length of block after block. Perhaps, his logical mind rationalized, his desire for her was so great that the thought of something preventing him from seeing it through to its culmination was the real issue. No, he thought with a snort. A portly gentleman in possession of an enviable set of silver whiskers frowned his disapproval of such an uncouth noise.

Clearing his throat to disguise what *had* been an unattractive sound, Sam shook his head. No. No amount of unfulfilled desire could explain his reaction at the thought of Miss Draper beneath the rubble of a collapsed tenement building or at the hands of an armed attacker. He shook that visualization out of his head and looked around to get his bearings.

Well, hell, he was practically in Mayfair, he realized. He may as well go and see his sister. He knew she and her new husband were preparing for a several month's long honeymoon, but he also knew Caroline would always make time for him.

It took him a bit of doubling back and wrong turns to find the right house. He'd only ever arrived by a coach driven by a man who knew London's streets much better than he did, apparently. By the time he arrived at the impressive grey stone manor with white marble colonnades, his stomach was growling. He hoped Caroline had her usual afternoon plates of finger sandwiches and biscuits. She had not yet acclimated to the English *ton* custom of eating supper at nine o'clock at night, though she had wholeheartedly embraced the English penchant for pot after pot of tea.

Ah well, perhaps he could induce her to have some coffee sent up, he thought as he waited for the butler to answer his knock. Or better yet, whiskey. The thought of whiskey awoke the memory of that potent distillation, shared in a noisy, smoky public house in Southwark. With Sarah. Right before he'd kissed her.

"You are a damned fool," he exclaimed, just as the door swung open.

The butler who was, rather fortunately, possessed of a rather wry sense of humor, bowed briefly.

"For which I apologize, Mr. James."

Sam grinned as he entered. "Not you, Chester. I'm referring to myself."

"Of course," Chester replied in a tone that said he quite concurred.

"There now," Sam said, handing over his hat and gloves. "Be a good, er, chap, and inform my sister I've come calling."

"Of course," the butler said again. "Might I inquire, sir..."

"Oh! I'm practicing my English lord dialect. What do you think?"

Chester merely raised his eyebrows and said, "Do you return to America soon, sir?"

Sam burst out laughing. "I do indeed. A good thing, I take it?"

"I only wish to bid you a bon voyage before you depart."

"I shall make sure to call for your blessings. Unless you'd like to go to America with me? It's a land full of adventures just waiting to happen, Chester."

Sam wondered at the glint in the butler's eyes. "Perhaps one day, sir," he said, turning to show Sam into a drawing room.

"I look forward to it," Sam replied and then noticing Caroline wasn't in the room said, "Oh Chester, can't you just show me straight up?"

"I must inquire if my lady is in, sir."

"She's always in to me!" he called to the departing butler's back. "I'm her brother!"

A few minutes later as Chester was showing him into the Trowbridge family's cozy upstairs parlor, Sam couldn't help but give Chester an "I told you so" look, which the butler blithely ignored.

"Sam!" Caroline exclaimed, coming to embrace him. "It's so good to see you."

He looked at her with a sideways grin. "It's not even been a fortnight since your wedding."

"Yes but as I'm accustomed to seeing you on a daily basis, two weeks is a long time. Besides," she said with a delighted smile. "This is the first time I've received you as Lady Trowbridge."

"Well I hope Lady Trowbridge keeps up the afternoon tradition of sandwiches. I'm about to perish from hunger."

A knock at the door behind him heralded the arrival of a maid bearing a tray laden with food.

"You say you're perishing from hunger if you've not eaten in two hours," Caroline said, fixing him a plate.

"Yes, well, it's occurred to me that I haven't eaten all day," Sam said wonderingly. He truly was a voracious eater. It was odd that he'd not realized he'd missed both breakfast and luncheon.

"Good heavens! What caused such an occurrence?"

"I was busy this morning. I've found a new ink supplier, by the way. And then I went for a walk and, well, I ended up here."

"What time did you start your walk?"

He shrugged as he ate an entire finger sandwich in one bite and reached for another. "Perhaps eleven o'clock this morning."

"Good heavens!"

"You need another English-sounding expression. That one is growing hackneyed. Ask your butler for assistance. He's quite impertinent."

"What are you talking about?" Caroline said with a frown. She looked as if she wished to check his temperature.

He waved his hand in dismissal and kept eating.

"Why did you walk so long? I take it something was on your mind?"

He was about to nod but stopped himself. He wanted Caroline's advice, but as her older brother, did not want to ask for it.

He poured himself a glass of lemonade and took a large gulp.

"Ack! That's sour!"

"Of course it is. It's lemonade."

"Yes, well, perhaps your cook should put some sugar in it.

Then it would taste like lemon cream."

Caroline gave him a look that said she feared for his sanity, but he was long since inured to such looks and finished his impromptu meal with a handful of biscuits.

"Caroline, you'll be sure to take care while you're traveling, won't you?"

"What? Why yes of course! Why would you ask such a thing?"

"Well there are plenty of dubious places throughout Europe. I should know as I publish travel journals."

"I hardly think Paris and Rome—which, as I recall, are your only published travel books—qualify as 'dubious.'"

"Two published *so far*," he clarified. I have several others in the editing stages."

Caroline threw her hands up in exasperation. "Yes, Lord Trowbridge and I shall be extremely cautious. Who knows, Vienna might prove to be a hotbed of dastardly plots."

Abruptly jumping to what he wanted to know, he asked, "What would you do if something happened to Trowbridge?"

"Wha—"

"How would you feel if, say, he were set upon by footpads and they took a dislike to him or he tried to fight them off and they stabbed him. How would you feel if he *died?*"

Caroline's eyes filled with tears and her face was deathly pale. He felt like a cad, but he had to know. He had to know if what he was feeling was like what Caroline felt for her husband.

"I would—I would wish to die as well!" she exclaimed. "I can't imagine having to live life without him by my side. Don't you remember how devastated I was those months before he arrived in Philadelphia when I'd had no word from him and thought he'd forgotten about me?"

"Yes," Sam said quietly. The spark had gone out of his vivacious sister for too long. If Trowbridge had not shown up when he did, Sam would have tracked him down and wrung his neck.

"That was before I was betrothed to him, before I was his wife, before—well before I knew just how vital he was to my happiness. To think of life without him does not bear contemplation."

Sam moved to crouch at her knee, taking her cold hands in his own and warming them. "I'm sorry. I didn't mean to upset you. I just wondered…"

"You did upset me!" she said, smacking his shoulder. "That was a horrible question to ask, and the way you did it?"

She blotted the tears from the corner of her eyes but dropped her hands suddenly. "Wait a minute. *What* do you wonder?"

"It's nothing," he said, rising to fetch another sandwich.

"Don't you take another bite until you answer me!"

He dropped the sandwich back on the plate and sat heavily on the sofa across from her, letting out a heavy sigh.

"Did you know Miss Draper has been held up at knifepoint thirteen times? Or is it fourteen? One of the times was with a broken bottle. Well really, she had the broken bottle so I'm not sure that counts. I can't remember if—"

"Who is Miss Draper?" Caroline interrupted loudly.

"Oh," Sam said, realizing that not seeing his sister everyday had its disadvantages. "She was the lady in blue you asked me about a few weeks ago. Her cousin is Lady Eleanor Chalcroft."

"Wait! Is this the Sarah Draper who runs an aid society?"

"Yes. In Southwark. The Mint, to be specific."

"Ah," Caroline said, steepling her fingers together and tapping her index fingers against her lips.

"You look positively diabolical when you do that," he said.

"Good," she replied, sounding more American than she had in months. "Now tell me everything. Miss Draper caught your eye at that ball or party, whatever the event was," she said with a flick of her fingers. "And then she captured your interest when she didn't immediately fall victim to your famous James charm." This last was said with no small amount of sarcasm.

"Now tell me, when did you see her next?"

Sam gave a condensed account of his visit to Southwark and then their encounter at the Chalcroft party.

"And you kissed her how many times?"

"I didn't say I'd kissed her," Sam said, because really, there were some things a younger sister did not need to know.

She gave him a look that begged him to deny it.

"Oh very well. Twice. Well, on two occasions."

"Multiple times each occasion," she said. It was not a question and he didn't deign to confirm it.

"And does she still antagonize you?"

"I wouldn't say antagonize," he argued.

"But she challenges you. Keeps you on your toes, so to speak."

"Yes," he said with a smile, remembering the way Sarah found a way to poke holes in his ego when he was a bit brash and made subtle jokes he had to pay attention to catch.

"You're in love!" she exclaimed.

"What? No! Of course—"

"You are! It explains everything!"

"And by everything, you mean…" he said, trying to sound blasé.

She held up a finger. "I haven't seen you in a month."

"Two weeks!" he protested but she ignored him and held up another finger.

"You didn't eat *all day.* That. Has. Never. Happened. Clearly your heart has taken over control of your body from your stomach.

"And," she said, holding up a third finger. "You all but asked me how I knew I loved Trowbridge."

"I did no such thing!" he said.

"You asked how I would feel if something dreadful happened to my husband. Which means you've been worrying about Miss Draper! Held at knifepoint thirteen times, eh? Sounds like you have plenty to be worried about, brother."

Sam slouched on the sofa. His little sister was too smart by half.

"Oh I wish I'd been at the Chalcroft's event to meet her!"

"Yes, why weren't you? I thought you sent a note round indicating you would attend."

Caroline blushed violently and affected an interest in the tasseled fringe on a pillow.

"Something came up."

"Indeed?" he asked sardonically and then shuddered in slight revulsion. There were some things he did not need to know about his sister and her husband.

She straightened her spine and said, "We are not discussing me. We are talking about you. What are you going to do next?"

"What do you mean?" Sam wondered if sitting up was worth the last of the sandwiches on the plate. He decided it was and thriftily polished them off.

"I mean, you have passage booked for home in a week. Clearly you need to cancel your ticket."

"In case you've forgotten, Lady Trowbridge, I have a rather large business to run. I've been away from it far too long as it is. There are decisions to be—"

"Sam, we're talking about the rest of your *life*. You have excellent managers. This business will survive another month without you. But if Miss Draper sets your heart on fire, you simply can't leave yet. You may never get this opportunity again."

Sam frowned at his sister's theatrics. Perhaps he had come to find out if his feelings for Miss Draper were…along the lines of what she felt for Trowbridge. But the idea that he was in love— that notion was too much. It was too—

He stood abruptly. "I must go," he announced.

"But you only just got here," Caroline protested.

"I just remembered I have a dinner engagement."

"You're fleeing because you're uncomfortable," she said flatly.

"Don't be ridiculous," he said as he bent to kiss the top of her head.

"You are the one being ridiculous. You're terrified of love because you've never allowed yourself to feel it before."

"Terrified," Sam repeated, struggling to look condescending.

"Don't you give me that look, Samuel Joseph James. I know you better than you know yourself."

"I'm sure you think you do," he said, and dodged the pillow she threw at him. The spoon that followed clunked off the side of his head.

"Ow!"

"Oh hush. That couldn't have hurt that much."

He rubbed his head and frowned at her. She visibly relented and came to inspect the damage.

"You have a hard head. You'll be fine," she said, not unkindly. She took his hands in hers. "Remember when you first met Miss Draper and she did not react to you as most women do?"

"I'm not likely to forget, especially as you keep reminding me."

"Remember I said get to know her? Let her get to know you?" When he refused to answer, she went on. "It turned out you very much enjoyed each other's company. All I'm saying is, she seems special. Give it some time to see what happens. You have your whole life to build your business, but a woman like Miss Draper only comes around once.

"I never did get the chance to warn Trowbridge you had the makings of a fishwife. Pity, he's stuck with you now."

"Yes, well, you might thank him. He's saved you from a life of listening to me tell you what to do."

"Who are you telling what to do now, darling?" Trowbridge inquired as he entered the room and kissed his wife soundly. "Not leaving yet, are you, James?"

"I am indeed."

"I hope we shall see you before we leave in a few days."

"I shall make a point of it," Sam said, shaking his brother-in-law's hand. He headed for the door, and paused in the opening. "Oh and Trowbridge?"

"Yes?"

"Thank you."

Walking down the hall, he grinned as he heard Trowbridge asking Caroline what he had been thanked for.

Chapter Seven

If Sarah had been preoccupied after her first kiss from Samuel James, she was so distracted after last night's garden encounter that her small staff at the kitchen commented on it.

"You must be feelin' puny to be starin' off into the distance like that," said Cora, the young woman who washed dishes.

Ida bustled into the kitchen carrying a load of empty plates. "She did the same thing last week. You did," the woman said when Sarah glanced over her shoulder.

"I've a great deal on my mind is all," Sarah said. "Miss Eleanor and I have received some additional funding and I'm trying to figure out how to make the best use of it here."

"Mm-hmm," Ida said, and then in a stage whisper to Cora, "The only thing sets a woman to day dreamin' like that is a man. Ain't no thought of new pots and pans gonna give a girl that far off look."

Cora's eyes widened and she hid a smile behind her hand.

Sarah frowned but realized the more she denied it, the more convinced Ida would become. Besides, the woman was completely right. With a sigh, she turned back to the list she'd been making of various supplies the families she helped needed. Decent clothing was always on the list as were shoes in every size. Blankets and bedding constantly needed replacing, and food was never in sufficient quantities.

"Poor Mrs. Sampson still shows no signs of delivering that baby anytime soon," Eleanor announced, dropping her basket and wrap on the wooden worktable and putting a kettle on to boil.

"Put a knife under the bed to cut the waitin'," Cora piped

up.

Ida shook her head. "No, the knife is to cut the labor pain. Set her on a horse to bring on the pangs."

Eleanor looked alarmed at both suggestions but pasted a game smile on her face. "Thank you, ladies, for your advice. She's not so late yet that I'm overly concerned."

Reaching into her basket, Eleanor pulled out a letter sealed with an impressive crest.

"What's this?" Sarah asked.

"It's from Lady Trowbridge." At Sarah's blank look, Eleanor clarified, "Lady *Caroline* Trowbridge. The newly wed Lady Trowbridge?" When Sarah lifted her palms in question, Eleanor said, "Goodness, you don't know very much about your Mr. James, do you? Caroline Trowbridge is his sister, you ninny."

"Oh. Well. We haven't talked much about our relations."

"No, too busy kissing, I'd wager," Eleanor whispered.

Sarah glanced at the other two women, but they were busy bickering over the best way to scrub burnt porridge out of a pot.

"Whyever would she write me? We've never even met."

"Clearly someone has mentioned you to her."

"How did you come by the letter? And what does she want?" Sarah asked.

"As I have met her recently, she thought to ask me to deliver it since she wasn't sure of the reliability of having letters delivered in Southwark. As to what's inside, I have no idea. And trust me, I tried to look, but the seal is affixed too tightly."

With uncertain fingers, Sarah broke the crested seal and unfolded the expensive stationary. Her eyes scanned the short missive and then she read it again.

"What does it say?" Eleanor asked.

"She wishes me to join her for a stroll in Hyde Park. She is most interested in learning more about our organization and the ways she and Lord Trowbridge might help."

"Is that all?" Eleanor asked, looking disappointed.

"She says Lord Trowbridge will escort us, as will her brother."

"Ahh," Eleanor said with a satisfied smile."

"I don't understand," Sarah said. "If she's interested in contributing to our organization and she knows you, why not just ask you?"

Eleanor grinned. "Because that's just an excuse. She's arranging a way for you to see Mr. James since it's nearly impossible to get you to attend society functions. Plus, I'm sure she wishes to meet in person the woman with whom her brother is enamored."

"Enamored? I wouldn't say—"

"I would," Eleanor interrupted.

"So you don't think she wishes to donate then?" Sarah asked with a frown.

Eleanor laughed. "I'm sure if you make a good impression on her, she will give you her blessings as well as her money."

"Blessings? That is assuming quite a bit, Eleanor."

"Fine. How about friendship?" At Sarah's hesitant nod, Eleanor continued. "Now I shall ask Juliette to loan you a walking gown. I shall bring a bonnet and pelisse. Or perhaps a Spencer. It hasn't been terribly cool lately, has it?"

"No. I shall wear my own gown."

"Sarah! Your gowns are practically threadbare."

"Nonetheless, a walk in the park does not require specific clothing as a ball does."

"Fine, but I'm still bringing you a bonnet. It's fine to look humble, but your current hat has seen better days and none of them recent!" Eleanor finished with a meaningful glance at the battered headgear hanging on the wall.

"It's never been the same since I was caught in that hail storm last fall," Sarah admitted, and allowed that the loan of a bonnet would be useful.

Two days later, Sarah found herself once again in Eleanor's plain coach, this time headed to Hyde park. Eleanor had insisted she wear the bonnet and Spencer she'd brought by this morning and as her fingers fidgeted, Sarah wished Eleanor had loaned her some gloves. These had a hole in the seam of the left index finger which Sarah hadn't noticed until the carriage was underway.

"Well," she announced to the empty seat opposite her, "At least the bonnet is cunning. I doubt anyone will notice my gloves."

Sarah had long since overcome any pangs of vanity caused by her meager wardrobe—it was a consequence of her vocation, after all. However, she couldn't suppress the thrill she received at wearing this hat. Finely braided straw was lined in a plum silk. A small feather plume and flower cluster matched the rich color as did the wide satin bow tied jauntily under her left ear.

Plum was also the color of the linen Spencer jacket and she had to admit, it rather brightened up her somber grey gown.

Sitting on her hands so she would stop picking at the hole in her glove, Sarah forced her attention to the carriage windows. They had crossed London Bridge and were making their way west along the Strand. It was a route that had become familiar in the time since Eleanor re-entered Society to save their funding. Once on Piccadilly, the buildings grew grander as they skimmed the edge of Mayfair where Eleanor's parents lived.

Sarah grew ridiculously nervous as the carriage pulled into the Knightsbridge entrance to the park.

"It's just a meeting with a potential donor," she told herself reasonably. Except that she knew that wasn't true.

"At least act like it is," she said sourly to her fluttering heart.

The carriage drew to a stop and Sarah waited impatiently for the coachman to open the door. Hopping down, she saw another, more elaborate carriage stopped ahead with a very fashionable couple standing outside of it. As Sarah approached, the gentleman stole a kiss from the lady and she rapped his arm with a fan, but judging from her laughter, she was not at all upset. The gentleman saw Sarah and at his word, the lady turned, a wide, welcoming smile on her face.

"You must be Miss Draper," Lady Caroline Trowbridge said, walking forward with both hands extended. She took Sarah's hand in a warm clasp and said, "It is so lovely to meet you! I hope you will forgive this rather unorthodox meeting spot. Having you to calling hours just seemed so formal."

"As I am a rather unorthodox woman, I don't mind a bit," Sarah said with a genuine smile. There was no way not to instantly like Caroline Trowbridge.

"And I quite admire you for it!" Lady Trowbridge said, linking her arm through Sarah's and guiding her to the gentleman who could only be Lord Trowbridge.

"Darling, allow me to present Miss Sarah Draper. Miss Draper, my husband, Lord George Trowbridge."

"Enchanted," said the handsome man, bowing over Sarah's hand and offering a smile, if not as effusive as his wife's, certainly as friendly.

"Shall we walk?" Lord Trowbridge invited, offering an arm to each of them.

"Oh darling, it's too hard to talk with you between us. Do be a dear and follow along."

Lord Trowbridge laughed shortly but acceded indulgently. Sarah glanced around but still saw no sign of Mr. James.

"My brother will be along shortly," Lady Trowbridge said. "He had a bit of business to attend to. I believe he was cancelling his passage to America for a later date."

Startled and absurdly glad, Sarah asked, "Why would he do that?"

"Oh he has obtained an appointment with a London publisher who is interested in reprinting some of Samuel's maps of America."

"Ah," Sarah said.

But before she could feel foolish for the surge of nameless emotion, Lady Trowbridge continued coyly, "I am certain there are other reasons as well. Now, tell me how it is you came to run your organization."

Sarah shared her well-rehearsed story of how she'd taken in interest in philanthropy, travelled to assist a missionary in his work, and taken over when he had abruptly died.

"How terribly brave of you! And what is the best part of your vocation?"

Lady Trowbridge—Caroline as she quickly instructed Sarah to call her—peppered Sarah with questions about Southwark and her work. Her genuine interest completely won Sarah over and she described her daily life in The Mint even as she deflected the more personal questions such as where Sarah had grown up and if she planned to have her own family in Southwark one day.

"Oh look! There is Sam!"

They paused by the shores of the Serpentine as Samuel James made his way across the grass toward them. His long legs ate up the distance and he strode with any easy, loose-limbed grace that made Sarah's mouth go dry with desire.

"He *is* a good looking man, is he not?" Caroline asked with sisterly pride.

Sarah gaped like a fish, unsure of how to respond.

"Oh he can be a bit of a blockhead, as most of the male species are, but he is a good man as well as a comely one," she finished. "Hello brother dear! I'd nearly given you up as a lost cause."

"You know you should never give up on me," he said, bussing his sister's cheek.

He took Sarah's hand. "Miss Draper. You don't know how glad I am to see you again," he said with a gaze that spoke of kisses and caresses.

"Mr. James," she murmured. She didn't know what her gaze might be telling him, but she was fairly confident her flaming cheeks gave her thoughts away.

She tried to collect herself as Mr. James and Lord Trowbridge greeted one another. They set off again, winding through the park, though this time, Caroline took her husband's arm which left Sarah to take Mr. James'.

"I've only just met your sister," Sarah said. "But something tells me she arranged this tableau so that you and I might, er, see one another."

"Miss Draper, I am insulted," he said with a frown and for a moment, Sarah thought she had said something offensive. "Insulted that you had to ask such a question. Surely a woman of your intelligence can recognize that *of course* my nefarious sister arranged this for that reason."

Sarah felt her lips twist wryly. "Whyever would you be insulted?"

"Well because it is a question unworthy of your canniness."

"Mmm. I think 'disappointed' would be the more accurate word. Surely my intelligence or lack thereof is no reflection on you, therefore you have no reason to be insulted."

They walked for several seconds in silence and Sarah wondered if this time she really *had* insulted him.

"You're right," he finally admitted. "Damn. And me a writer and publisher."

She smiled in delight and patted his arm in consolation. "Well, you *are* American. It is to be expected."

He burst out laughing at that and Sarah felt a warm glow fill her that was completely different from and yet equally as powerful as the hot flush that normally accompanied her reaction to him. It was as if she'd accomplished something great by making him laugh.

"Miss Draper, have you any aspiration to be an editor? I would hire you in an instant."

She felt her smile broaden and she contemplated what it would be like to work in a publishing firm, her only daily concern the appropriate usage of words like "insulted." She could even envision writing her own treatise, going to work dressed smartly, interacting with intellectuals and professionals. People like Mr. James. Well, specifically Mr. James.

But then she thought of Ida and Cora, even Mr. Thackery and the hundreds, perhaps thousands of children she had fed over the years and knew that no work would be more vital for her.

Still, it was fun to tease Mr. James.

"I'm not sure you could afford me."

"Indeed?" he asked, a delighted spark in his eyes. "Are you certain of that? I am rather well off."

"American," she accused flatly and he laughed loudly enough that the Trowbridges glanced over their shoulders, indulgent smiles on their faces as if they were an old married couple delighting in the antics of youngsters.

"Shall I hurl 'English' at you to imply that your tastes are so rich that you require an exorbitant salary?"

"Oh indeed," she said, holding up her left hand and wiggling the finger with the split seam. "Clearly my penchant for frivolous wardrobe expenditures has grown out of hand."

He captured her hand and ran a thumb over the tear. "Why do you not buy yourself a new pair of gloves?" There was no judgement in his tone, only curiosity and Sarah answered candidly.

"Oh I shall eventually. Though not pretty, these still have a bit of wear in them."

"Well I shall make a requirement of my donation that part of the money goes to such things as gloves for the head of the organization."

"No you will not!" she exclaimed, genuinely upset. Men only paid for clothing for their wives and mistresses. "That would be inappropriate in the extreme. I never use donation money for my own expenses. I have a small annuity which I use for such things. Besides—" she stopped abruptly.

"Besides what? Tell me," he persisted as she cursed herself for uttering that word. "I shall nag you mercilessly until you confess. I can tell it's something important and I've learned nagging from my sister who is a master."

Sarah frowned and bit her lower lip, but before she could respond, Mr. James held up a finger asking her to wait.

"Say Trowbridge," he called out and his sister and her husband paused to turn and look at him.

"I suppose it is a bit too late to warn you that Caroline nags like a fishwife."

"It is favorite of her many qualities," her husband said gallantly.

"I beg your pardon, George?" Caroline said with raised brows.

"Only someone who cares very deeply for me would harry me to do things like take care of myself and be a better person."

"Good answer," Caroline said, patting her husband's arm approvingly.

"Here, here," Mr. James agreed but when he glanced at Sarah, she could see he was uncomfortable. She wondered if it was because he didn't want her to think he cared…or did. The thought made her stomach clench nervously. Caroline had been watching their suddenly awkward interaction and took pity on them, gamely stepping into the conversational chasm with an animated description of her and Trowbridge's upcoming honeymoon.

They continued their walk along the Serpentine, chatting and laughing until Caroline declared that she needed a rest.

"There is a pavilion not too far away," Trowbridge said. "It has many benches and if we're lucky, the sweets vendor will be about and we can sample her iced cakes."

"Your sweet tooth is incurable," Caroline proclaimed as they made their way to the large white-columned structure.

Trowbridge bent his head and whispered in his wife's ear something that made her turn a brilliant shade of pink and giggle.

Having an idea of what he must have whispered, Sarah cast a sideways glance at Mr. James and found him studiously inspecting the low-lying clouds.

A nursemaid with her charges and a small group of young men and women were enjoying the benches beneath the pavilion and under the watchful eye of several chaperones and the structure hummed with the murmur of voices.

Caroline led them to a row of benches with the best view of the water and Trowbridge set off to find them refreshments. He returned shortly with a paper cone of small, bite-sized iced cakes, which they shared as conversation roamed from the cities Caroline most looked forward to visiting to the types of employment Sarah tried to help people find.

Lord Trowbridge had clearly never considered the plight of London's poor, growing up as he had in a life of wealth and privilege. But to his credit, he seemed duly horrified that, as he put it, "The greatest city on earth should have citizens so ill-served."

Sarah choose not to debate the merits of the "greatest city," as it was ever helpful to have members of the aristocracy feel a sense of duty to their fellow citizens.

"You see, Robert, this is why I wish to contribute to Miss Draper's cause."

Lord Trowbridge suddenly looked uncomfortable and Sarah cast a glance at Mr. James who quickly said, "Caroline, that would be a perfect way for you to spend the money in the discretionary account I set up for you. Besides, it will give you something to focus on besides shopping."

Trowbridge's face eased and Sarah realized that Caroline's dowry must have come not a day too soon, obvious love match though they were.

"Yes, of course!" Caroline said quickly. "That's a splendid idea."

The sugared treats devoured, Mr. James left to wash sticky hands in a nearby fountain, having eschewed the wooden skewers that accompanied the treats for his bare hands. Caroline and Trowbridge wandered a short way off and Sarah spied them stealing kisses beneath the low-hanging branches of a chestnut tree. She smiled at their obvious happiness but did not wish to be caught watching and so wandered down to the water's edge where several well fed ducks swam up to see if she had any offerings. She crouched down and tossed the last crumbs of her cakes to them.

It was a quiet day, with that muted heaviness that comes with low-lying clouds. Lost in her thoughts, Sarah did not immediately recognize the man's voice beside her. It was only when the man's companion laughed rather shrilly that she returned her attention to her surroundings and when next the man spoke, it was as if a goose had walked over her grave.

She looked over her shoulder slowly, willing her memory to be wrong, but as she saw Peter Greene, her heart sank in recognition.

Feeling her gaze, he glanced at her and visibly started.

"Ahh...Sar—Miss Draper," he said, and his companion looked at him expectantly.

Sarah stood and turned to face him fully, her fingers going coldly numb, her face feeling wooden.

"Evangeline," he said and cleared his throat. "Allow me to introduce you to Miss Draper. We both grew up in Aylesbury Vale in Buckinghamshire." The woman smiled politely and Sarah forced her head to nod.

"Miss Draper, this is, ah, my wife. Lady Evangeline Greene."

"It's lovely to meet someone from Peter's childhood," Lady Greene said, shaking Sarah's fingertips gingerly. "He speaks so rarely of Aylesbury."

"You don't live there?" Sarah asked.

Lady Greene tittered behind her finely-gloved hand. "Good heavens, no. We live in London year round, though I should like to visit the country at least once a year. It is so healthful, you know. Mr. Greene says he won't step foot in Buckinghamshire until his father passes, which is terribly maudlin of him, as I remind him frequently. But my dear husband is quite stubborn when he sets his mind to it. Confide in me, Miss Draper, was he like that as a young man? I'm sure he must have been."

Overwhelmed by the woman's rapid-fire discourse not to mention Peter Greene's actual presence, Sarah felt unable to respond. Finally, she forced herself to say, "I'm sure I don't know, Lady Green. I didn't really know him at all."

"Oh?" Lady Greene said uncertainly. "Well..."

"If you will excuse me," Sarah said. "I must finish my walk."

"Of course. Don't let us hold you up," Peter said quickly. His wife looked a bit put out but nodded politely.

"It was nice to meet you, Miss Draper."

Sarah turned and stumbled out of the pavilion. Behind her she heard Caroline Trowbridge calling her name but she didn't stop. She all but raced up the gentle incline, her heart pounding more from emotion than exertion. Cresting the hill, she gathered her skirts in her hands and started running. She ran until she could not breathe. Bracing a hand on a tree, she pressed the other to her side, willing her heart to slow.

Five years since she'd left Buckinghamshire. Six since she'd last seen Peter Greene. Since he'd destroyed her life with a single sentence. She could see him, full of the certainty of his freedom, able to walk away from everything they'd done without a backward glance, with no repercussions. He'd gone on to marry well—if his father was not yet dead, then Lady Greene bore a courtesy title from her noble father.

"Sarah!" Samuel James was sprinting toward her. She pushed away from the tree to flee but her legs were shaking.

Mr. James took her arm. "What's wrong? What happened?"

She swung her arm to free it from his grasp. "Leave me be!" she sobbed, seeing not Samuel but a man of privilege. A man who would leave England as easily as Peter Greene had left Buckinghamshire.

"Tell me what has happened?" he implored. "Did that man say something to you?"

Sarah laughed, the sound hysterical to her own ears. She laughed at herself as much as at the irony of his statement. Oh yes, Peter Greene had said things to her: wonderful things, sweet things. And then those brutal words: "I can't marry you," after she'd given him her very life for safekeeping.

She looked now at Mr. James and realized she was doing the same thing with him, imagining a happy ending based on a few stolen intimacies. Neither man had actually said anything about emotions, about the future, about...love.

The only difference this time, she thought wildly, was that she hadn't yet given herself to him fully. She had no doubt she would have succumbed to his charms sooner, rather than later, and her own experience as well as those of the women she worked with in Southwark should have set the warning bells off in her head immediately. Well, at least they were clanging now.

"Sarah, let me help you," Mr. James urged, again reaching for her hand.

She jerked away from him. "Leave me alone."

"But—"

"I don't want to see you again. Go back to America! I've had enough of your pretty words and pretend interest. I know what kind of man you are with your looks charm and ability to make me forget myself." There was more she wanted to hurl at him—six years of hurt she wanted to unleash, but instead she turned and ran to her carriage, tumbling in as soon as the driver scrambled down to open the door. Once it was closed behind her, she collapsed against the seat, dry sobs wracking her body.

Though she'd not done so in six years, Sarah prayed—prayed that Eleanor would not be in their small flat when she returned. She wanted only to strip off her borrowed finery, close the shutters, and crawl beneath the covers of her bed. Perhaps after a healthy dose of medicinal brandy.

But like her last prayers, this one also went unanswered, for Eleanor was in the tiny set of rooms they had shared for two years, sorting through a large pile of clothing.

"The Quakers brought by clothing and food," she said, gesturing to the stack of crates filling the small kitchen area. "I thought it a dreadful shame they carried all these boxes upstairs when we'll just have to—Sarah! What happened? What's wrong?" Eleanor jumped to her feet and crossed quickly to Sarah, putting a hand to her forehead before guiding her to a straight-backed chair.

"I'm fine," Sarah said dully, wishing her cousin would return to her parent's house.

"You're quite clearly not. Weren't you at the park with—"

she gasped. "Did Mr. James do something?" She scanned Sarah from head to toe. "Did he say something to you?"

The words were the exact ones Mr. James had uttered not an hour before, said with the exact same concern. Sarah felt her stomach clench sickeningly because as she'd calmed down on the ride home, she'd realized how wrong she had been to pin Peter Greene's flaws on Samuel James. The two men were nothing alike, and Samuel had given her no reason to suspect him of the same crimes Peter had committed. She'd cursed her foolishness as she realized that she'd crushed the tender shoots of feeling that had been growing between them.

"Please Eleanor," she said hoarsely. "Leave me be. Go to your parents' tonight."

"I don't think you should be—"

"Go!" she implored.

Eleanor's face went blank and then she turned and gathered her things. She paused at the door. "I will be gone for three or four days. My parents and I travel with Lord Reading and his father to their country estate. Will you please keep an eye on Mrs. Sampson?"

"Yes," Sarah whispered. Her cousin left and shut the door quietly behind her.

"What a bloody awful day," Sarah cursed. For now she'd not only pushed away Samuel James, but she'd hurt the only person to serve as friend, confidante, and family since she'd come to Southwark.

She paced the confines of her small rooms as it seemed the only action that kept her from jumping out of her skin. She'd always prided herself on remaining calm in times of stress—hadn't she kept her head when Mr. Thackery had a knife drawn on his wife and Dr. Kendall?

Running a charity in an area as poor and dangerous as Southwark had long since cured her of reacting emotionally to the constant stresses of life here.

When she'd first arrived two years before, Eleanor had even commented on it.

"How do you remain so serene? I am constantly on the verge of tears! People are so cruel here. *Life* is so cruel here."

"Crying and ranting will do no good here, and it very well could endanger you. You must keep your wits about you, Eleanor, not only for yourself, but for those we seek to help. People are no more cruel in Southwark than anywhere else. It's just that they live so close to the edge of survival, it is a little more obvious. Do you not think they don't see how bitterly difficult and unfair their lives are? If they think *you* consider it a hopeless situation, it will only make matters worse. And if you're in a dangerous situation—which you eventually will be, I assure you—then losing your head may cost you your life."

She didn't know if her words had helped Eleanor or not, but if her cousin had suffered from despair since, she kept it hidden well.

As for herself, Sarah hadn't shed a tear since the night Brother Joshua—the monk she'd come to The Mint to help—had died and she realized that if she didn't wish to go home, she would need to take over his charity. She'd learned self-control, cultivated an unwavering equanimity that had served her well in the turbulent streets of Southwark.

Then Samuel James had entered her life and suddenly her emotions were barely contained beneath the surface of her skin.

She stopped in the middle of the room and scrubbed her hands over her face. The late afternoon light was weak, battling clouds and smoke to barely illuminate the room. The light was grey and in its pale glow, everything else was grey as well.

Staring bleakly out the window, Sarah thought how she'd forced herself to relive the memory of Peter Greene's to squelch her feelings for Samuel James. And yet she had not turned away that night he'd kissed her in the pub. Rather, she'd drunk him in like the Scotch whiskey, only he'd been more intoxicating, bringing her body to life in ways she'd shunned for years.

After their embrace in the Chalcroft garden, her defenses had lowered even more. Who knew what might have grown between them. His sister had said he'd postponed his passage home. Eleanor had speculated that he could even be seeking to move here because of her.

But it didn't matter now, for just when she was at her softest, her most open after hours spent with Mr. James and the very much in love Trowbridges, when daydreams and fantasies had been buzzing in the heavy soft air of the park, Peter Greene had arrived to remind her what became of fantasies.

A sob tore from Sarah's throat and she doubled over, for it was not only her life he had ruined that day...

"No!" she cried, and dashed the tears from her face. Peter Greene had made a muck of her life six years ago, but she'd ruined any chance at whatever might have developed between Samuel James and her.

Overcome with the need to expend the frenetic, hopeless energy roiling inside her, she grabbed up one of the crates of food delivered by the Quakers. It was heavy and it banged against her hip, but she lugged it downstairs and for the two blocks to the building where her kitchen was located. Her arms were burning and her lungs heaving by the time she set the box in the pantry, but she returned to her flat and made six more trips.

By the time she was done, she was drenched in sweat and physically exhausted. But she had exorcised her bitter regret, at least temporarily She took a sponge bath and fell into bed where she quickly sank into a heavy, dreamless sleep.

Chapter Eight

Sam tossed back another whiskey and barely felt the burn at the back of his throat. He hadn't set out to get drunk, but as he'd downed the first glass, he couldn't help but remember drinking whiskey with Sarah in a shabby pub in Southwark. No, he corrected, that's not what first came to his mind; though he tasted whiskey in his glass, in his mind he remembered the taste of it on her lips, on her tongue. *That* memory had led to a second drink. Then his traitorous mind had brought up images of the multiple kisses they'd shared in the Chalcroft gardens. Who knew where those would have progressed had they not been interrupted by Reading and Lady Eleanor, for Sarah set him ablaze like no other woman ever had. Perhaps because his attraction was to more than just how her mouth fit so perfectly against his, her lips full and lush and mobile. It was more than how their bodies had melded together, there in the quite dark of a London garden. Though it was as if his hand had been made to fit the curve of her lower back; the softness of her breasts was a perfect counterpoint to the contours of his chest; the strength of her arms around him a perfect match for how closely he wanted to hold her. The taste of the soft skin of her neck, sweeter than any ambrosia. It

Sam surged to his feet, a remote part of his brain pleased when he maintained his balance with only the merest wobble. Eschewing his glass, he grabbed the bottle and headed for his bedchamber. Depositing the bottle on his nightstand, he crossed to the washstand and splashed water on his face to cool his ardor. He stared at the drops of water on his nose in the mirror, and forced away fantasies of Sarah lying beneath him in the soft grass of Lord Chalcroft's garden from his whiskey-soaked brain.

Because for all of the delicious physical attractions Sarah Draper held for him, the greatest pull was her very presence. The way she talked to him about real life issues, the way she was completely honest in her responses—guarded but honest. There was no coyness to her, no affectation. From the beginning, she had not been afraid to unleash her rapier sharp wit upon him, teasing him for being an ignorant American or...well, mostly for that, he thought with a half grin.

Then there was her courage: leaving a comfortable upbringing to live and work in one of London's toughest slums. But her bravery was not just about facing dangers, it was about helping people that society had cast aside as unworthy, seeing them with all their warts and flaws and still committing everything she had to trying to improve their lives.

Pushing away from the mirror, he made his way to the bed. He picked up the half-empty bottle, but paused with the neck just inches from his mouth.

Why *had* she left a comfortable upbringing? She'd said she'd been inspired to help by a priest, but that didn't ring true. No, he corrected himself, it didn't seem to be the *whole* truth. He wondered again about the man at the park today, feeling sure he'd had something to do with her past. He wished he'd been able to track the man down after he'd chased after Sarah, but he was gone by the time he walked back to the pavilion.

Then there were Sarah's words she'd flung at him like knives. He took a long pull from the bottle, then tugged and kicked until he freed himself from his boots. He sprawled back against the pillows, remembering her anguished plea to leave her alone, to go back to America, her accusations that he'd seen her as nothing more than a freakish diversion, her insistence that he was no more than a handsome face and a glib tongue. He paused, staring blearily at the canopy. *Had* she said he was handsome? He laughed humorlessly.

His reflective mood turned sour. "I know when to take a hint," he mumbled. Curse Caroline for her insistence that he try to get to know a woman's mind, try to appeal to more than a flirtatious interest. He knew where he stood with a woman who was simply interested in his looks and quick charm.

So what if those relationships burned out quickly? he thought petulantly. They were pleasant and mutually enjoyable. Unlike this wretched position he found himself in, longing for a woman who clearly did not want him around.

"To hell with it," he grumbled. He took one last swig from the bottle and snuffed out the bedside candle.

There were times he cursed his penchant for waking up early—mostly when he'd overindulged the night before. How much less uncomfortable it would be to be able to sleep off the pounding headache, pasty mouth, and general sluggishness of too much liquor. But no, he thought, swinging his legs over the edge of the bed, he was awake with the dawn.

Picking up the bottle, he was surprised to see barely an inch of liquor left in it. He'd drunk more than he'd intended and far more than he normally did. And why? he asked himself, putting the bottle down with a thunk. Because a woman he barely knew had fallen into a snit and told him to pack off to the States. Yes, they'd shared a half-dozen—oh very well, a dozen—passionate kisses. (Did anyone actually keep track of details like this when indulging in a garden tryst?) Yes, they'd been rather ground shaking. But still, he rationalized, it was just a harmless flirtation in the end.

He padded to the washstand and poured a glass of water.

Thank God he'd not made it round to the ticket offices yesterday to change his return passage. He'd been stuck in a meeting most of the morning and then it was either see to his ticket and be exceedingly late or run straight to the park and be only a little late.

He'd been ridiculously excited to see Sarah again, had even planned how to get her alone for some more stolen kisses. Surely groves of tress were to be found at the park and barring that, he could escort her home and take advantage of the long drive to

Southwark. His preference was to enact both scenarios.

Shaking his head at his reflection in the shaving mirror, he wondered what madness had possessed him these last few weeks. Well, no matter. He had come to his senses and within a week would be boarding a ship for the States where he would throw himself back into his business. Digging in his trunk, he fished out a packet of headache powder and scarcely noticed the bitter taste as he poured it down his throat. A cold bath and a hot shave did much to make him feel human again and once he was dressed, he vowed to have a productive day.

He spent the rest of the day writing down his ideas to grow his publishing house, as well as editing the travel journal he had been writing about London. If he thought about Miss Draper throughout the day, it was with a shake of his head and a forced gratefulness that he'd discovered her mercurial nature before anything had progressed too far. If he didn't entirely believe that, well, it merely required repetition. He knew how to convince himself of practically anything.

When his sister called the next day to bid him farewell, he was back to himself and completely unperturbed by thoughts of Sarah Draper.

"What happened to Miss Draper?" Caroline asked immediately upon entering the room.

"And so nice to see you too, sister," he replied dryly.

"What did she say when you caught up to her?" she demanded. He'd left the park shortly after Sarah had and he knew his sister had been dying with curiosity to ask him about it. He was frankly surprised that she hadn't beat down his door yesterday.

"She told me to take my sorry hide back to America. Which I am doing, by the way. Two days after you and Trowbridge depart."

"No! You changed your booking to remain in London longer, didn't you?"

Remaining excessively calm in the face of her rising agitation (it was a time-honored older brother practice, after all), he said, "Never got around to it. I don't really see a need to hang around once you're gone, though."

"You weren't going to stay for me! You were going to stay to further your relationship with Miss Draper! To get to know her better. To see if you two suited."

"As to that," he said, affecting an interest in a stack of papers on his desk. "Turns out I know all I wish to about Miss Draper. And no, we don't suit."

Caroline tugged her hat off and cast it onto a table, heedless for once of the mess the action left of her coiffure.

"But I don't understand! What else did she say? Why did she run off like that?"

"I have no idea."

"Something must have been terribly wrong," Caroline said, pulling off her gloves to chew on her thumbnail.

"She didn't deign to share it with me if there was," he said tightly.

Caroline stopped at his tone and stared at him. "Did you two have a quarrel?"

"A quarrel? What on earth would we have to quarrel about? We scarcely knew each other."

"You scarcely—what on earth are you talking about? You're in love with Sarah. You all but admitted it the other day."

"I assure you, I'm not," he said crisply. "Now if we may change the subject?"

But if Caroline heard him, she did not acknowledge him. She tapped her finger against her mouth as she paced in front of him. "If you didn't quarrel, something else must have upset her. Did someone else approach her at the park? Perhaps in the pavilion? Maybe someone recognized her and said something unkind. There are certainly plenty of horrid people in the *ton* who look down on her for leaving her position in society to work with the poor."

Sam frowned at his desk. He had seen that man talking to Sarah, of course. He'd even asked her about him. Had he said something unkind or inappropriate? Or perhaps commented on her relationship with Sam himself? What if he'd seen them kissing in the Chalcroft garden?

Some of Sam's righteous indignation faded at the idea that Sarah's lashing out had had nothing to do with him. He'd wondered as much during his drunken reverie, but he'd allowed his —well, his hurt pride, dammit—to turn her behavior since then into simply an irrational woman's snit.

"Did you escort her home from the park?"

"What? No, I—"

He'd stormed off after seeing that the man in the pavilion was gone. Sam hadn't wanted to face Caroline and her questions.

"You didn't?" his sister practically screeched. "You let her go home, as upset as she was, without finding out what was wrong and without making sure she arrived safely?"

It had been a while since he and Caroline had had a good sibling row and Sam jumped into the fray blindly.

"I asked the bloody woman what was wrong—I chased her halfway across the park, for God's sake! She didn't want to tell me. What was I supposed to do, tie her to a tree until she confessed?

"And she had a coachman to see her safely home! I made sure she got to the carriage, but yes, I assumed the man would do the job for which he's being paid."

"Hmmph," was all Caroline said. They glared at each other for several moments in prickly silence and Sam saw when his sister's expression melted from anger to something like compassion.

"I'm sorry, Sam," she said. "It's only that I liked Miss Draper very much and it's clear to anyone with eyes that you're quite taken with her."

He scowled at that comment, but did not correct her.

"And given our conversation a few weeks ago about how easily you give up on a woman—"

"Alright, Caroline, stop. You've made your point."

To her credit, his sister abruptly changed the subject, prattling on about a farewell dinner Trowbridge's mother was hosting in their honor.

"Good heavens, you'll be back in a few months," he growled. "You'd think the two of you were trekking off to India for four years."

An hour later, Caroline stood to leave. Sam hugged her tightly and promised to be a better correspondent.

"You're a *writer*, for goodness' sake," she chided. "Just pretend you're writing one of your travel articles."

"Yes, yes," he placated, opening the door for her.

She paused in the hallway, a small frown creasing her brow. "And Miss Draper," she began.

"Caroline—"

"Just make sure she's alright."

"I'll think about it," he said, giving her one last kiss goodbye on her forehead.

The next day found him wrapping up the last of his actual business in London. In addition to the new ink supplier, he'd set up a trade with a fellow publisher who wished to reprint Sam's maps of America and in return would give Sam exclusive distribution rights of their world maps in the States.

He was debating putting a bit more money into Caroline's bank account when he realized he'd never given Sarah Draper his promised contribution.

"Well dammit," he muttered, staring at the lockbox in which he kept his currency. He debated just going to the bank and forcing the manager to deposit the funds in Sarah's account, but Caroline's words had been clattering around in his brain since the day before.

Also, he was feeling a bit like a heel for not making sure Sarah was well. What if something was truly wrong and he'd let his ego keep him from helping her?

That settled it. He opened the lockbox and withdrew a stack of banknotes, paused, and then added a few more. He wrapped them securely in a sheet of parchment and tucked it in his breast pocket. Leaving so quickly he forgot his hat, he ran down the three flights of stairs and called for a hackney cab.

He tried not to dwell on what he would say to her—pursuing a woman after she'd given him the brush off was new territory for him—and he didn't want to overthink it. But the closer his cab drew to Southwark, the more anxious he grew to see her. He'd missed her, dammit, and they hadn't managed to sneak away for a kiss at the park as he'd planned. Perhaps if they had, she would not have encountered whatever had upset her.

If that man he'd spotted with her had said something to her, he would track him down and—

The cab drew to a stop in front of Sarah's building. As soon as he handed up a few coins to the driver, the man urged the horses on, unwilling to linger in The Mint.

Sam's heart pounded like a nervous schoolboy's, and he tugged his waistcoat in place and smoothed his hair before striding purposefully into the building. He realized immediately he had no idea which set of rooms was Sarah's and so he pounded on the first door he came to. There was no answer, nor did anyone open the second door. Finally the third door opened to his insistent pounding and a frazzled woman holding a wailing toddler on her hip opened up.

"Which is Miss Draper's door? Sarah Draper?" he clarified when the woman stared at him mutely. "She runs the aid organization here."

"I know who she is," the woman said. "I just don't know why I should be tellin' ye where she lives."

"I have something for her. Something important."

"That doesn't sound like anything good. I don't think she'll want anything you have to give." She moved to close the door and Sam stopped it with the flat of his hand.

"Hey! Wot do you—"

He held up a gold sovereign. "I assure you, what I bring is for Miss Draper's benefit."

The woman hesitated a moment and Sam cast a quick glance behind her at the squalid room. It was no surprise to him when she took the coin and gestured with her chin to the staircase. "Third floor."

"Is there a number?"

"Brown door," was all she said and closed her door firmly.

Sam fully expected to have to knock on every door on the third floor, but once there, he found one painted brown door amidst a half dozen doors of various shades of grey.

"Right," he said to himself under his breath, and strode the few steps to her door, where he rapped smartly.

A few seconds later the door opened. Sarah must have been expecting someone, for she said, "I'm so glad you—oh! Mr. James. I—what are you doing here?" Her expression, so open when she answered the door, shuttered as if someone had drawn a curtain across it.

Sam made to remove his hat and remembered he'd forgotten to put it on. "I, er, came to deliver the donation I promised. We somehow never completed the…transaction."

"Oh," she said, now seeming flustered. She tried to tidy her hair, but Sam found the escaping tendrils incredibly erotic, as if she'd just arisen from bed.

"Also I wanted to make sure that you were alright. You seemed upset the other day at the park…" his voice trailed off as he felt foolish for bringing it up. Of course she'd been upset and angry, any fool could have seen that. But he was desperately curious what had caused it. From the floor below he heard a rapid clomping sound but ignored it.

"Oh," she said, biting her lower lip. He could tell when she decided to tell him and he leaned forward slightly. "I must apologize for my, well my extreme rudeness."

"You needn't apologize. You were clearly bothered by something. I should like to assist you if I may. If that man said or did anything—"

"No, it's not that," she interrupted. "That is to say, I was upset because of him but—"

"Who is he?" Sam hissed. "American though I may be, I do not suffer offense to any woman."

A half smile tugged at her mouth but she shook her head.

"He neither said nor did anything offensive. It was simply seeing him that—"

"Miss Sarah! Miss Sarah!" A young boy, perhaps eight or nine darted up the stairs. His face was dirty, his hair stuck out in all directions, and he was wearing mismatched shoes several sizes too large for him, no doubt the cause of the clomping sound Sam had been hearing.

"Thomas! What is it? What's wrong?"

"It's me mam! The babe is coming. She sent me to fetch Miss Eleanor."

Sam glanced at Sarah and saw the color drain from her face. "Miss Eleanor is gone for a few days. You must fetch the midwife."

"She's nowhere to be found!"

"Then Dr. Kendall," Sarah insisted.

The boy shook his head. "Mam don't want 'im. She wants Miss Eleanor. Ye must come, miss," he said, grabbing Sarah's hand.

She pulled back. "I can't!" she whispered, and Sam put a hand out to catch her elbow, worried she might faint. Her eyes were huge, her pupils dilated. Her skin had a waxy sheen to it.

"Are you unwell?" he asked worriedly.

"I can't do this!" she said, shaking her head repeatedly.

"Miss, please! Mam's screaming her head off. I think something's wrong. She ain't never had pain like this before."

Sarah turned anguished eyes to Sam.

"What can I do," he asked.

She shook her head and closed her eyes briefly. When she opened them, she looked resolved, if still pale. Turning, she crossed the small room to collect a battered leather case and her basket. She closed the door behind her and followed Thomas as he clattered down the stairs. Once outside, she turned to Sam.

"I must go."

"I'm coming with you," he said firmly.

"You needn't—"

"I'm coming," he repeated and saw some of the tightness

leave her expression as she nodded.

He took the case and they raced down the street.

"I thought you were an accomplished healer," he said when they waited for a dray cart to pass so they could cross the street.

"Eleanor," she panted. "She always assists with the births."

"But surely you—" he paused as she turned terrified eyes to him. Clearly she had attended a birth that had gone wrong.

"All will be well," he said, willing reassurance into his voice though he felt nearly as much trepidation as she was obviously experiencing.

She nodded shortly and they took off again, following young Thomas who, despite his flopping, oversized shoes, was remarkably fast. He turned into a narrow alley, across a refuse-filled courtyard, and through a battered door. A shallow flight of stairs led to a dark hallway and as they ran down it, they could hear the screams of a woman in pain.

Once in the room, Sam was buffeted by a wave of heat, humidity, and the heavy smell of blood.

Suddenly calm and focused, Sarah set her basket near the pallet on which the laboring mother lay. She took the woman's hand in her own.

"It's alright, Mrs. Sampson. I'm here to help you."

"Miss Eleanor?" the woman said weakly, then moaned as another contraction hit. Sarah talked her through it, reminding her to breathe, praising her efforts.

"Miss Eleanor is away, dear, but I shall help you," Sarah said with forced easiness. Sam could hear the strain in her voice but thankfully the laboring mother was in too much pain to notice.

She looked over her shoulder to Sam. "The case," she said. He brought it immediately and she opened it, withdrawing a roll of wool felt in which a sharp knife, scissors, and needle and thread were wrapped.

"Fetch some water—we'll need to boil it," she instructed as he looked around for a vessel.

"Here, lad," he said to Thomas, but the boy was frozen in place as another contraction pulled a wail from his mother. Sam grabbed the boy's shoulder and gently shook him. "Thomas! We must help your mother."

At those words, the boy's attention snapped to Sam, who said, "We need a pot—a large one."

The boy scrambled to find one. It wasn't large and it was dented in several places, but it was clearly the best to be had.

"We need to fill it with water. Where's the nearest well?"

"I'll get it," Thomas said.

"It will be too heavy, lad."

The boy flinched as another moan tore from his mother's throat.

"I can do it!" he insisted and Sam realized he needed to fetch the water, to leave the room and the terror of his mother in pain.

Sam nodded and watched the boy run out of the room. He turned and saw Sarah struggling to move Mrs. Sampson.

"What do you need? Let me help."

"I need to sit her up a bit. It's too hard for her to push lying flat on her back."

Sam slid his arms under Mrs. Sampson and gently lifted her, but the movement brought on another contraction and he had to wait, bent over, while she dug her nails into his arm and groaned loudly.

"Will it be soon?" he asked, looking for something to prop behind the laboring woman. There was not so much as a spare blanket and so he sat on the bed and supported her against his chest.

Meanwhile Sarah had arranged the woman's skirts above her knees. She bent to examine Mrs. Sampson, gently pressing on the woman's distended belly as her other hand searched beneath the bunched skirts. After a few moments, she straightened abruptly, her eyes full of tears and terror.

"What is it?" he whispered.

She lowered a shaking hand and visibly forced her face to

smooth. "It's breach. The baby is backwards."

"Is that bad?"

Her face crumpled and she nodded her head.

"Mrs. Sampson?" she called, dashing a hand roughly across her face to wipe away the tears. "Mrs. Sampson, you must listen to me. No, no, you mustn't push!"

Sam had no idea how Sarah knew the woman was pushing, but Mrs. Sampson said, "I *have* to!"

"I know it feels that way, but you must wait as long as possible.

"Why?" Sam asked, as Mrs. Sampson clenched his hand so tightly it went numb. "There, there," he murmured to her. "You're doing a wonderful job. That's right, yank my damn hand off. There you go!"

He turned back to Sarah who was watching him with an absorbed expression on her face. "If she's not fully ready, if the —" she hesitated. "If the—if she's not open enough," she shook her head, looking at Mrs. Sampson, but the woman was lost in her own world. Nonetheless, Sam gently pressed her ear to his chest while covering the other with his hand.

"If it's not open enough, the baby's head could get stuck. Or the cord could wrap round its neck. Or—oh God, why can't the midwife be here?"

"You can do this," Sam said. Then more sharply, "Sarah! You can do this. I believe in you. And I'm right here with you." He lifted his hand from Mrs. Sampson's ear. "We'll get through this together. The three of us."

Sarah stared at him for a moment and then nodded, her expression hardening with resolve.

"We need to turn her over," she instructed.

"On her stomach?" he asked, surprised.

"No. On her hands and knees. It...it may make the delivery easier.

He nodded and then said cheerfully to Mrs. Sampson, "Come on dear, let's get you up."

"What?" she mumbled, frowning.

"Yes, yes. I fancy a dance and you shall be my partner."

Mrs. Sampson's eyes opened and she stared at Sam as if he'd gone mad. "Who are you?"

"I'm your dance partner, don't you know. Now let's roll you over."

"I can't—" She hissed a sharp inhale. "I can't dance, you fool."

"Fool? Did you hear that, Sarah? Mrs. Sampson called me a fool. Very well, then well shall simply turn you over."

Mrs. Sampson shook her head no, but with Sarah's gentle instructions and Sam's insistent tugs, they got Mrs. Sampson situated on her hands and knees. Sarah sat beside her on the bed and checked her progress. Mrs. Sampson yelled again, but Sam thought it sounded less pathetic this time and more determined.

"The baby! I see it. Gently now, Mrs. Sampson. I know you want to push, but wait as long as you can."

"Easy...for you...to say," the woman grunted and Sam patted her back consolingly.

He watched Sarah's face, intent with concentration as she tried to guide the baby out. Sweat streamed down her face in the sweltering room. He fumbled in his pocket and withdrew a handkerchief, reaching over the laboring mother to mop Sarah's brow.

"Thank you," she said without looking up. "Here it comes, Mrs. Sampson! Almost—wait! No wait! Don't push!"

But Mrs. Sampson was past hearing. Sam felt the tension in her body as he helped support her.

Sarah's hands were full of slippery baby and she struggled to hold it with one hand while she did something he couldn't see with the other.

"Please," she mumbled. "Oh ple—oh no."

Sam craned his neck to see Sarah holding the baby, its eyes scrunched tight. It had a bluish cast to its complexion and Sarah kept whispering, "Oh please, oh please," as she unwound the cord from its neck.

"My baby?" Mrs. Sampson asked wearily.

"Yes, yes, dear. You did splendidly," Sam said, helping the woman on her side.

Sarah briskly rubbed the baby's back and then delivered a dull smack with the heel of her hand and then another.

A moment of tense silence was followed by the shrill wail of the child.

Sarah released a gasping sob, which she quickly bit off, and began wiping the baby down and tying off the cord, while Sam helped Mrs. Sampson to a more comfortable position.

By the time he'd settled her, smoothing her skirts down and fetching her a cup of water, Sarah had swaddled the baby and was laying it in Mrs. Sampson's arms.

"It's a girl, Mrs. Sampson. A healthy girl."

Mrs. Sampson nodded, her eyes closing as she instinctively cradled the baby.

"Where is Thomas with the water?" Sarah wondered as she returned to the bed to deliver the afterbirth.

"I'll find out," Sam said. He stepped outside the door and nearly tripped over the boy, who was huddled on the floor, the full pot of water next to him.

Sam quickly delivered the water to Sarah and returned to Thomas.

"Is she dead? Is mam dead?"

"What? No!" Sam said, crouching down beside the boy. "She's fine. And you have a baby sister."

"A sister?" Thomas said, looking less than pleased.

Sam smothered a laugh and laid a consoling hand on the boy's bony back. Feeling the knobs of his spine, Sam frowned. He reached into his pocket and pulled out a handful of coins.

"Thomas, I need you to do something for me. I need you to take this money and fetch some food. Your mother will be hungry after working so hard and I'm sure you could do with a good meal, eh?"

"Gor blimey!" The boy said, staring at the money in his small, grubby hands.

"Run along now. Your mother will be wanting supper."

"Yes, sir," Thomas said, tugging on his forelock before running off.

Back in the small set of rooms, he found Sarah tidying up, wrapping the bloodied linens in a bundle to be washed. She took the water from him and began sponging off the baby and Mrs. Sampson. She wrapped the tiny girl in a length of linen and settled her again in the mother's arms where she began nursing enthusiastically.

Sam helped straighten the room and after Sarah brought the new mother a cup of medicinal tea, he urged her to step outside for a bit of fresh air.

He turned to her once they were in the hallway. Sarah looked like a violin string stretched to its limit, on the verge of breaking. Her dazed gaze aimlessly surveyed the landing before coming to rest on his face. They stared at one another for an infinite moment and Sam fancied he could hear when her violin string snapped. Her face crumpled and her body slowly collapsed as great wracking sobs shook her.

He had her in his arms in an instant, holding her against him as he pulled the door closed behind her. Gathering her more tightly against him, he kissed her hair and her brow in between whispered reassurances and endearments. He stroked her back soothingly, feeling each of her sobs as if it were a lash on his heart. He squeezed his eyes tight and held her for all he was worth.

When he felt her finally stir, he dipped his head to her ear and murmured, "Let me take you home."

She nodded but paused one step toward the stairs. "My basket," she said.

"I'll fetch it," he assured her, returning shortly with both basket and medical case.

"Wait," she said as they were about to exit the building. "Someone must stay with Mrs. Sampson. There," she said, gesturing to a door. Sam pounded on it until a woman answered.

"Mrs. Sampson has just delivered her baby and requires your assistance," he said, shoving the last of his coins at the open-mouthed woman.

"What's wrong with Miss Sarah?" she asked.

"She's not feeling well. Now will you see to Mrs. Sampson?"

"Of course," the woman replied. She glanced at the money in her hand. "You needn't pay me to help her. She's my friend," she said, trying to hand the coins back to him.

He shook his head. "Keep it. There may be supplies the babe needs."

The woman nodded and headed up the stairs.

Sam guided Sarah outside and down the street. He hoped he remembered the way back through the maze of streets and alleyways, for Sarah was lost in her own world, heartbroken sobs escaping her from time to time. They were only a few blocks away from her building when she stumbled. Handing her the basket and leather case, he caught her and swept her up into his arms.

"No," she protested. "I'm too heavy."

He chuckled and ignored her, striding faster down the street. "I have boots that weigh more than you. Hush, now."

He wondered what experience in Sarah's past had brought this despair on. The birth was challenging, but she'd clearly known what to do and in the end, both mother and baby were fine.

Perhaps too often in The Mint, babies and mothers were not fine and Sarah was just experiencing the relief of avoiding such a situation. Perhaps, he thought, carrying her up the stairs to her rooms, but he didn't think so. There was something deeper here, he was sure of it.

He set her down gently and opened the door. He wondered if it was pointless to lock homes in Southwark or if Sarah had just forgotten in the rush to leave.

She moved woodenly into the room, glancing at the meager furnishings as if seeing them for the first time. Finally, her gaze fell on him and the distance in her eyes focused, the lines of her face conversely softening.

"I cannot thank you enough for your help today," she said hoarsely. "I—I could not have done it without your support."

"I'm sure you would have managed just fine," he said, tucking a strand of hair behind her ear. "But I'm glad I was here for you."

She nodded distractedly, her gaze never leaving his.

"Are you alright?" he asked, his palm moving to cup her cheek. She closed her eyes and rested her head in his hand.

"No," she said shakily. "But I will be." She opened her eyes and smiled at him.

"What—" He paused, not wanting to cause her more grief, but suddenly desperate to know what was hidden in her heart. "What happened to you? Before today, I mean."

She continued to stare at him and he wasn't sure how, but he could tell the moment she decided to tell him.

"Won't you sit?" she said, gesturing to one of two straight-backed chairs.

"I don't suppose you have any of that medicinal whiskey about?"

She shook her head. "I used the last of it two days ago on a patient."

"Might one of your neighbors—"

"Wait!" She knelt on the floor and pulled a trunk from beneath her bed. Rummaging through the few items of clothing, she said, "There's medicinal liquor, Mr. James, and then there's *emergency* liquor." She held up a half-full bottle of brandy, a wobbly but triumphant smile on her face.

Her eyes were red and puffy, her hair bedraggled, and there were smears of blood on her dress. But at that moment, she was the most beautiful woman he'd ever seen and he knew, without a thunderclap or earthquake, he knew that he loved her. She was strong, smart—incredibly smart—witty, independent, and by God, she set his blood on fire with her dark hair and eyes and her lush mouth and that long, elegant neck that begged for him to nibble it.

"Perfect," he breathed. She thought he meant the brandy

and he did not disabuse her of the idea as she climbed to her feet and fetched two cups. Though his awareness had occurred as suddenly and naturally as waking up, it was still a momentous realization. He'd never been in love before. Not like this, not where he knew that not a day would go by without her being the first thing he thought about upon waking and the last thing before falling asleep. And how he wanted to make sure that when *she* slept, it was in his arms. Every night. All in all, it made him feel a bit lightheaded.

She handed him his cup and he was glad to see she'd been generous in her portions. He took an initial slug just to feel the soothing burn, then resolved to sip the rest. He wanted to concentrate on what she was going to say, because he knew it was going to be monumentally significant.

Chapter Nine

Sarah took a gulp of the brandy and willed herself not to cough. She'd had the bottle for four years and only brought it out in times of the direst need. Today definitely qualified. And if she was going to tell Sam her story, she would need all the courage she could muster. She took another sip and then a deep breath. Sam looked at her expectantly and there was a wealth of compassion in his eyes. Compassion and…something else. Something new. Something that made her heart pound faster than normal.

She shook her head to clear it of such thoughts. She needed to concentrate as she told her story. The story she'd not told another soul.

"There was a man at the park the other day," she began.

He nodded shortly. He'd asked her about Peter that day.

"His name is Peter Greene. We grew up together."

"Where?"

"Aylsebury Vale. In Buckinghamshire. We were childhood friends. We played together, kept each other's confidences. Peter had always dreamed of joining the army. His father bought him a commission and he went to India. When he came back, he wasn't the same. His parents thought he'd been a commissary officer, but he had volunteered for the front lines. He was… different when I first saw him. He had seen, and I suppose done things that haunted him."

Sam nodded in understanding, rolling the glass idly between his hands.

"His first night back he had a, well I suppose you would call it an attack. I stayed with him until it passed." She stared past Sam's shoulder, seeing again that evening with the gaiety of the party behind them so at odds with the terror and panic Peter was suffering just a few yards away. Rousing herself, she told Sam how she'd convinced Peter to share his experiences with her, how she'd brought her dog on walks with him so Peter could tell him the things he couldn't bear to tell her.

She paused to take another sip of brandy before describing how Peter had kissed her, how the halcyon summer days had slipped by, how she'd thought herself so in love with him that she didn't hesitate to give herself to him. She was immersed in the memory, but for the first time she felt removed from it. As a result she was able to focus on Sam's reaction as well. She saw his fingers tighten on his glass but when she glanced at his face, he forced the tense muscles of his face to soften into a small smile of encouragement. There was no judgement in his gaze and she relaxed slightly.

"I assumed we would marry, of course. We'd been friends since we were children. My family is not noble, but we are established gentry and related, as you know, to the Chalcrofts. There was no reason to suspect I would not be a suitable bride. His father was only a baronet, not so very high above us. But he said he couldn't marry me. Or anyone, I think he said, but then he admitted his father had plans for him."

"He turned you down because you couldn't elevate his family?" he asked incredulously, his blue eyes flashing with indignant fire.

"I don't think that was his primary reason, though he said it was his father's."

"Did he tell his father what he did to you?" Sam said sharply, standing and clenching his fists. He looked ready to pummel something and Sarah smiled that he was so indignant on her behalf.

She shook her head and caught his hand, tugging until he sat again.

"Let me finish," she said gently.

"I apologize." He reached for the brandy and splashed

more in each of their cups.

When he was settled, she continued. "I think he was still greatly shaken by the war. I believe I helped him, of course, but perhaps there were things he'd never been able to tell me, terrible things that prevented him emotionally from being able to be—" her voice cracked, but she forced herself to finish. "To be a father."

"Didn't he consider that before he—wait! Do you mean to tell me…did you become pregnant?"

She nodded, her inner gaze looking back six years to that grassy meadow where she'd met Peter Greene for the last time until three days ago.

After their initial kiss that day, she'd stopped him as he'd moved to unbutton her gown.

"What's wrong?" he'd asked. "Oh bother, is it that time already?"

"No, it's not that. Peter, wait!" she said when he resumed trying to undress her. "I must ask you something."

"You know I find you beautiful," he said, nuzzling her neck until she finally pushed him away.

"Peter, we are going to be married, aren't we?"

That brought him up cold. "Someday," he finally said, hesitantly

"Well, we need to make it someday soon," she said with a joyful smile. "Because we're going to have a baby. Everyone knows we've been courting since you came home. A short betrothal will raise no eyebrows and it won't be the first eight-month baby in Aylesbury."

She took his hands and gazed up at him with all the love in her heart. She felt the tremors in his hands before she realized his whole body was shaking.

"What's wrong Peter? I admit, I am a bit nervous as well, but it was to be expected with all of our 'afternoon walks'."

"I can't," he said, his voice a dry rasp. "I can't be a father. I can't bring a baby into this world. If you knew what I'd—oh God!" he cried, flinging her hands away. He turned to the nearest tree and bashed his head against it.

"Peter! Stop! What are you doing? Why are you saying this? We can't take it back! I'm pregnant. Don't you understand?"

"We'll give it away. Find a family to take it in."

"I'm not giving away our child!" she cried hoarsely.

"I can't—I won't," he stammered. Then, "My father—"

"But if you told him—"

"I can't marry you, Sarah," he said, his despair crystallizing. "I can't. And even if I could, my father would never allow it. He hopes to marry me off to a woman with a title. Someone who will aid his social climbing aspirations."

"Son of a bitch!" Sam cursed through his teeth, surging to his feet again, too full of ire to sit still. "Goddamn son of a bitch. But—"

Sarah held up her hand to stop him. "That's not why I… broke down today." She took another sip of brandy.

Sam paced back and forth to expel some energy. Then he sat back down yet again, clearly prepared for the worst.

"I wandered the woods after Peter left. I was so distraught, I didn't know what to do. How would I tell my parents? I was their only child. They would be devastated." She remembered how terrified she'd been—not just of the darkening woods, but of the future which only this morning had seemed so bright and yet now felt as terrifying as the wild animals she imagined were lurking behind every tree.

"It started to rain. I'd walked much further than I'd realized. A priest from the next shire over found me." She smiled, remembering Father Gregory rooting around in the woods for truffles, his brown robes blending into the forest. He was the first priest she'd ever met, having been raised in the Anglican church and she had no idea how to address him. She had stared at him mutely, knowing her horror was evident in her face.

"Are you alright?" he'd asked in a low melodious voice.

"I—he—" she'd choked, the tears streaming down her face.

"Come, sit down, child," he said, gesturing to a moss-covered stump. He rummaged in his basket and withdrew a stone bottle of ale that he handed to her. "Drink."

She shuddered at the taste but he urged her to drink a little more before handing her a chunk of dark bread.

"I'm not hungry," she gasped.

"I know. Take a bite anyway. You look thoroughly done in."

She nibbled a bit and he nodded approvingly.

"Are you lost?" he finally asked.

"I—I suppose so. I hadn't really thought about it, but—" she glanced around. "I have no idea where I am."

"You're in the woods just east of Lower Hartwell. Where did you mean to go?"

"Oh! I...I live near Aylesbury Vale."

"You've had a good long walk then. There's no need to cry. I'll see you safely home."

"That's not why I was crying," she burst out.

"No?" he asked and she realized he already knew that. "What can upset such a lovely young lady on such a beautiful summer day?"

She burst out crying again and though he was a stranger and a priest who would surely judge her for her sins, she found herself unburdening her story to him. He patted her consolingly on the back as she told him about Peter, about the baby, and about him claiming he could not marry her. She couldn't seem to stop the words from pouring out. When she was done, she felt exhausted and a bit amazed that she'd so readily confessed her shame to this priest.

Father Gregory sat silently for several long moments and she braced herself for a sermon on sins and pride, knowing she deserved it and yet dreading it nonetheless. And yet nothing in his expression indicated judgment. When he spoke, his tone was thoughtful.

"And you say he spent several years in the Army?"

She nodded, bending over to wipe her nose unceremoniously on the hem of her skirt.

He sat in quiet contemplation a while longer, nodding

now and then to himself.

"We shall have to inform your parents, of course," he said gently.

This brought on a spate of new tears as she considered how devastated her parents would be. They'd assumed Peter would marry her as well, though they'd had no idea that marriage would become a necessity.

"They'll be so ashamed. I'm ruined. I shan't be able to show my face in public again!"

He nodded some more. "As for that, let's take one step at a time. First, let's tell your parents. They may have some ideas you've not been able to consider."

"They won't! They'll despise me—"

"Let's reserve judgment on that front. They may yet surprise you. However, if they do not have any ideas for this delicate situation, I may be able to help."

"How could you possibly help?" she'd cried. And then, "Forgive me. I'm not myself."

"Of course you're not," he said, patting her hand.

"I'm such a horrible person! I knew better. I should have—"

He shook his head. "You are simply young and in love. And perhaps a tad naive, but there is certainly nothing evil in that."

At the surprised look on Sam's face, Sarah nodded. "Yes, I'd been expecting fire and brimstone as well. But Father Gregory was different. He took me back to my parent's house and helped me explain everything. My mother reacted much as I'd expected. She grew faint and then looked at me as though she didn't recognize me. I knew she could not believe a daughter she had raised would have acted so improperly. My father wanted to call out Peter—"

"Damn right," Sam interjected.

She shook her head. "The scandal would have been even worse. And my father was not—there's no way he would have survived such a thing. No, Father Gregory convinced them to keep me at home and act like nothing had happened. I was to conceal my pregnancy for as long as possible and once I could hide it no longer, they were to send me to his care. Lower Hartwell is a much poorer, smaller village. There is scarcely any interaction between it and Aylesbury Vale. He would put out that I was his widowed sister, come to keep house for him."

"Is that what you did?" he asked, scarcely believing that such a plan would work.

She nodded. "I was scarcely showing, but my parents didn't want anyone to suspect, so they sent me off several months before the baby was to have been born. They...well I suppose they just couldn't reconcile what had happened to who they thought I was. I'd never caused them trouble, always behaved exactly as I should."

"It's not like you killed someone," Sam said scathingly.

She smiled. "I may as well have for the scandal that would have ensued if word got out. My parents wouldn't have been able to show their faces. Their position in Aylesbury Vale was so important to them. They rarely traveled to London for the season. Their church and their friends was everything to them."

"But you were their daughter!" Sam protested.

She smiled sadly. It was nothing she hadn't thought time and again. Her parents were who they were and she'd had to let go of her disappointment long ago or suffer miserably every day.

She took a sip of brandy and continued her story. "I helped Father Gregory feed the poor in the area. His was the first charity kitchen I'd ever heard about." She smiled grimly. "I was terribly ignorant of the plight of many of England's poor before then."

"I imagine it was quite a shock," Sam said.

She laughed humorlessly. "After Peter's pronouncement, nothing seemed to shock me. But yes, it did take some getting used to, the idea that a child might go to bed hungry because their parent didn't earn enough to feed them. I realized just how sheltered a life I had lived up until then. It made me feel terribly guilty."

Sam opened his mouth to speak but she forestalled him. "Let me finish while I have the courage," she pleaded. He nodded shortly. "I worked there for three months until—" her voice cracked again and she waited a moment, collecting herself.

"The reason I knew how to deliver Mrs. Sampson's baby is because my baby was also breech. The midwife—she was so kind. She worked so hard. She had me in every conceivable position. She fed me herbal teas. She even—she even reached inside me trying to turn the baby. But in the end—"

Sarah broke off, suddenly pulled to that sweltering tiny room where she had spent so many hours laboring. The midwife had been so calm and so reassuring. She talked Sarah through each contraction, urging her not to push as long as possible. She had counseled and cajoled, encouraged and pleaded endlessly. Eventually, however, Sarah's body had taken over and she had pushed for all she was worth. Even now she didn't know how long it actually took; it could have been an hour, it could have been all night. All she remembered was how quiet the midwife became when the pressure finally released and the babe was out. Sarah had waited for the tell-tale cry but she didn't hear anything. She tried to push herself to her elbows but she was simply exhausted and fell back against the sweat-soaked sheets.

"My baby," she'd mumbled through dry lips.

The midwife was hunched over the baby, chafing its feet, rubbing its back. After several minutes, she wrapped it gently in a blanket but she did not bring it to Sarah.

"What's wrong?" she cried. "Why won't you bring it to me?"

The midwife turned then, a sorrowful expression on her lined face. She brought the tiny bundle to Sarah. "The child is with God now," she said gently.

"What? No!" Sarah tore back the blanket and looked down at the perfect little face searching for movement but it was still and peaceful, waxy pale like a porcelain doll with perfect little lashes against rounded cheeks. She could not believe that after all that work, all that pain, after everything she'd been through the baby was—

"It happens sometimes when the babe comes backwards,"

the midwife said sadly and tucked the blanket back over the babe's face before tending to Sarah.

With a visible start, Sarah pulled herself back to the present. Samuel was looking at her with a look of intense grief. She forced herself to smile reassuringly. It had been five years ago, after all, though the ache was always there, waiting to be recognized.

"The rest you know. Father Gregory asked if I wanted to help a fellow monk establish an organization in The Mint. When Brother Joshua died so suddenly, I stayed on. There was nowhere else for me to go and it felt good to be helping people. I learned how to cook for a hundred people. I began learning the healing arts. We could never keep a doctor longer than a few months.

"But I was never able to deliver babies. When Eleanor arrived, she was fascinated with childbirth and she became such a good midwife. She can even handle the ones that don't end well, but I've never been able to do it."

"Until today," he reminded her, reaching out a hand to her. She took it and clung to it like a lifeline.

"Thank you for helping me," she said.

"I didn't do anything."

"You did," she insisted. "You kept me…present. You helped me focus."

"You were amazing. You *are* amazing, Sarah."

Tears filled her eyes but did not spill over. "I'm not—"

"Shh," he said, and gently pulled her to her feet. He stepped closer until he was only inches away. He could see the rapid rise and fall of her chest as she clutched his hand tightly. He tilted her chin up with his other hand and waited until her eyelids fluttered open.

"You are amazing and strong and beautiful. God, you're so beautiful."

Her lips parted on a sigh and he slowly lowered his head, touching her mouth with his own in a kiss that was infinite in its slowness and tenderness.

She remained still as a statue for several moments and then her lips began to move under his, tasting, caressing, exploring. He drew her more tightly to his body, feeling the length of her against him, fusing them together with heat.

Slowly, oh so slowly, he drew his tongue along the seam of her lips, dipping in to sip her sweetness. Her hands slid around his waist, and up his back while he cradled her head in his hands, his thumbs stroking along her jaw.

He tasted of brandy and wet warmth, the hot press of his mouth stimulating and comforting at the same time. One kiss melted into the next in a slow, languorous dance. Eventually, inexorably, the fire grew, stealing their breaths so that they had to pause, panting, between kisses.

Sarah felt her heart racing in time with her labored breath. She felt overwhelmed with sensation, as if suddenly the very weight of her clothes was too much to bear, the air too thick to inhale. She opened her eyes and studied his beautiful face: broad brow, spiky golden lashes, laugh lines at the corners of his eyes, full, firm mouth still damp from her kisses.

As if feeling the weight of her gaze upon him, he opened his eyes and she was lost. It was as if time froze. There was no world outside the connection between them. His eyes were dark blue, faceted with lighter shards, sensuous beneath heavy lids. But there was more—she felt like she saw her very own soul in the depths of his eyes. The connection was so powerful and so startling that it brought tears to her eyes.

So this is love, she thought. It was so much more than the infatuation she'd felt for Peter Greene. It was based on a connection so much deeper than what she could do for him. It made her feel as if she knew everything about him, as if she could read what was at the core of him and knew that it fit the core of who she was like a puzzle piece. She knew that their bodies would fit perfectly also. She realized suddenly that the physical and emotional craving she was experiencing need not be denied.

She drew back from him slightly and began to undo the long row of buttons that ran from her neck to waist. She heard his breath catch, saw his lips part as he watched, transfixed as she reached the last button.

His gaze sought hers and he whispered, "Are you sure?"

She nodded. She had never been more sure of anything in her life.

Chapter Ten

Sam froze when she pulled back from their embrace, cursing himself for moving too quickly when she clearly needed space after her heart-wrenching confession. But then she started unbuttoning her gown and he stopped breathing. His eyes were transfixed as each tiny button slipped free of its moorings. She reached the last button and her fingers parted the placket slightly. He gasped. Or perhaps he sucked in a breath. He wasn't sure. He looked up into her beautiful dark eyes and said, "Do you mean—No, Sarah. I won't risk you—I mean, you needn't—" he stammered.

She smiled, a tiny smile, really, but one filled with power and knowledge and a hundred other emotions he hoped he was reading correctly. "I know," she said, and turned to rummage in her medical case. She withdrew a small sponge and a dark brown bottle, the contents of which looked like an oil of some sort as she applied it to the sponge.

"Turn around," she whispered and he complied. He heard the rustling of skirts behind him. "Is that—"

"It should prevent a babe. I learned of it from an old midwife who had, I believe, been a prostitute in her youth."

"Do you dispense it to many women here?"

She touched his shoulder and he turned around.

"Not as many as you would think. Preventing pregnancy is seen as wrong as having a baby out of wedlock. It is judged more of a sin than having a dozen children who will starve for want of adequate food. But since I'm already as damned as a soul can be—"

"You're not—" he began, but then saw she was smiling.

"Are you sure?" he asked again.

She nodded and he was lost.

He closed the small gap between them and drew a finger delicately down the gap of her gown, feeling her shiver deliciously. There were only a few inches of bare skin before he encountered her threadbare chemise and he brought his other hand up to spread the fabric of her gown apart, gently nudging it off her shoulders. She wriggled a little bit and the dress puddled to the ground.

They'd not lit a candle or lamp, but a stray shaft of setting sun cut through the gloom outside to bathe her in its golden glow. It had been cloudy for days and the soot of Southwark ensured a haze even on sunny days. Sam took the radiant beam as a clear message that he was meant for this woman.

She pulled the pins from her hair and thriftily set them on the table.

"I can't afford to lose any," she said with a wry grin. "I have just enough to keep my hair in place. If I lose anymore, I'll have to wear braids like a little girl."

She shook her hair down around her shoulders in a dark cascade of silk. Sam ran his hands through the strands, letting the thick locks spill from his fingers like water. If he had his wish, she would never put this wealth of hair up again, but since that wasn't possible, he made a mental note to buy her a dozen racks of hairpins so she wouldn't have to worry about losing one again.

"You are so incredibly beautiful," he murmured, mesmerized by the sight of her flushed cheeks and kiss-swollen lips. She looked so different than when she was in her somber gowns, dispensing aid around The Mint or even when she was bedecked in satin at a *ton* event. And yet she was still those women as well as this tempting seductress and Sam loved every single facet.

She started to say something but hesitated.

"What is it?" he urged, tracing the soft wings of her brows with one finger.

She licked her lips and he felt his body's response in every muscle.

"When you look at me like that...I feel beautiful."

"I will never let you doubt that feeling," he said before he kissed her again. With each touch of his lips against hers, he better learned the contours of hers, more quickly discovered what brought her pleasure. Sarah turned her head after a moment to whisper huskily, "I fear you may be overdressed."

"I fear you may be right," he agreed with a grin.

Stripping his jacket off so energetically his arms got stuck, he flapped about like an overlarge bird and she giggled while she unbuttoned his waistcoat.

"Here, let me help," she said, straightening his sleeves and freeing his arms.

He slowed down while unwinding his stock—no sense in choking himself, but tore his shirt off so rapidly he split a seam.

The shirt had not even hit the floor before her hands were on him, tracing the muscles of his chest, caressing the hard contours of his shoulders and upper arms.

The slow sensuous spell that had captivated them just moments before was suddenly eclipsed by a fiery need to touch and kiss and consume.

He took her lips in a desperate open-mouthed kiss while her hands gripped his back and tugged at his waist, pulling him closer against her.

He grabbed the strap of her chemise too roughly and the shoulder seam split.

"I'll replace that," he said against her mouth as he pulled the torn garment from her body. But then all thought fled his mind as his hands found the satin skin of her breasts.

She tore at his breeches, shoving them to the floor, then pulled him to the low bed. He followed her down, his lips never leaving hers.

He felt a shiver of pure delight at the skin-to-skin contact and paused for just a moment to savor the exquisite sensation. But then she ran her tongue along the rim of his ear and he lost control. He'd never experienced that before in any of his previous sexual encounters, but suddenly his hands were shaking as he ran them down the length of her body and he could not kiss her deeply enough. He needed more of her. He needed all of her. He shifted so he was atop her and felt her legs part in welcome.

She must have been in the same feverish grip for her hands traced the muscles of his back and buttocks frantically, her fingernails scratching him in a sensation that was a bit pain and even more pleasure. Her lips kissed every part of him they could reach, her teeth grazing his shoulder and neck with a sting that made him shudder with desire.

He could wait no longer. He surged forward, but in their passionate slipperiness, he missed. And missed a second time. He felt like a green lad with his first woman, but when she smiled at him and took him in hand, he laughed softly and waited while she guided him home.

That was different too.

Never had he enjoyed laughter amidst passion and never had he experienced the sensation that he was home, seated deep inside the woman he loved. He stared at her and she too must have felt the intense connection, for her eyes glistened and she reached up to caress his cheek.

He could wait no longer at that. He surged forward again and again and she met his every thrust. Their bodies were new to each other and they hadn't yet learned the nuances of moving together, of most efficiently finding pleasure, but there was an intensity to their union, a pure, passionate joining that far outweighed any awkwardness.

Within minutes he felt her body tense, her face a beautiful mask of ecstasy before she convulsed with pleasure, a keening cry that was his name escaping her lips. With a guttural groan, he pulled out, spilling himself in the most soul-wrenching release he'd ever experienced.

"Just in case," he murmured into her hair and he felt her nod.

He collapsed against her and she wrapped her arms and legs tightly around him. A moment later he started to move. She hugged him tighter.

"I don't want to crush you," he whispered in her ear.

"Stay," she murmured. And he did.

"Very well, move," she laughed a minute later.

He chuckled as he rolled to the side and gathered her close to him. "I told you I was heavy," he murmured into the silken hairs at her temple. She snuggled up against him, her head resting on his shoulder and her arm around his waist. She draped a leg over his hip and sighed in obvious contentment.

He felt a silly grin curve his mouth, but he couldn't contain it. Everything about her just felt so *right*. He'd never encountered such a feeling before and he wanted to savor every moment. But it had also been a rather intense day, what with helping deliver a baby followed by amazingly passionate lovemaking, and as Sarah's breathing slowed and deepened, he felt his own eyelids droop. Funny that, he thought, he was usually never able to sleep with an empty stomach, but what with helping deliver a baby and some amazingly passionate lovemaking, they'd never got around to actually eating anything...and in spite of his hunger he fell asleep.

It was his stomach that woke them several hours later. Or rather, it woke Sarah.

"What was that?" she asked, lifting her head and straining to listen.

"Wha—" he mumbled, still mostly asleep. Then his stomach grumbled again. Loudly. "Oh, that."

She giggled and he smiled, pleased to have been the reason for her mirth. Somehow he didn't think she'd had much reason to laugh over the last six years.

Another rumble of complaint renewed her laughter and she said, "Very well, we can't have you starving to death." She crawled over him to get out of bed and at the feel of her naked limbs sliding over his, Sam was tempted to ignore his hunger pangs for a few more minutes. But then she was out of bed and he could only listen for her movements in the pitch black of the room.

He heard her light a candle and the room was bathed in a pale glow. Not enough to read by, but just enough to admire her naked form as she rummaged through the cupboards for food. Her skin was golden in the feeble candlelight, her only covering the dark silk of her hair. He felt his body respond to her, and it was all he could do not to cast aside the plate she brought back to the bed.

"There's not much," she said apologetically. "I usually eat at the kitchen."

"It's perfect," he said, and again he did not refer to the food she offered.

She crawled back in bed and Sam was delighted that she appeared unselfconscious of her nakedness, though her long hair cloaked her breasts and sitting amidst the rumpled bedclothes, the rest of her was lost to sight as well.

They split a small meat pasty, a bit of cheese, and an apple.

"Here, I'll eat that," he said when she moved to put the core back on the plate.

She laughed as he devoured the last of the apple. "What are you, a horse?"

"My sister claims my preference for apple cores is because I'm an ass, not a horse."

She laughed again and he felt his heart swell with the sound.

He reached to brush a crumb from the corner of her mouth, but thought better of it and used his tongue instead.

She caught her breath, then turned her head to match her lips against his.

She tasted of apple and he couldn't get enough. The metal plate clattered unheeded to the floor as they joined together in a union of heat and desire.

It was the early light of pre-dawn when next Sam awoke. Sarah was tucked against him, her hands curled under her cheek, a stray tendril of hair obscuring her eyes. He gently smoothed the hair back and marveled at the spiky dark crescents of her lashes as they lay against her cheeks.

He would never tire of staring at her, he decided. The smooth oval of her face, the faint scattering of freckles on her nose, the silky straight slashes of her eyebrows, the delicate pout of her lips; he was mesmerized by all of it and he wanted a lifetime to study it.

A lifetime, he thought again, his caressing hand stopping abruptly. Did that mean—he waited a moment, holding his breath, listening for the answer.

Yes, his heart said. Then again more loudly in case he hadn't heard it the first time. *Yes!*

His hand as it resumed stroking her hair trembled a bit, but he'd never felt steadier.

Another hour passed during which time he watched her sleep, holding still so he wouldn't disturb her, even as his right arm went to sleep under her head.

His mind whirled with plans and ideas, his heart full of thoughts for the future.

He flexed his hand, trying to restore the feeling to his arm and the bunching of his muscles caused her to stir. He froze, watching as her eyebrows lifted just before her lashes fluttered and she opened her eyes.

"Good morning," he murmured.

She smiled a slow sleepy smile that made his heart contract.

"Good morning," she replied, her voice husky and warm.

He kissed her slowly then pulled back to watch her finish waking. She yawned and stretched, her breast popping up over the sheet. And he just couldn't help it. He had to have her one more time. He caught the errant breast in his hand and she squeaked as he lightly pinched her nipple. The eyes she turned on him were dark with need, her pupils dilated pools of black in the dark brown of her irises.

She grabbed his head and directed it down. He obliged, laving her breast and nibbling the tender underside. She gasped at that and pushed him onto his back, climbing atop him

He was willingly at her mercy and gave himself over as she took the lead and rode him. With her atop him, it was harder to pull out in time. He had to physically lift her when all he wanted to do was bury more deeply inside her and stay there forever. Nonetheless their culmination was intense and sweaty, and afterwards, Sarah collapsed against him, panting as heavily as he was.

They dozed a few more minutes before Sarah stirred, lifting herself up to gaze down at him. She dropped a final kiss on his nose before reluctantly sliding off him. She poured water from a pitcher into a shallow basin and began washing.

"I've got to get to the kitchen. We received a big food donation from one of the Quaker groups in the city and I've got to see that none of it goes to waste."

He watched her gather up her torn chemise and fetch a needle and thread.

"I'm sorry about that," he said, sitting up. He had assumed she had a spare and felt bad he wasn't able to replace it before she needed to wear it.

"You needn't be. It's not the first time it has torn. At least this was in the pursuit of something enjoyable." Despite her worldly statement, she was blushing and didn't meet his eye as she quickly repaired the garment.

"Nonetheless, I intend to replace it. With silk, I believe."

"Silk? That won't last me a month!" she said, finishing her stitching. She bit the thread off and pulled on the chemise, which was nearly transparent it was worn so thin.

"I'll buy you a dozen then. Two dozen! And a crate of hairpins," he continued as she retrieved her carefully stored pins and bound up her long locks.

"That's really not necessary," she said shortly.

"Oh but it is," he replied, pulling on his own clothes and envisioning an entire wardrobe that would best suit her coloring. Perhaps all those hours accompanying his sister for her trousseau fittings were going to pay off. "I've unwittingly become quite the expert on ladies' fashion thanks to Caroline."

"I don't want you to buy me anything!" she snapped.

He looked up from his failed attempts to tie his cravat. "What? Why not?"

"Despite my actions, I'm not a—a prostitute whose favors need to be bought," she said, her voice hoarse with suppressed tears.

He dropped the cravat and looked up at her in shock. "What do you mean? Of course you're not. That never even—I would never think—oh, blast it!"

He stared at her and she looked down, fingering the worn folds of her chemise.

"I apologize," she said in a low voice. "I—I'm a bit sensitive about such things."

He crossed the few steps to her and took her hands in his.

"You've nothing to apologize for," he said. "I just want to take care of you. I won't buy you hairpins or chemises if you don't want me to."

She glanced up with a wry quirk to her full lips and it was all he could do not to kiss her. "I never said anything about not buying me hairpins."

He laughed and then gave into temptation, kissing her thoroughly.

A short time later found them both dressed and standing awkwardly outside her building, trying to delay their separation as long as possible.

"I shall—" he began at the same time she said, "You must—"

They laughed and he said, "You first." She shook her head.

"It was nothing. What were you going to say?"

"I want to know when I can see you again. May I come this evening?"

She bit her lower lip and for a heart-stopping moment, he thought she would say no. But then she nodded, her eyes bright with anticipation.

"Damn," he said.

"What is it?" she asked with a frown.

"I should have kissed you goodbye upstairs."

"There wasn't a goodbye kiss amongst all of those earlier?"

"Certainly not! Those were good morning kisses and getting dressed kisses and because-you-were-standing-there kisses."

She smiled a wide, beautiful smile that lit her entire face up. "Of course they were," she agreed. "Yes, it is a pity one of them wasn't a goodbye kiss. Still, perhaps it's for the best."

"Oh? Why is that?"

"Well this way, we won't say 'goodbye.'" She leaned very close to him and whispered, "We'll simply say, 'I can't wait to see you soon.'"

He grinned at that, feeling as if the world were the most perfect place just then. "I can't *wait* to see you very soon," he murmured in his deepest, huskiest voice.

She shivered visibly. "Me either," she whispered, staring at his lips.

They were frozen in place, staring at one another until a man driving a cart yelled at a group of boys who'd run across the street in front of him, startling his nag.

Sarah jumped and blinked rapidly. She looked at him one last time and then turned and walked quickly down the street. Sam watched the sway of her hips until she was lost to sight, then took off in search of a hackney coach.

His day was a whirlwind of planning and arranging. And no small amount of shopping. He scarcely stopped to eat, but by the time the sun was making its way to the western edge of the city, he'd accomplished all he'd set out to do and was looking forward to presenting his achievements to Sarah.

Once in The Mint, he gathered his armload of packages from the coach and struggled not to drop them as he made his way to her door.

"Good heavens!" she exclaimed upon opening the door to the pounding of his booted foot. "What is all of this?"

"Supplies," he said succinctly, looking around the room for

the largest horizontal surface. Deciding on the bed, he quickly crossed the room and dumped his armload.

"What kind of supplies?" she asked, standing beside him.

His hands now free, he turned and grabbed her to him, kissing her with an intensity that felt like he'd not seen her for months instead of hours.

She held still for a moment in surprise, then returned his embrace with equal fervor. Several long minutes later, they surfaced for air, their faces flushed, their eyes sparkling.

"Now *that* is a proper hullo," he said with a grin.

"Indeed," she replied primly and he laughed aloud. He stared at her face, soaking in her beauty, delighted to see that the tenseness he'd noticed before about her eyes and mouth was gone, the former soft and happy, the latter lush and damp from his kisses. He grinned at her, absurdly pleased to think he was the reason for her relaxed and open expression.

He finally, reluctantly, released her to show her what he had brought.

"Where is that—aha! Here it is." He opened a tin and presented her with a delectable assortment of sugared biscuits.

"Take one," he urged, gesturing with the tin. She reached a hesitant hand forward to select one. He grabbed three and popped them in his mouth as she slowly nibbled hers. She closed her eyes in enjoyment but they flew open as her tongue registered the flavor.

"Lemon!" she exclaimed.

"Yes," he said, grabbing two more. "I was inspired by that lemon cream dessert at the Chalcroft's. However, unlike that night, we can eat as many as we want!"

She laughed and he took advantage of her open mouth to feed her another biscuit. This caused her to laugh harder, spraying crumbs everywhere, which elicited still more giggles.

His love for her swelled to the point he could scarcely breathe. He wanted to make every day like this for her, full of laughter, free of worry.

She struggled to chew the mouthful of sweets while stray

giggles escaped. While she did so, he reached into another packet and pulled out a bottle of wine, which he uncorked. He found the cups they'd used the night before and filled them. He handed her one and she took a swallow, her eyes widening at the rich taste.

"Good, isn't it?" he asked, and she merely nodded as she sampled it again, letting it roll over her tongue, smooth and fruity.

He watched her, taking a greater delight in her enjoyment of the treats than he was in the actual taste of them. He couldn't wait to pamper her every day. He caught her in between sips and stole a kiss, finding the wine even sweeter when tasted on her tongue. He chuckled at that. He was completely besotted.

"What do you find amusing??

He smiled at her. "I'm happy."

She lifted her eyebrows. "Is that such a rare occurrence?"

"No, of course not, but this is a different kind of happy."

She gazed at him, a soft smile curving her mouth. "I understand. I'm happy too."

Tell her, a voice in his head urged. *Tell her you love her now.* He didn't doubt the feeling, and was reasonably sure she felt the same. Still...he'd never said the words to a woman before. It was a bit unnerving.

"What else is in these packages? Don't say it's all wine and biscuits!"

He sprang into action, simultaneously relieved and disappointed to have been distracted from his thoughts.

"As promised, a rack of hairpins," he said, presenting the papers of crimped metal.

"This isn't a rack," she exclaimed. "It's—well I don't know what it is, but it's at least a lifetime supply!"

"You have a wealth of beautiful hair," he said, tugging a tendril loose from her chignon. "I wanted to make sure I got enough. Besides," he finished sheepishly. "I have no idea how many pins a lady actually needs to do her hair. It is perhaps the only thing I didn't learn while I accompanied my sister on the endless shopping trips leading up to her wedding."

Sarah still seemed amazed at the multitude of pins, but she laughed and said, "I thank you for these. They shall come in handy." She studied him for a moment. "That was kind of you to take your sister shopping. Most unusual, as well."

He shrugged. "She didn't really know anyone here other than Trowbridge himself and I couldn't bring myself to send her out on her own."

"Lord Trowbridge's mother couldn't lend guidance?"

Sam grimaced. "She wasn't initially supportive of their engagement. I didn't trust that she would give the best advice."

"What possible fault could she ascribe to your sister? Caroline is perfectly lovely!"

"Well, she can be a pain in the arse as well, but the dowager had never even met Caro when she voiced her opposition." He briefly explained about Lady Trowbridge's objection to an uncouth American until she had realized she needed that American's hefty dowry to save her estate.

Sarah grimaced. "It's ridiculous, the nobility's abhorrence to marrying anyone other than a fellow Englishman. We are all essentially the same people, after all."

"I'm glad to hear you say so," he murmured under his breath.

"How many shopping trips did you accompany your sister on?"

"At least a thousand," he said with a heavy sigh.

"One thousand?" This with a disbelieving raised eyebrow.

"Easily a hundred."

"One hundred shopping trips? That must have been quite a trousseau."

"Well it felt like a hundred," Sam said with an unrepentant grin.

"I'm sure it did. Perhaps you can take heart in the knowledge that you undoubtedly know more about current ladies' fashion than I do."

"As it so happens," he said, reaching yet for another package. "I do know a thing or two."

He quickly unwrapped the bundles, revealing a pile of chemises and undergarments, three ready-made gowns, and an assortment of hair brushes, perfumes, gloves, and shawls.

He turned to look at her expectantly, but her expression was not at all like when he'd handed her the hair pins.

"What is all this?" she asked in a low, hoarse voice.

"Uh…just a few things I picked up. For you," he clarified, and then felt like an idiot. They clearly weren't for him.

"I asked you not to buy me garments. I am able to clothe myself." There was no inflection in her voice and he was starting to wonder if he had made a crucial judgment error. Striving to keep his voice soothing, he said, "I know that you do. I simply wanted to give you a gift. I thought you would want them for when we travel. To, er, the States."

At that her blank expression cracked and she looked at him in shock.

"I beg your pardon?" Her voice was like the crack of a whip. "What do you mean, 'When we travel to the States?' When did we make plans to do such a thing?"

He saw her fists clench and in his head, he could hear Caroline chiding him for arranging people's lives without their permission. Trying to backtrack, he said, "It's only that I, er, assumed we would marry after…" his voice trailed off as he glanced at the bed.

"But you didn't assume you would need to ask me?"

"Well of course I was going to ask you," his own temper sparking. "I just didn't expect you to overreact to a few pieces of clothing quite so strongly."

Her eyes widened and she sputtered, "Overreact? Overreact?! Do tell me what I should have done when you purchase personal items for me after I specifically told you not to, and then offhandedly toss out that I'll be leaving my home for another country and, oh yes, we will be marrying. You're right. I don't see how I could have reacted to all of that with anything but delight!"

Put that way, Sam decided, she had a point. He felt a bit of a fool and no small part of the bullying boor his sister had accused him of being time and again.

"Look, this all came out wrong. Allow me to begin again. What I should have started with was telling you I lo—"

"Telling me again!" she shouted. "May God save me from another man telling me what to do. You are all alike."

He knew she was referring to Peter Greene and the comparison to that gutless cad infuriated him. "All alike, are we? What, did Greene ask you marry him, then? Did he intend to save you from yourself?"

"Save me from myself?" Tears sprang to her eyes and though it seemed she wasn't even aware of them, they hit Sam like a punch to the gut and he instantly regretted his impetuous words.

"Sarah—" he said, reaching for her. She knocked him away and covered her face with her hands.

"Please just go," she said.

"Sarah, I love you," he said urgently. "Please let me—"

She jerked her head up at his confession, but he could see in her eyes that she didn't believe him. She thought he was only saying it to convince her to do his will.

He turned his hands up in supplication, at a loss for what to say to untangle the mess he had made of his proposal.

She stared at him with eyes that bespoke pain and betrayal and for the life of him, he couldn't understand how he had earned such a look.

He picked up his hat and left the room.

He attempted to contact her the next day, sending a carefully worded letter trying to explain his intentions, but she returned it, crumpled and unopened.

Two days later he left England.

Chapter Eleven

For Sarah, the next weeks passed in a fog, and she went through her days like an automaton. If the ladies at the kitchen noticed her distraction, they must have realized it was not the same as when she'd been lost in sensual daydreams of Samuel James, because they said nothing, just stirred the porridge she'd begun cooking before it boiled over, and fetched the bread she'd put in the oven before it burned.

She alternated between two emotions: there was the anger at the high-handed way Sam had tried to take over her life. Buying her clothes after she'd specifically asked him not to was bad enough, though she probably would have gotten over that rather quickly. She fingered the frayed cuff of her grey dress. Her wardrobe *was* in a deplorable state and it was only her pride that had made her balk when he first mentioned buying her a silk chemise. She'd taken care of herself for five long years, pouring every cent she raised into her work and relying on the annuity from a tiny inheritance she'd received from an aunt for her personal living expenses.

She thought of the silk chemises with a shiver of longing. She had packed away all of the clothing he'd brought and the memory of the way the chemises had rippled against her fingers, nearly transparent in their delicacy, had made her long to try one on. But the notion seemed to smack of hypocrisy and so she'd folded them neatly and tucked them into the trunk with the other garments.

She should have distributed all of the items to those women she knew who needed new clothes more desperately than she did. She knew she should have and she hated herself for keeping them. She just…couldn't part with them. Not yet, anyway.

But when she thought of how he'd planned an entire life for her—in America, no less—without even consulting her. Her blood still boiled when she thought of that. She had barely recognized that she loved him when they tumbled into bed. And if that wasn't the most reckless thing she'd ever done, she didn't know what was. With Peter Greene at least, she'd been a naïve young girl certain her childhood sweetheart would marry her. She frowned as she bound the twisted ankle of one of her kitchen helpers.

What on earth had made Sam think that he could present her with marriage and leaving her home as a *fait accompli*? Did he really think she would jump for joy and so readily turn her back on everything she had built here?

And that led her to the emotion that had been battling the anger in her heart and in which she spent as many hours: bitter regret.

She regretted her instant indignation; she regretted her angry words. She regretted not giving him the chance to propose to her properly, and she regretted not opening that letter. Mostly she regretted not telling him she loved him in return.

As the days progressed into weeks, the anger had less and less a hold on her and the regret spread like a bruise over her heart, not actively painful, but an ever present ache. She would be fine all day, focused on her work or one of the dozen new projects Eleanor had suddenly acquired funds for, and then something, some memory or sound, a scent would bump that bruise and her eyes would flood with tears.

For a woman who had prided herself for five years on maintaining a stoic front, it was humbling to suddenly become an uncontrolled watering pot. "Oh bother!" she said on one of those inconvenient occasions. "It's not as if I even knew him that long," she chided herself. She'd been taking inventory in the storage room of the kitchen. The influx of donations thanks to Eleanor's work with the Ladies' Compassion Society meant that they were now able to put food boxes together for families instead of only feeding them at the kitchen, but she was still figuring out a system to ensure that each box had complementary ingredients.

Suddenly she recalled the first time Sam had kissed her in the back of the pub, and before she knew it, she was wondering what life would have been like if they'd not had such a ridiculous row...if they had figured out a way to be together. To marry.

"Dammit," she said, wiping a tear away with her knuckles.

"Goodness, Sarah!" Eleanor exclaimed, entering the room. "Did you hurt yourself?" Eleanor appeared to be looking her over for injuries.

Sarah turned aside and cleared her throat. "No, of course not. I simply got something in my eye."

"Of course," Eleanor said, unconvinced. She'd never mentioned the tiff they'd had—or rather, the spat of foul temper Sarah had vented on her cousin—and if Eleanor wondered what had become of Mr. James, she forbore from asking. Still, she had been unusually solicitous of Sarah lately, which unfortunately had the effect of making Sarah feel even more maudlin.

She simply had to snap out of this mood. She shook her head and turned a bright smile on Eleanor.

"There now. I seemed to have blinked it out. What brings you in today? I thought your mother had conscripted you for wedding business?"

"I am here on official wedding business," Eleanor declared. "I am here to officially invite you to the festivities. There's even an engraved card here somewhere," she said, digging in the rather large reticule on her wrist.

"Oh and to inform you that you are to accompany me to the modiste on Thursday. My mother insists that you have your own new gown for the wedding instead of borrowing another of Juliette's. Not," she added hastily, "that Juliette minds one bit. She insisted I relay that message."

Sarah smiled. Lady Chalcroft had always been uncomfortable around Sarah when she would donate old gowns and jars of jam, but since Eleanor's two-year absence and recent return to her family, Lady Chalcroft had been positively maternal toward Sarah, insisting she dine with them weekly and urging Sarah to take better care of herself.

It had been years since Sarah had experienced a mother's concern and the effect was as unnerving as it was heartwarming.

"Very well, but it must be something I can wear more than once. It must serve—"

"Yes, yes," Eleanor said, laughing. "It must serve many purposes to be worth the expense."

Sarah smiled grudgingly. She supposed she *had* become a bit of a stick when it came to economizing.

Giving into a spontaneous urge, she hugged Eleanor tightly.

"Good heavens! What is that for?" her cousin asked, a delighted grin on her face.

"To thank you for being a wonderful cousin and even better friend. And to apologize for my mercurial moods of late."

"Firstly, you are welcome and the thanks are returned. And please don't even mention the latter—we are all entitled to the occasional mood swing. Although," she added, needlessly straightening the jars on the shelf in front of her. "If there's anything you'd like to talk about, I'm always here to listen."

Sarah reached over and squeezed Eleanor's hand. "Thank you," she said, surprised to discover her throat had tightened with emotion. "Perhaps...soon. Now tell me all your wedding news while I finish my inventory lists."

As Eleanor chatted about where she and Lord Reading would live—*not* in Mayfair they had agreed—and how Reading had been so supportive of Eleanor's work here and a dozen other details that only a woman deeply in love would think to remark on, Sarah found the angst that had been plaguing her releasing. The tension in her brow softened and she felt a sort of peace settle over her heart. She couldn't quite explain how it happened, but for the moment at least, her regret eased even as her heartbreak softened.

By the time Eleanor finished, Sarah was able to turn a genuine smile on her cousin and say, "I am so very happy for you."

She could tell Eleanor wanted to mention Samuel James, and Sarah appreciated her restraint. She had meant it when she said she would open up to her cousin soon, she just wasn't quite ready.

Distracting Eleanor with one of her favorite topics, Sarah said, "Now tell me what style of dress I should order for your wedding." And so their next hour was filled with talk of muslin and lace and waistlines and hems.

Three weeks' time found Sarah in St. Paul's Cathedral, dressed in her very own stylish gown, the most lovely shade of pale aqua. Long white gloves encased her arms and aqua slippers peeped beneath her hem. It was a gown she would never be able to wear in Southwark, but she would be able to wear it to the weekly family dinners Lady Chalcroft insisted would continue after Eleanor's marriage. And she would perhaps be able to wear it to the meetings with donors Eleanor insisted were important.

Since Eleanor's return to society when she single-handedly saved the funding for their charity, she had become an unstoppable force in taking their organization to another level of service and efficiency. She had nearly doubled their contributions and tripled their staff. Sarah actually now found herself with the occasional free day, something to which she still wasn't entirely accustomed.

Sarah wasn't exactly sure how Eleanor did it all. Certainly she'd reduced her time spent in Southwark, but she was still there three or four days a week, assisting Dr. Kendall, working in their kitchen, and checking in with those families with whom she had developed a particularly close bond. The remainder of her time was spent in the city, meeting with other aid organizations and potential donors.

And then there was Eleanor's betrothed, Alex Fitzhugh,

the recently named Lord Reading. She didn't know when Eleanor managed to spend time with him, but as he took his place in front of the altar, Sarah could tell he was not a man deprived of love. He stood as if he were ten feet tall, watching the back of the church with a hungry intensity that reminded Sarah of how Sam had looked at her the night they made love.

She swallowed back the tightness in her throat, blinking rapidly to avert any dampness in her eyes. Today was about Eleanor, not for memories of a fleeting love.

And yet, as she stood with the rest of the congregation to watch the bride walk down the aisle, she felt the whisper of her silk chemise against her skin and all she could think about was him. It had seemed a crime to wear her old chemise beneath the beautiful new gown and so she allowed herself to wear it this once. And as she'd slid it on, she felt as if he were embracing her.

Sarah wrapped an arm around her midriff and closed her eyes as Eleanor and Reading said their vows. For the millionth time, she wondered what would have happened if things had been different between her and Sam. If he'd not been so bloody managing, if she'd not been so proud.

She found herself in the same pose that evening at a ball hosted for the newlyweds by Eleanor's father-in-law, the Earl of Southampton. She was standing well back from the dance floor, having turned down an invitation to waltz. Nonetheless, she had a perfect view of Eleanor and her new husband as they swirled around the floor, their bodies in perfect time. They gazed at each other as they danced as if there were no one else in the room and the sight brought tears to Sarah's eyes. She quickly shut them before they spilled, and as a result did not see Eleanor's mother approach.

"Your time will come, dear," Lady Chalcroft said in a gentle voice.

Sarah's eyes snapped open and she lowered her arms.

"I—I only...That is, the sight of them is quite moving."

Lady Chalcroft watched her daughter and Reading as they finished their dance. "Yes, they are happy. But two years ago it was quite a different story, as you know." A shuttered look crossed Lady Chalcroft's face and Sarah knew she was thinking of the years Eleanor spent hidden in Southwark, and her parents thought her lost for good. The elegant lady took a deep breath and turned back to Sarah.

"The point being, that I'm sure during that time, Eleanor despaired of any relationship between her and Reading—Mr. Fitzhugh at the time—working out. And yet look at her now." She gestured across the room where Eleanor was now sipping from a glass of champagne under the adoring gaze of her husband.

"I suspect all is not lost with Mr. James," Lady Chalcroft said, her gaze still on her daughter.

Sarah started and stared at Lady Chalcroft's serene profile. She wondered just what the woman knew—Sarah hadn't even confided her feelings for Sam to Eleanor...

"But he's returned to America," she finally said.

"Good heavens, do ships only sail in one direction? His sister lives here now, after all. I'm sure he'll find himself on this side of the ocean soon enough."

Sarah smiled. Lady Chalcroft made "this side of the ocean" sound like "the proper side of the ocean."

"And if he does not or if he finds himself too stupid to realize what he's lost, there are any number of eligible men in London, dear."

Sarah started to protest but Lady Chalcroft kept talking.

"Perhaps not a nobleman—not that you aren't worthy of one, mind you, but they can be a trifle high in the instep about their wives, er, running a business, as it were."

Sarah smiled at Lady Chalcroft's euphemism.

"But there are any number of men who should count themselves lucky to have a wife such as yourself, and who will be tolerant of your activities."

This time Sarah had to bite the inside of her cheek to contain her giggle.

"Now, no more turning down invitations to dance. You

must get out there and at least pretend to have a good time. Then one day, you'll find you actually are." Something in Lady Chalcroft's voice made Sarah think she spoke from experience, but before she could ask her about it, the woman patted Sarah's arm and sailed off.

Sarah was impressed that Lady Chalcroft—Cousin Elizabeth, she reminded herself—had noticed her turning down invitations, then realized there was probably very little Lady Chalcroft failed to notice in her little kingdom of the *ton*. Deciding it was best to follow her directive, Sarah smoothed her face into what she hoped was an inviting expression and began a slow perambulation around the room. She was halfway through her first circuit when she heard her name called.

"Miss Draper! I say, Miss Draper!"

She turned to see Lord Trowbridge approaching her, a wide smile on his face. She felt a moment's hesitation at seeing Samuel James' brother-in-law, but as he stopped in front of her with a proper bow, Sarah saw nothing but sincere good will in his face.

"Lord Trowbridge," she said with a curtsey. "How lovely to see you."

"Indeed," he agreed. "Caroline and I have missed seeing you. My wife was quite taken with you. She felt she'd met a—how did she phrase it? —ah yes, a kindred spirit."

"Oh...I've been, er, quite occupied with the aid society."

"Oh yes, of course. Quite the undertaking, that."

"It is," Sarah agreed, just to keep the conversation going. She wasn't sure why he had sought her out. "Where is Lady Trowbridge?"

"Oh she's about here somewhere," he said with a wave of his hand. "She is the most sociable woman I've ever known. I say, would you care to dance?"

Sarah hesitated a moment, but recalling Lady Chalcroft's admonition, smiled and took Lord Trowbridge's hand.

The song was a quadrille, which involved much promenading about the dance floor, making it possible to keep up the conversation.

Lord Trowbridge asked her about Southwark and the people there. He seemed genuinely interested and mentioned how Caroline had expressed a desire to volunteer.

"You've quite won her over with your devotion to your vocation, Miss Draper. Although," he continued with a slight flush and a grin. "I am afraid my lovely wife will be unable to contribute physically as she is, ah, in a delicate condition. It is the reason we returned early from our travels, you see."

Sarah smiled warmly, having just caught sight of Lady Trowbridge dancing on the other side of the parquet floor. "I am very happy for you both. May I assume you've not made the news public?"

"Quite right," Lord Trowbridge said. "Although I've privately told so many people, I very much fear it will soon be public knowledge."

Sarah smiled again. Lord Trowbridge was so clearly besotted with anything having to do with his wife. It was very touching and caused that same funny little pang of longing she'd felt when watching Eleanor and Reading.

"Caroline will, however, contribute to your works, as she promised. Her brother insisted on providing for her quite handsomely in addition to her dowry. Caroline calls him a dreadfully managing sort, always trying to fix things for other people." If Lord Trowbridge felt her physically start, he did not indicate it. "But I can't help but think that such actions are simply demonstrations of his caring."

Sarah studied Trowbridge's face, looking for any hint that he was trying to deliver a message, but his classically handsome face was devoid of any subterfuge.

As the dance drew to a close, he said, "Oh! Look who we've ended up next to!"

Caroline and her partner were just bowing to each other and as she looked up and saw her husband, a beaming smile broke across her face.

"Darling," she cooed and then seeing Sarah, exclaimed,

"Miss Draper! How delightful to see you! Oh I am so glad to meet you here. I had hoped you would attend."

Trowbridge offered an arm to each of them and escorted them to a quiet part of the room.

"Trowbridge, be a dear and fetch us some lemonade? The dancing has quite worn me out." They shared a private smile and Trowbridge departed.

"Do tell me how you've been, Miss Draper. Or may I still call you Sarah?"

"Of course," Sarah murmured. Caroline was slightly overwhelming with her energetic friendliness, not unlike her brother.

"I have quite missed furthering our acquaintance. Although we did have a perfectly splendid honeymoon, since we've been back, I've been at a loss as to how to contact you. I scarcely know my way around Mayfair—I have no idea where Southwark is. That is the correct name, isn't it?"

"It is, but Lady Trowbridge, you should not venture into Southwark."

"Please call me Caroline. And whyever not? You're perfectly safe there, aren't you?"

Sarah ignored that question and instead said, "I shall give you the direction of my kitchen and you may send word to me there should you like to meet here in the city."

"Very well, but one day I should like to see you at work."

Sarah hesitated. "Lord Trowbridge suggested that perhaps you should take extra care just now."

Caroline laughed. "You'd think he was the first man to father a babe! I told him not to mention it until I was further along, although according to my mother-in-law, we should not speak of it at all until long after the babe is born. As if we found the poor thing under a cabbage leaf!"

Sarah laughed at that and they fell into an easy conversation about one lady's gown and another gentleman's dancing abilities, sipping lemonade delivered by Trowbridge who tactfully left them to their tête-à-tête.

Several minutes later and quite out of the blue, Caroline said, "So since my brother is not here and you are not in America, I can only assume he did something asinine."

Sarah choked on her lemonade and the resultant burn in her throat made her eyes water.

"Ah...," she began, at a loss as to how to respond.

"Oh you needn't worry about offending me. My brother has long had asinine tendencies. He just usually does a better job at keeping them under control. Now do tell me what he's done so I may berate him."

"Oh no! That is to say—" Sarah broke off, her cheeks flaming, but decided she was tired of always denying her feelings. Ever since her experience with Peter Greene, she'd closed off her heart, refusing to allow herself to truly get close to others. She'd even kept part of herself hidden from Eleanor and she was heartily sick of the effort it took. Deciding to take a risk, she said, "To be fair, I have a few, er, asinine qualities myself."

"Oh good. Otherwise Sam would run roughshod over you." Caroline turned more fully in her chair and Sarah realized again that Sam and his sister shared the same intense blue eyes. The sight made her heart clench with longing for him.

"Now," Caroline said, as if there weren't two hundred other people in the room. As if they weren't celebrating Eleanor's wedding. As if there was nothing more important than listening to Sarah's story. "Tell me everything."

And to her surprise, Sarah did.

Caroline was outraged at Peter Greene's actions, horrified at Sarah's parents washing their hands of her. Caroline's eyes filled with tears as Sarah skimmed over the loss of her baby—there was no way she could tell that full story in a crowded London ballroom.

She confessed to falling in love with Sam, which made his sister smile in delight, and she described his announcement of their impending removal to America amidst the armload of gifts. At that, Caroline closed her eyes and shook her head.

"That man," she sighed. "He really is very intelligent normally. And he's generally attuned to other people's feelings. It's what makes his travel books so interesting to read; he doesn't simply describe the places he's visited, he describes the people. But when he gets an idea in his head, or should I say, in his heart, he sometimes forgets to consult those very people he most wants to include.

"This is not, mind you, an excuse of his idiotic habit. Why, when Trowbridge and I were courting, you would not believe what Samuel did."

Sarah knew she shouldn't pry, but suddenly any story of him was dear to her so she said, "What did he do?"

Caroline shook her head as she smiled. "Trowbridge and I met in Italy. He was on a Grand Tour and I had accompanied Sam. It was love at first sight for us and we both knew it. Sam, however, was afraid Trowbridge was simply indulging in a bit of holiday romance, so he had one of his friends pretend to court me."

Sarah half-laughed, half-gasped. "He didn't!"

"Oh I assure you, he did," Caroline said with a sour expression. "He later said it was just to test Trowbridge. If his interest was not genuine, one rival would have shooed him off, or so he thought."

Caroline glanced at Sarah as if reading her mind. "Do *not* agree with that idiotic idea!"

Sarah felt her cheeks flame. "Oh, I wasn't!"

Caroline looked unconvinced but continued, "The point I'm trying to make is that if Sam had simply *asked* me, or good heavens, asked Trowbridge, we could have assured him that nothing in the world would prevent us from marrying. And his ridiculous subterfuges were unnecessary."

"Clearly," Sarah said.

"Again, I'm not excusing my idiot brother's behavior. I'm simply giving you some insight into his thoughts so that you can more easily berate him for his high-handedness."

Sarah frowned. "While I appreciate your consideration, I—well the fact of the matter is, your brother is in America and I am here."

"Yes, and I am pregnant. If you think he won't be here to welcome his first niece or nephew…" Caroline let her words trail off with a raised eyebrow.

"You are utterly diabolical, my lady," Sarah said.

"Caroline," she corrected.

The strains of a waltz began and Lord Trowbridge came to claim his wife for it. As Sarah watched them dance, she couldn't help but wonder how far along Caroline was. No more than two or three months, she estimated which meant it could easily be six months until Samuel James was back in England, she thought with a sigh.

Eleanor's father-in-law, the Earl of Southampton claimed Sarah for her second dance of the evening. The older gentleman —who had been the cause of Eleanor's estrangement with Alex Fitzhugh two years ago—gallantly declared he was the luckiest man to secure her for the final dance. She laughed as he led her to the dance floor and caught sight of Lady Chalcroft, whose raised eyebrows clearly said, "When I advised you to dance, I meant with *eligible* gentlemen." Sarah grinned sheepishly in response, but she figured small steps were in order for a woman who could count the number of balls she'd attended on one hand.

The evening came to an end with a tight hug from Eleanor.

"Thank you for everything, Sarah. You've made me who I am today."

"Pish tosh," Sarah said. "You made who you are today. I just allowed you to discover yourself while working your fingers to the bone."

The two women stared at each other with happy tears in their eyes speaking more than words could convey. Finally Eleanor spoke, "I told Alex I couldn't be away too long, but he's planned a fortnight-long honeymoon. I shall be back to work the day we return."

"Eleanor, we shall be fine. With all of the staff you've hired, we shan't even notice you're gone!"

Eleanor poked her tongue out like a five-year-old and they

both laughed.

As Sarah turned to leave, Eleanor called out, "Have a care for my mother. She's determined she'll have you wed within the year."

Sarah shook her head and waved, but she couldn't help but notice the devious look in Lady Chalcroft's eyes as they returned to Chalcroft House.

Chapter Twelve

It was amazing, Sam reflected, how productive a man could be when his brain wasn't preoccupied with a woman. Since his return two months ago, he'd thrown himself into his work, catching up on the things that had occurred in his absence, finishing the edits on his travel journal of London, and overseeing the production of a new series of maps on each of the twenty-one states.

He, of course, thought of his sister from time to time. They had been each other's only family for many years, after all, but he knew she was obviously happy, as her many letters sent from her honeymoon travels assured him. If he had to skip the parts of the letter where Caroline asked about his courtship of Miss Draper and admonished him to write to her of all the juicy details, well, his sister should know him better than to expect a response, much less a detailed accounting of a non-existent courtship.

Sam roughly folded the latest letter from his sister and shoved it in his desk drawer. He stood abruptly and went to check on the repair of his oldest printing press, needing something to do to wipe those last words he'd read from his mind.

"I know you will roll your eyes unbecomingly, elder brother that you are, when I say how very proud of you I am that you have chosen to fall in love with a woman of conviction and vision, one who will stand up to your often tyrannical tendencies and challenge you to improve yourself."

Improve himself, he thought with a snort. Caroline was mighty free with her judgements for a chit barely twenty-four years old. Who did she think she—

"Mr. James, we need to send someone to the docks to fetch a tympan," said his shop foreman, Mr. Beckwith. "It should have arrived a few days ago, but the shipping company hasn't delivered it and we can't coax this old one through one more run."

"I'll go," Sam said abruptly.

"We can send one of the boys," Mr. Beckwith protested. "Ye needn't waste your time on such an errand."

"I said I'll go," Sam said shortly, and then embarrassed at his tone, said, "I need to stretch my legs. Been at my desk too long today."

Mr. Beckwith nodded in understanding and Sam turned to fetch his coat and hat.

He walked the four miles to the shipping office his foreman had mentioned, forcing himself to notice the increasing Philadelphia traffic, the new shops that had opened, the chill of the breeze. None of it helped. Despite his best efforts, his sister's words clanged in his brain and awoke his memories of his aborted courtship of Sarah Draper.

He knew he'd made hash of his proposal, knew he'd handled the whole episode in the worst possible manner. His sister had long berated him for what she called his high-handed, inconsiderate meddling (she'd repeated the phrase often enough over the years that he was never likely to forget it). He didn't mean to be managing—oh very well, he amended, he did like to manage things. He was a born problem solver and so far his success rate at problems as diverse as handling a skilled labor shortage to reworking the plumbing of his Philadelphia home was fairly high. He'd even nudged Trowbridge to confess his feelings for Caroline back when they first met in Italy, though to hear his sister tell it, she'd managed just fine on her own.

The point being that when it came to Sarah Draper, he had to admit that he had embodied every adjective Caroline had hurled at him over the years. The problem was that he'd never loved a woman as he loved Sarah He had been completely out of his element on how to progress their relationship, especially since they'd skipped many of the formalities in a courtship and progressed straight to the physical delights. Then too, he admired her. He laughed humorlessly as he picked his way across a muddy street near the docks. He was well aware that his admiration of her abilities should have made him even more respectful when it came to her wishes and opinions. His purchasing those gowns and other sundry items in his mind were a paltry way for him to help her and to show her how he felt. It had never occurred to him that she would view his actions as some sort of statement that she couldn't take care of herself.

He shook his head as he entered the shipping office. This was why women were so infuriating, he thought. They had to read meanings into things that didn't have meanings. They misinterpreted simple gestures into hugely complicated statements.

It was a delight to deal with the surly old shipping clerk inside the cramped, smelly office. By his grunt, Sam clearly understood he'd been instructed to state his business. When, without a word, the man turned and left the small room, Sam knew the package was being fetched. And when the grizzled man grunted at the customer behind Sam after handing over the box, Sam knew he'd been dismissed. Easy, clear, uncomplicated communication. That was all he asked for.

With renewed determination to put frustrating women from his mind, Sam spent the walk home planning his renovations for his warehouse.

Two days later, he was walking the streets again, this time with no errand to run, simply a mind to clear. He'd dreamed of Sarah again, damnit. He dreamed of her frequently, but last night he'd had the most intensely erotic dream about her and when he'd awoken—long before dawn—he'd been unable to stop thinking of her. Again. Time, it seemed, was not doing its purported job in solving matters. If anything, it was making matters worse.

The hackneyed phrase, "Absence makes the heart grow fonder," flitted through his brain and he sighed heavily in disgust.

A cry of distress was a welcome distraction from his thoughts. He dashed down the street toward the sound and careened around a corner into a sort of alleyway between two buildings.

A woman was huddled on the ground, a broken basket at her side. Sam saw two young men fleeing down the narrow passage and made to give chase. Nothing would have pleased him more than to take out his frustrations by pummeling two bullies who sought to prey on a woman. He took a step in their direction, his muscles bunched to sprint when a broken sob drew his attention and he realized that it was more important to aid the criminals' victim.

Crouching, he laid a hand on her shoulder. The woman cried out and jerked away.

"Easy, easy," Sam said. "I'm here to help. I mean you no harm."

The woman stared at him, wide-eyed, for a moment before saying, "*Sie namen alles.*"

"I'm sorry," he said, recognizing the language as German but not understanding a word. "*Ich spreche kein deutsch.*" That and ordering a beer was the extent of his vocabulary in German.

The woman nodded and gestured to her broken basket. A few small packages remained inside—a small bag of beans spilling open, a loaf of bread, worse for the wear for its travails.

Sam gathered the basket together and offered the woman a hand up. She rose gingerly, dabbing gently at her cheek, where a bruise was already forming. She peeked inside the basket and moaned.

"What was in here?" Sam asked, needing to say something.

She stared uncomprehending at him, but as he pointed into the basket and turned a hand up in question, she nodded, then gestured eating and feeding a baby.

He nodded, his expression grim. He thought of Sarah's stories of being robbed and fury at the assailants who would threaten and steal from people weaker than themselves filled his chest even as he ached with longing for Sarah.

"Come," he said gently, urging the woman out of the alley.

She looked at him suspiciously, clutching her broken basket to her chest.

He sighed in frustration, trying to figure out how to convey his meaning. He'd always been terrible at charades—Caroline had long said so. She claimed his only use at a charades party was to provide a bit of hilarity due to his ridiculous gesticulations.

Sam reached into his pocket and pulled out a two-dollar note. The woman frowned and a storm of angry German met his ears.

"No! That's not what I meant!" Sam protested, having an idea of what she suspected. Why hadn't she yelled like that at her assailants? Surely they would have fled if only to save their ears. He rubbed his forehead and tried again.

"Money," he said, holding up the note. "Food," he said, making eating motions. "Shop," with a point at her basket. "Oh for the love of—here, take the money. You buy the food yourself. He considered the two-dollar note. Though he knew what ink and paper cost in bulk, he had no idea the cost of bread and milk. He pulled out another bill and added it to the first. "Food," he said again. Warily, the woman took the money and edged around him. Once she was out of the ally, she darted around the corner and down the street.

Sam followed more slowly, not wanting her to think he was following, but also full of vim and vigor from not being able to chase down the two thugs. Once he saw the woman enter a shop, he lengthened his stride, determined to burn off his jumpiness through sheer miles.

Over the next month, Sam walked so many miles he had to visit his tailor to take in his trousers and sent two pairs of shoes to the cobbler for new soles. He was returning from one such long walk when his housekeeper handed him the day's mail.

He shuffled through the stack of invitations as he walked

upstairs for a hot bath. Twenty minutes into his walk, it had begun to rain—a cold, sleety kind of downpour. He should have turned back immediately, but he'd had another dream about Sarah. It had started off with the same erotic undertones of kissing and touching, but before it woke him with steamier images, suddenly he was wandering dark empty streets. He supposed it was Southwark, but wherever it was, he was searching for Sarah and with each passing step he became more frantic to find her. He'd lurched awake, his heart pounding, his hand searching in the sheets for a missing Sarah.

He'd known he was going to need a particularly long walk to exorcise that dream and so even though he'd left the house without an umbrella, when the rain started, he'd simply jammed his hat down further and turned his coat collar up. Now, however, he was chilled to the bone and wanted nothing more than a hot bath, a hot toddy, and a hot fire, preferably all at once. He entered his bedroom and shuffled to the last envelope, smiling when he recognized Caroline's handwriting. Tossing the other missives onto a bureau, he began tugging at his cravat.

The maid who'd been sent to draw his bath and tend the fire came out of the bathing room. "It's all ready for you, sir."

"Thank you," he said. A knock at the door heralded a footman with his toddy and as soon as he left, Sam stripped down and eased himself into the steaming water. His frozen toes tingled painfully as feeling returned to them, but it was worth it to be immersed in warmth. He reached for his drink and Caroline's letter and began to read about her return to England, the upgrades she and Trowbridge had begun to make on Heathmark Manor—"ah, already spending the dowry," Sam murmured with a grin—and the various events she planned to attend. Or perhaps had already attended. He rather skimmed over that part and was about to turn the page when Sarah's name caught his eye. He backtracked and read the entire paragraph more carefully. Tea with the dowager Lady Trowbridge, yes, yes…shopping…wedding ball of Lady Eleanor Chalcroft and Lord Reading. Aha, Sam thought, this must be it.

"The wedding was perfection, as one would expect from the union of two earldoms—really though, if they weren't so obviously in love, one might resent that they did not spread such earlishness around to those of lesser status. I don't refer to myself, of course, completely besotted as I am with Trow—"

"Yes, yes, Caro. Get to the point," he muttered, but did not skip a word lest she say something of Sarah.

"And despite the obvious love match, there are those envious young ladies who even still make such a complaint. I suppose the gentlemen may think it too, but if so, they don't voice the opinion, at least where I can hear it. I shall have to ask Trowbridge if he's heard any such talk among the bachelors."

Sam gritted his teeth and kept reading.

"Instead of the usual wedding breakfast, or perhaps in addition to it, for there is every chance they had a wedding breakfast and simply didn't invite everyone, the Earl of Southampton hosted a ball in honor of the newlyweds to which we were invited. The earl has not hosted an event in nearly thirty years, or so Trowbridge's mother informed me, and he clearly had decided to make up for his deficiency in grand style for if there was a cut flower left in London afterwards, I will be surprised. The food was divine too! My favorite being the lemon cream—" at that, Sam smiled.

"Though it was a crush, Southampton was rather exclusive in the guest list and as a result, one could actually stroll through the beautiful rooms without having to squeeze between people and carry on a conversation without shouting.

"The dancing was divine, as the orchestra—"

"Caroline," Sam growled. The damn bath water was growing cold. He quickly stood, dried off, and wrapped himself in a brocade robe before taking a seat in front of the fire in his bedchamber. He scanned the letter to find his place and resumed reading.

"And it was after a particularly lovely quadrille that I noticed Trowbridge had partnered with Miss Sarah Draper."

Sam sat up straighter, intent on the page in front of him.

"She looked beautiful, as I'm sure you can imagine. She wore the most cunning gown of pale aqua."

Sam smiled. When he thought of Sarah looking beautiful, it was when she had not a stitch of clothing on, her only covering the fall of silky dark hair. Shaking that distracting image from his head, he focused again on the letter.

"She was quite the belle of the ball and in fact was claimed for the last dance by a high ranking member of the nobility. As I am still new to England, I took it on the good faith of my mother-in-law that he is considered quite an eligible bachelor."

It was ridiculous, really, that Sam's fingers tightened into fists, crumpling the edge of the letter. Preposterous that his blood surged, pumping his muscles as if in preparation for a fight. He'd been away from London for more than three months. He and Sarah had parted in anger. There was absolutely no reason for him to feel jealous. None! And yet he found himself smoothing the creases of the letter to see if Caroline mentioned Sarah's reaction to this would-be suitor.

But Caroline, ever the annoying younger sister, had already moved on to another topic. He skimmed through the words, barely registering her announcement that she was expecting.

"I still have months to go, of course, but I do so wish you were here, brother dear. You have ever been a source of comfort and support for me and while there is certainly nothing you can actually do for me, I should find your very presence comforting."

And then the last line of the letter: "Sometimes we need people not because they can fix everything. Sometimes we simply need them because of who they are to us."

Sam stared at that last line. While it could certainly be interpreted to support her request that he return to London for the birth of her baby, something told him Caroline did not refer to herself in that sentence. She was rather more blunt about her requests.

He surged to his feet and paced in front of the fire. What was Caroline trying to tell him? Damnit, he knew what she was trying to say. She'd chided him often enough on his overweening desire to fix things. But why would she phrase it in such a way? Had she spoken to Sarah? Had Sarah told her what happened between them? The idea that his sister knew details of his failed love life was disturbing, but ultimately, he knew Caroline only had his best interests at heart and he knew she had very much approved of the notion that he was in love with Sarah.

He re-read the last line, then went back and re-read the paragraph describing Sarah. Surely if Caroline thought Sarah had moved on and was allowing herself to be courted by some—what was it? "high ranking member of the nobility"—she would have said so. Or better yet, not mentioned Sarah at all, fearing it would bother him to hear she was moving on with her life. Despite her love of tormenting him, Caroline was actually very protective of him.

No, Caroline was definitely sending a message. While she was generally not so subtle in her messages—correction, he thought with a smile as he poured himself a drink, generally not so subtle with *him,* as she considered him a bit of a dunderhead when it came to emotional astuteness—she generally always had a point. He sipped the rich brandy and considered what it was Caroline thought he should do. Clearly she wished him to return to England so she must believe there was a chance of patching things up with Sarah. But is that what he wanted? He stared out his bedroom window, though he could see nothing except his own reflection in the rain-spattered darkness.

"Damnit," he muttered again. Of course he wanted to patch things up with Sarah. It didn't matter if he'd only known her a short time, if he'd been away from her an even longer time. The fact of the matter was, she was in his blood. She'd reached down to his very soul and entwined herself around it and life was just not going to be right without her in it. But what would that life look like with her in England with a vocation that was so important to her and him here in Philadelphia with a thriving business?

He tossed back the last drops of brandy and absently

browsed through the rest of his mail. He'd thought them all invitations to various society events, but there was another envelope from England. His heart sped up. He didn't know what Sarah's handwriting looked like and while he would say these letters had a masculine slant to them, still…

It was not, in fact, from Sarah, which in all fairness, had been a ridiculous notion, and he felt equally ridiculous for being so disappointed. He focused again on the words. Ah, another disappointment. The printer he'd met with in London, who'd contracted to reprint some of his maps of the States, was facing dire financial straits and would not only not be able to proceed with the reprints, but was in fact going out of business by the end of the month.

"Fuck," Sam muttered, dropping the letter on top of the others. He crossed the room to pour another drink, but paused with the decanter in mid-air as he stared unseeing at the plaster in front of him. "I'll be damned," he said as a truly outrageous idea occurred to him. Without even quite realizing it, he set the decanter down, though he tossed the heavy crystal stopper carelessly from hand to hand as he paced the length of the room, thinking furiously. He never heard the soft knock of the housekeeper or the sound of her entering with a tray of food, didn't notice when she glanced sideways at him in concern as she set the tray on a table and set out the food.

He paced for many minutes until he decided he needed to put pen to paper to make any sense of his ideas. He fetched both from his leather case and only as he looked about for a flat space on which to write did he notice the table of food.

He pushed the covered plates aside and dipped his nib in ink before absently grabbing a roll and chewing on it while he scribbled figures and notes. He paused at some point to pull a ledger out of his case, consulted some numbers, and then returned to his note making. Several hours later he stood and stretched, twisting his upper body until he got a satisfying crack out of his spine. Only then did he realize how hungry he was and lifted the lids from his plates to devour the now-cold beefsteak and roasted vegetables.

He glanced at his stack of paper, now neatly organized, with some corners turned down to mark particularly important ideas. As he shoved a chunk of potato in his mouth, he realized his fingers were ink-stained, but he smiled because he had a plan that. Two plans, really; one to enable him to return to England and another to win back Sarah.

He paused, mid-chew. Truthfully, he only had one very sound plan that would take him to England and that's what was outlined on the sheets in front of him. The plan to regain Sarah's favor was more of a bone-deep, heartfelt conviction. He really hadn't the faintest idea how to go about the actual practice. Always before in his *affairs du coeur* when things had soured, even briefly, he took it as his cue to make a speedy departure. Never before had he actually sought to solve the problem. But never before had he cared so deeply.

He glanced up at a rumble of thunder and caught sight of himself in the full-length mirror. He'd forgotten to shave in the bath and his beard, several shades darker than the hair on his head, left the lower half of his face shadowed. His hair was a rumpled mess from running his hands through it distractedly while thinking, and it stood on end, adding to his crazy appearance. But his eyes, as he thought about Sarah, were full of steely determination. Never before had he loved a woman as he loved her, he reminded himself. Never before had the rest of his life felt as if it was on the line.

He looked for his waistcoat and pulled his pocket watch out. It was nearly midnight and while he was invigorated with his business plans and his hopes regarding Sarah, it had been a long day, followed by his near-marathon walk in the sleet, and then his brainstorming session. All in all, he was done in, but as he climbed in bed and blew out the candle, he decided it had been one of the most productive days of his life and he couldn't wait to implement his plans.

As his eyelids grew heavy, he now welcomed instead of dreaded the idea of dreaming about Sarah.

Chapter Thirteen

Three weeks later, across the Atlantic and staring out an equally rain-spattered window, Sarah was not feeling so positive. It had been a night full of dreams about Sam and birthing babies, some of whom turned out to be hers, but then instead of Sam being there, Peter Greene was present, demanding she give him a baby since his wife couldn't bear one.

As a result, she hadn't got much rest and she felt groggy and out-of-sorts. At least she didn't have to be at the kitchen first thing this morning. Eleanor's ever-improving gift for raising money, added to the organizational skills she'd honed while helping Sarah for two years, had led to a large paid staff that took care of the actual cooking and serving at the kitchen. Sarah still went in everyday to make sure new people were trained properly, to pay bills, and to plan for future projects, but it had been weeks since she'd pared a potato or kneaded dough.

Turning from the window, she finished winding her hair into a knot at the base of her head, smiling wistfully as she used way too many hairpins to secure it.

She buttoned the collar of her dress, a wine-red muslin, one of the gowns Sam had purchased. She'd kept them packed away after he left, loathe to wear them, loathe to part with them. But then she'd had to wear one of the silk chemises when her old linen one simply couldn't be repaired any longer and after that, it just seemed silly not to wear the dresses. Though they could not be further apart and she would never have admitted it to another soul, wearing the gowns somehow made Sam feel closer to her. Then, too, it felt wonderful to wear a day gown that hadn't been turned twice, whose cuffs and collar were frayed, and whose hem was marked with random stains that no amount of soaking would remove.

She would never have chosen a gown of this color on her own and somehow that made this dress all the more special. She only wore it for important errands.

Today she was on her way to make an appearance at a ladies' luncheon where Eleanor was giving a speech, ostensibly about "Remaining a lady in every situation," but which was, in actuality, a subtle reminder that *"nobless oblige required those descended from kings and queens do all they could for those servants of the of the crown less fortunate than themselves."*

Sarah had rolled on the bed with laughter at that line when Eleanor had practiced her speech in front of her yesterday.

"What's so funny?" Eleanor asked, clearly confused and yet delighted to see Sarah overcome by the giggles.

Sarah finally sat up and wiped the tears of mirth from her eyes.

"I'm sorry. It was the 'descended from kings and queens part.' Half of the nobles in the *ton* only have a title because their twice-removed cousin from their father's aunt's half-brother died before he could manage to convince some equally blue-blooded woman to marry him in the hopes of providing a blue-blooded heir." At that, Sarah erupted into more giggles and the occasional snort. Eleanor tilted her head and frowned with an expression that was at once perplexed and amused. Seeing her cousin that way set Sarah off on another spurt of hilarity until Eleanor, with a little frown, said, "But that's how father came into the earldom."

Sarah choked as she stifled a laugh, horror seeping through her veins. "Eleanor, I'm so sorry. I didn't mean—that is—"

At which point Eleanor herself shrieked with laughter, giggling so hard she had to hold her stomach and gasp for breath as she said, "Oh Sarah, you should see your face! I thought you were going to expire from mortification! Oh!" she whooped.

Sarah threw a pillow at her cousin but couldn't hold back

a smile.

After Eleanor's laughter trailed off (not without a few snorts of her own), Eleanor said, "Forgive me, but I simply couldn't resist. You are quite right, of course, but I've found certain ladies of the *ton* respond far more generously when I let them pretend they are direct descendants of Queen Elizabeth rather than reminding them they are probably more closely related to the people in Southwark."

"Queen Elizabeth didn't have any children," Sarah said. "She never married."

Eleanor's left eye twitched. "Dear, are you being deliberately obtuse?"

"Sorry," Sarah said, biting her cheek to keep from laughing again.

"Perhaps tomorrow it will be best if you simply smile and nod and allow me to do all the talking."

"Of course," Sarah murmured with a small smile. It was all she ever did at these luncheons Eleanor dragged her to. Though she'd grown more comfortable at the society events in the last months, she'd not been brought up in that level of society, and especially after years in Southwark, she was never completely at ease with the members of the *ton*.

Now she gathered her gloves and hat and glanced out the window to see if Eleanor's plain, unmarked coach had arrived. It was just turning the corner and she turned to leave, picking up her umbrella as she did so.

Sarah's cheeks ached from smiling so much throughout the luncheon, but true to her word, Eleanor had coaxed a dozen substantial donations from the ladies present.

"I promised Alex I would be home early today," Eleanor said. "Do you mind taking the drafts to the bank?"

"Of course not," Sarah said. Though she'd had more outings to the city in the last three months than she had the previous five years, it was still nice to have a day away from Southwark and her endless responsibilities there.

She followed her trip to the bank with a visit to two of her favorite apothecaries and then a walk down Bond Street. A few months ago, she'd have viewed the exclusive shops selling fine clothing, jewels, and tobaccos as the epitome of excess and wastefulness. She smiled to herself as she thought of how judgmental she'd been. Now, however, with the financial worries she'd long battled eased by the influx of donations, Sarah could simply enjoy the displays of fine lace or beribboned hats as she might enjoy a sunrise or a garden of flowers. There was still a great deal of excess amongst the rarefied wealthy members of the *ton*, but she had also met some genuine people and made, dare she say it? a few friends.

By the time she returned to her flat that evening, she was pleasantly worn out. It wasn't the bone weariness that came from a day of toiling in the Southwark kitchen all day, cooking, serving, and cleaning. Nor was it the mental exhaustion that followed setting a bone or stitching a wound or helping a patient battle a fever. It was simply a relaxed peacefulness of just enjoying a day to herself and walking miles in the fresh air. She'd been fortunate the rain had stopped and while it had been cloudy, it was a quiet kind of overcast, peaceful in its own way.

The bothersome mood with which she'd awoken had disappeared and as she climbed the stairs to her set of rooms, she thought of Samuel James for the first time since this morning. Now, however, with a newfound tranquility, she could view her short time with him from a position of peace and equanimity, grateful she'd had even a short time of love.

She shook her head and laughed at her whimsy as she entered the darkened rooms. She'd had a few such bouts of peaceful thoughts and they were inevitably followed by equally strong feelings of regret or anger, but for some reason this time, she thought the peaceful feeling might last a bit longer. She lit a single candle—influx of donations notwithstanding, she would always be frugal in her own life—and undressed for bed.

As she lay beneath the covers, waiting for the sheets to warm, she allowed thoughts of Sam to fill the darkness around her. She remembered the feel of his body next to hers in this narrow bed, the smell of his neck as she nuzzled it, the taste of his skin as she kissed it. For once she refused to chase away such memories with thoughts of the terrible way they had parted, refused to wallow in regrets or what ifs. Instead she simply enjoyed her memories as she had enjoyed her walk along Bond Street today. And with that philosophical mindset, she fell into an easy slumber.

"Sarah! Sarah!" Sam yelled, which was strange because in her dream she'd been right beside him and there was no need for him to raise his voice.

"Sarah, wake up!" This was accompanied by a loud pounding, which was also at odds with the tenor of her dream. With tremendous effort, Sarah dragged her eyes open, only to have them burn from the smoke seeping into her room. She sat up as the door burst in, allowing a billow of smoke to pour in from the hallway.

"Sarah?"

"Sam?" she called, convinced she was still dreaming. When he rushed across the room and grabbed her, however, she'd never felt anything more real in her life. "Sam! What are you doing here?" she asked, then coughed as the smoke thickened.

"We've got to get you out of here! The building is on fire."

Sarah allowed him to pull her out of bed and across the room.

"Wait! I must dress!" she said, tugging her hand out of his grasp and turning to look for her gown.

"There's no time! Come with me!"

"But—" When she hesitated, confused and disoriented, he swung her up into his arms and strode from the room. The smoke in the hallway was so thick, Sarah didn't know how Sam could see. She buried her face in his neck and smelled not burning wood, but the achingly familiar scent of him.

Above her, he coughed and she pulled a length of her

nightgown up to cover his mouth and nose. The move exposed her legs well past her knees but such a concern was completely irrelevant now. Sam made a slow descent, carefully feeling for the next step down and Sarah realized that between her in his arms and the billowing smoke, he had no idea if the step below him was still there or had been burned away. She wondered how long ago the fire started. Holding her breath, she glanced over his shoulder and saw bits of burning building falling into the landing outside her rooms. The tinder dry flooring and old walls quickly burst into flames. The heat was oppressive, pressing in on them, as if trying to convince their very skin to accept the flames.

It normally took her perhaps a minute or two to descend from her floor to the front stoop of the building but this time it felt like hours as Sam carried her to safety. Her eyes burned from the smoke and her ears were filled with the roar of the fire that screamed and roared about them like a living thing. Once outside, the heat and oppressive smoke was replaced with fresh air—bitterly cold air pushed by an unforgivingly sharp wind. Sarah's teeth chattered and she burrowed as close as she could get to Sam's body heat as her body went from being baked to being frozen in a matter of seconds.

Sam strode across the street and set her inside a waiting coach, wrapping her in the lap blanket before pulling off his jacket and tucking that around her as well.

She looked through the open door to see the windows of the top floor illuminated with the blaze inside. The feeble light of daybreak made it's tepid way through the low hanging clouds and Sarah scanned the crowd of people in the street.

"Mrs. Bidwell! The children!" she cried, moving to get out of the coach.

Sam restrained her. "Everyone from the top floor is out and safe," Sam said.

"What of the other residents? Has everyone been accounted for?"

"I'll go find out if you'll promise me you will stay in the

carriage."

"But—very well," Sarah said as a shiver of cold made her clutch his coat more tightly around her. He touched her cheek briefly, and moved to close the door.

"Wait!" She tore a strip from the hem of her nightgown for him to cover his mouth and nose. He tied it about his face as he sprinted to the building entrance. She watched him talk to the other men there before going into the burning building. Sarah held her breath as long as she could as if that would help, hoping Sam wasn't choking on the thick smoke billowing from the doorway and upper windows of the building. A figure emerged from the building and then another, but neither was Sam.

She glanced at the crowd of people huddled in the streets again, trying to tally up her neighbors and see if anyone was unaccounted for, but the light was still too dim and even with the cold wind, the smoke made discerning faces too difficult. She tried to imagine where Sam was in the building, how long he could remain in there. It felt too long—his life wasn't worth her need for reassurance. She was about to get out of the carriage and go in after him when Sam staggered out of the building. He doubled over coughing and Sarah jumped out of the carriage and ran to him, heedless of the frozen ground beneath her bare feet or the bitter wind cutting through her thin nightclothes. She pulled his arm around her shoulder and urged him to lean on her as she helped him back to the carriage. A heavy rain started to fall as they climbed in and she prayed it was enough to keep the fire from spreading to other buildings. There was no fire brigade in The Mint.

Once inside, Sam coughed again, deep racking gasps as his lungs tried to expel the smoke he'd inhaled. She looked him over for injuries in the dim light but could see nothing other than a rent in his shirt and a nasty scrape on his forehead. She tore another strip from the hem of her gown and dabbed at his brow. He started, as if coming out of a trance.

"I'm fine," he said in a raspy voice.

"You've a cut here," Sarah replied, dabbing at the blood.

"It's nothing," he said. He gave direction to the driver and then pulled her to him, collapsing back against the squabs.

Sarah relaxed completely against him, relieved he was well, still discombobulated by being awoken by a fire and his rescuing presence. She smiled wearily; she wasn't sure which occurrence was more shocking. How had he come to be there at just the right time? How had the fire started?

She felt the coach lurch into motion and sat up. "Wait! I must see if anyone is injured."

"Doctor," Sam mumbled. "There's a doctor there. Kendall."

Sarah pressed her face to the window. "Oh," she said. Dr. Kendall would have things well in hand. As the driver eased the coach through the crowds of humans, animals, and carts, she saw people from neighboring buildings helping the displaced residents into their homes.

The rain began to come down harder and Sarah could see that the fire was either completely out or soon would be.

She turned back to Sam and her heart surged at the sight of him. His eyes were closed and in the pale light filtering through the clouds she thought he looked leaner and a bit wearier than he had when she last saw him; but his face was every bit as dear to her. She reached out to touch his cheek, but stopped an inch away, suddenly shy and uncertain of what his presence meant.

The cold, which the initial shock of the evening had blunted, sank into Sarah's bones and her teeth chattered before she was able to clench them.

Sam kept his eyes closed—she imagined they still burned from all the smoke—but he reached his hand out and found hers easily, pulling her to him gently. Despite the chill air and the fact that she still had his coat, his body radiated heat. She nestled in the crook of his arm and draped herself against him. Within minutes, she was toasty warm and despite the terror of the last hour, she found herself dozing off.

She awoke to find Sam lifting her out of the carriage.

"I can walk," she protested and he chuckled hoarsely.

"You don't have any shoes, sweetheart."

Having no response to that—and quite enjoying being in his arms—she glanced around, surprised to see they were at the Chalcroft's home, though she didn't know why she should be. She supposed if she'd thought about it, she would have assumed Sam would take her to...wherever he was staying.

As he carried her up the stairs and pounded on the front door, Sarah was simultaneously disappointed that he hadn't done just that and embarrassed that her thoughts should take such a scandalous bent.

She knew that in a moment she would be engulfed by the efficiency of Lady Chalcroft's servants. The countess herself would probably be awoken to see to Sarah. She pressed her face into Sam's neck and clung to his shoulders, trying to impart the smell and feel of him into her body.

The door swung open and Sarah allowed Sam to handle all the explanations as the butler efficiently ordered rooms and medical supplies to be prepared.

Sarah felt Sam ascend the stairs, carrying her with ease despite the fact he coughed every few steps. Before she was ready to relinquish her grip on him, she felt him lowering her to a soft bed. She forced her eyes open and tried to read his expression beneath the layers of soot and weariness. He smiled and seemed about to say something when Lady Chalcroft burst into the room.

"Good heavens! Sarah? What is this I hear about a fire?" Lady Chalcroft rushed to the bed and laid a soft hand on Sarah's forehead, which brought a smile because it seemed like such a maternal thing to do, even though Sarah had escaped a fire, not a fever.

Lady Chalcroft sat on the edge of the bed and peered closely at Sarah. "Do you have any injuries?"

Sarah shook her head and croaked, "No."

"She inhaled a bit of smoke as we were getting out of the building," Sam said in his own smoke-husky voice.

Lady Chalcroft turned to him. "I understand we have you

to thank for saving Sarah's life, Mr. James."

"I was glad to be of assistance."

Though Lady Chalcroft turned back to Sarah, her next question was still directed at him. "What on earth were you doing in Southwark so early in the morning?"

Sam seemed at a loss for words and though Sarah desperately wanted to know as well, she could tell he was rather embarrassed to speak in front of Lady Chalcroft so she faked a cough which, given the smoky state of her lungs, turned into a real coughing fit. As a diversionary tactic it was effective, although it did leave her rather gasping for breath.

Lady Chalcroft filled a glass with water and held it for Sarah as she drank. "I've sent for the doctor. He'll be here soon. Mr. James, do you require medical attention as well?"

Sarah glanced up from the glass of water to find Sam's gaze on her. He started at Lady Chalcroft's question.

"No, my lady. I am fine, I assure you."

"I imagine you'll want to go and change then. Perhaps we might invite you to dinner later this week to thank you for your assistance this morning."

Sam seemed to regain himself, for he smiled at Lady Chalcroft's obvious dismissal and bowed correctly. "I would be honored. My lady. Sar—Miss Draper." And with that he turned and left.

A series of housemaids brought pails of steaming water and proceeded to fill the tub in the adjoining room. As soon as they left, Lady Chalcroft said, "I shall leave you to your ablutions and then I am sure you will wish to rest until the doctor arrives."

Sarah nodded, feeling exhausted even though her only exertion had been being carried downstairs and sitting in a cold coach.

"Oh!" she exclaimed. "Will you let Eleanor know I am well? She was to meet me in Southwark this morning. I should hate for her to worry."

"Of course," Lady Chalcroft replied. "I shall send a note round later this morning."

"Er...if you wouldn't mind sending it now, my lady, I fear it may miss her if we wait too long."

"But it's scarcely seven o'clock in the morning."

"Eleanor is usually at work by eight."

"Eight o'clock? In the morning?"

Sarah clenched her teeth to prevent her smile from showing. Lady Chalcroft had uttered that question in the same tone she might have asked of the cannibal, "He eats people?"

When she had her features under control, she said, "Indeed, my lady."

Lady Chalcroft shook her head as if amazed by the knowledge. She finally said. "How many times have I asked you not to call me that?"

At that Sarah did smile. "I'm sorry, Cousin Elizabeth. I fear the shock of waking up to a house on fire has affected me."

"Of course it did!" Lady Chalcroft said, standing quickly. "A nice soak will help restore you, I am sure." She crossed the room but paused at the door. "I may not wish to know the answer to this, but how was it that Mr. James was at your...home this morning?"

Again Sarah suppressed a smile and was glad to be able to answer honestly. "I'm sure I don't know. I awoke to his pounding on my door yelling that the building was on fire."

Lady Chalcroft's face cleared and she smiled. "Well we shall have to interrogate him when we have him to dinner."

Sarah nodded, wondering if she should warn Sam before he accepted Lady Chalcroft's invitation. The elegant woman sounded positively ruthless.

But as she bathed and put on a clean nightgown, Sarah couldn't help but wonder herself just why Sam was in London and why he'd been at her building so early this morning. They'd not spoken in the carriage, but it was obvious their bodies didn't need words as they'd fit together like two pieces of a puzzle as they'd shared warmth and solace after the terror of the fire.

Clean, though still smelling faintly of smoke, she sank into the pressed linen sheets and pulled the covers up to her neck. As she allowed sleep to pull her into its embrace, she imagined herself back in that carriage, safe in his embrace.

Sarah awoke suddenly a couple of hours later, worried about her neighbors. She forced herself to take a deep breath, reminding herself that Sam had mentioned Dr. Kendall. Surely, he would have made sure everyone was well cared for. She did a quick physical inventory and realized that she felt completely restored, aside from a bit of residual sore throat. She feared Sam would have suffered greater effects and wondered if anyone else had been injured or killed. Fires were all too common an occurrence in the crowded slums of Southwark and Sarah had treated innumerable patients with burns from minor to fatal. She knew how lucky she was and knew she had Sam to thank for her life, for she'd been too deeply asleep to have awoken in time to save herself. The odd thing was, she never slept that late. She was always up before dawn, even on days she didn't have to be at the kitchen. Shaking her head in wonderment, she threw back the covers as a maid was entering.

"Oh miss! I hope I didn't wake you!" the girl said.

"Not at all. I was just getting up. What have you there?" she asked, for the girl's arms were full of fabric.

"My lady sent word over to Lady Worthing and Lady Reading asking to borrow a few clothes until you could have new ones made," the girl explained.

"That was very kind of everyone," Sarah said. "I take it Eleanor, er, Lady Reading was informed why I had need to borrow a gown?"

The girl's eyes were wide as she said, "I'm sure I don't know, miss."

Sarah realized the girl herself probably wondered how she came to be here without a single garment to her name. "I escaped a fire last night. Unfortunately the circumstances were dire enough that I was unable to collect any of my gowns. I simply had to flee."

The young maid gasped. "In your unmentionables? In

front of everyone?"

Sarah suppressed a chuckle. "Are nightgowns considered unmentionables? Very well then, yes, I did. But I doubt anyone noticed seeing as how many of them were in similar attire."

The girl's eyes widened further, if that were possible. "Blimey!" she said, clearly fascinated and appalled at the notion of a bedclothes party.

"We were all fleeing for our lives," Sarah felt compelled to remind her. "One doesn't worry much for rules or modesty when one is facing a fiery death."

That seemed to reach the maid and she rushed forward to spread the gowns on the bed. "Of course, miss. I'm so very glad you weren't harmed!"

Sarah smiled at the girl's obvious sincerity and turned to look through the gowns.

"You don't know me, miss, but I know you."

"Oh?" Sarah said, glancing at her warily.

"You helped me mam a few years back. Me da had died and we couldn't work our land, so mam left us with a neighbor and came to London for work but she had no references and no skills to offer, 'cept one and she didn't hold for that."

Sarah nodded. It was a brutal choice forced on many women at their wits' end in the uncaring streets of London.

The girl continued, "She found your kitchen, she did. And you let her sleep there at night, taught her about cooking for loads of people, helped her get hired as a scullery maid. Right here in this house!"

Sarah had a hazy memory of the woman. "What is your mother's name?"

"Alice Parsons," the girl said proudly. "She's the cook now. Moved right on up 'cause she was such a hard worker and so good at cookin', thanks to you."

Sarah smiled. "I remember her. But her talent is her own. I merely showed her the basics—we haven't fancy ingredients in Southwark."

"That may be, miss, but mam says she'd be nowhere if it

weren't for you. She even got me and my sister hired on, her ladyship sets such a store by her skill."

"That's wonderful," Sarah exclaimed, seeing Cousin Elizabeth in a new light. "I shall look forward to seeing your mother again."

"Shall I help you dress, miss? Many of these gowns fasten up the back."

"Do they?" Sarah asked. "How very impractical. I suppose you'd better, then. But first, please tell me your name."

'It's Martha, miss."

"Very good, Martha. Let's see what you've brought."

When she was dressed, Sarah made her way downstairs and sought out the butler to ask for a carriage or hired hackney to take her as soon as possible to Southwark. With a precise nod of the head, he informed her a light luncheon had been laid out for her.

"Lord and Lady Chalcroft are occupied, Miss Draper, so I took the liberty of setting a place for you in the yellow drawing room. It overlooks the gardens, which are still quite lovely, even at this time of the year."

"Thank you, Mr. Dawson. That sounds far less lonely than the formal dining room."

"Indeed, miss," Dawson said, leading her into the yellow parlor. "Will there be anything else you— "

"Sarah!" Eleanor exclaimed, bursting into the room and rushing to embrace her cousin. "Good heavens, what happened? Mother said there'd been a fire. Are you all right? How did you escape? When—"

Sarah held up a hand to stem the rush of Eleanor's questions and turned to smile at the butler. "Thank you, this is lovely."

Dawson bowed and withdrew, and if he had any natural curiosity himself about Sarah's adventures, it remained firmly hidden behind his impassive butler's expression.

"Sarah!" Eleanor demanded impatiently.

Sarah lifted her eyebrows and gestured to the table.

"Would you care to join me? No? I'm sure you won't mind if I eat then, seeing as I haven't had a bite to eat since yesterday's luncheon."

Eleanor regained herself. "Of course. I'm sorry, I've just been a bit frantic since mother's note came. I, er, couldn't make out some of her writing."

Sarah nodded in understanding.

"Well at least have a roll while I eat and I shall tell you everything."

It didn't take long, when all was said and done. It had been a remarkably short time from when Sam first pounded on her door until Lady Chalcroft was tucking her into the guest bed.

Eleanor stared in amazement as Sarah finished her account, the half-eaten roll forgotten in her hand.

"But…I don't understand. How did Mr. James come to be there? I thought he'd returned to America months ago."

"And so he had. I'm not sure when he returned. I saw his sister, Lady Trowbridge just last week and she certainly gave no indication that she was aware of any travel plans."

"You saw Caroline Trowbridge? Last week? Why?" Eleanor appeared flummoxed and Sarah couldn't blame her. Sarah had ever been a bit of a social recluse before Eleanor's arrival and even since then, she'd been hesitant about her forays into society.

"She and I have become…friends. She wished to volunteer at the kitchen but as she is expecting, her husband has requested she limit her volunteering to things she can do from her home."

"How on earth can she assist from her home in Mayfair?"

Sarah smiled. "She has been making bandages for us and putting together packets of herbs and simples for the families in The Mint. She's been quite helpful, really. I needn't spend hours tracking down all the supplies and you know we are forever short of bandages. "

Eleanor looked grudgingly impressed but came back to the original subject. "Very well, but then what did Mr. James say had brought him back to London so soon after his departure?"

"He really didn't say," Sarah said.

Eleanor frowned. "Did you ask him?"

"Well, no," Sarah said, thinking again of their drive into Mayfair. "We didn't really talk."

Eleanor's eyebrows lifted and a small smile curved her lips. "Do tell."

"No! Eleanor, it wasn't like that. It was—well, you just can't imagine the terror of fleeing a burning building. Once we were safe in the carriage, we just couldn't talk. We rather collapsed to be truthful, and actually, I believe I dozed off." She didn't see the need to mention that she'd done so in Sam's arms. She still wasn't sure how she felt about that. No, that wasn't accurate. She'd loved it. It had felt so right to give and take comfort in a simple embrace. What she was unsure of was how she felt about Samuel James' return and certainly how he felt about her.

Eleanor sat, deep in thought, her fingers absently tearing the rest of the roll to crumbs.

"You need to call upon Caroline Trowbridge," she finally said, coming out of her reverie.

"What? Why?"

"She and her brother are purported to be quite close, despite his apparent lack of communication about his travel plans. She will know what has brought him back to England."

"I told you," Sarah said, distinctly uncomfortable with the idea of visiting Caroline simply to gain information about her brother. "Lady Trowbridge is expecting. I'm sure Mr. James simply wishes to be near for the arrival of his niece or nephew."

"Mmhmm," Eleanor said, with an unconvinced expression. "And he was so worried about missing the event, he arrived, what, five months early?"

"Perhaps four and a half," Sarah mumbled.

Eleanor gave her a speaking glance. "You must call on her. This afternoon."

"I can't! I must return to The Mint and take stock of the damage, see if anyone needs assistance."

Sarah could tell Eleanor wanted to argue but she also was

obviously worried about their neighbors, none of whom had a Mayfair house in which to seek refuge.

"Very well. I'll go with you."

"Thank you," Sarah said.

"Let me raid mother's linen closet first. We'll need as much bedding as we can get our hands on, I'm sure."

They set out shortly after under the disapproving gaze of the housekeeper who eyed their armload of linens as if they'd stripped them from her bed.

They spent the afternoon tracking down neighbors, making sure everyone had found shelter, and treating the few injuries Dr. Kendall had not yet attended—generally mild ones that hadn't required immediate attention.

"It seems your Mr. James was remarkably effective in waking the other residents in addition to carrying you to safety," Eleanor remarked as they left their last stop where they had heard tales of Sam pounding on doors and urging people to flee as he made his way to Sarah's door.

"He's not *my* Mr. James," Sarah said, but she was incredibly proud of him as well as thankful he'd been there.

Eleanor gave her a sideways glance accompanied by a small smirk, but forbore from commenting.

They made their way to their kitchen where dinner was being served. Sarah felt almost like a stranger as she watched the team of employees and volunteers serve the food. It had been just her and then just her and a couple of assistants for years before Eleanor came along, but now there was a full staff working and Sarah felt almost superfluous.

Eleanor linked her arm through Sarah's and guided her through the tables.

"It's still yours, you know."

"What?" Sarah asked.

"All of this. The whole institution. It's still your baby, your creation."

"Oh I don't want credit," Sarah protested and it was true; it just felt strange to be removed from the actual *work* of the place.

"I know you don't. But I also know how vested you are in these people. I just want you to know that they realize it too."

And as they made their way through the room, Sarah was greeted by men and women alike. She was hugged by small children. Everyone expressing relief and thanks that she was not harmed in the fire.

"How silly of me," she said as she dabbed at a tear that escaped her eye. "It's not like I haven't seen most of these people every day for five years!"

"It's not silly at all. You've had a great fright, escaping a fire like that. It's perfectly natural that you should be a bit emotional," Eleanor said matter-of-factly.

Once in the kitchen, they organized several boxes of food and set out with a small cart to deliver the supplies their neighbors most needed.

They returned to Eleanor's parents' house long after the sun had set, having found everyone from their building and distributed the food, linens, and medical supplies.

"I shall ask Alex about rebuilding. He will have no end of good ideas, I'm sure, though we may be hard-pressed to get a penny out of that horrible landlord," Eleanor said. Sarah smiled at her cousin's absolute confidence in her husband and allowed her own thoughts to flick briefly to Sam, wondering where he was at that moment.

"Eleanor!" Lady Chalcroft exclaimed as they made their way up the stairs. "Where have you been? I've been worried sick."

"I left word that Sarah and I had gone to The Mint to check on our neighbors."

"Yes, but it is nearly seven o'clock. Surely you didn't need to be gone quite so long."

Sarah felt her lips twitch with a smile and quickly pressed them together to stifle it. She glanced at Eleanor who either was not as successful at hiding her grin or, more likely, didn't bother pretending not to laugh at her mother's comments.

"Mother, we weren't making social calls, you know. It wasn't a case of arriving, eating a cucumber sandwich, and departing precisely twenty minutes later."

"Well I know that," Lady Chalcroft said, a trifle defensively.

"We had to track everyone down and make sure they had a place to stay until permanent accommodations can be found. Some people required medical attention. Poor Doctor Kendall is only one man, after all."

"Who is Doctor Kendall?" Lady Chalcroft asked, duly distracted from the lateness of the hour.

"He is the most brilliant doctor! I've yet to see a medical case he couldn't help, have you Sarah?"

"Has he a practice in the city? Perhaps we should consult with him about your father's gout. I've not been pleased with the treatment Dr. Finswith has provided of late."

"Oh, he's much too busy with his practice in Southwark, mother, but I do commend your willingness to consider him as a practitioner."

"Despite what you may think, Eleanor, I am considered to be rather open-minded."

Eleanor smiled as she kissed her mother's cheek. "I don't think I'll come up after all," she announced. "I'm sure Alex is home by now and wondering where I am." She turned to hug Sarah.

"It is customary to refer to your husband by his title, dear. Especially now that he has one."

Eleanor laughed. "I loved him as Alex long before he was Reading, mother." At her mother's pursed lips, Eleanor relented. "I shall promise, however to call him Reading in public."

"I suppose that's the most I can hope for at this point," Lady Chalcroft said dryly. As Eleanor turned to leave, she called out, "Oh Eleanor, Please check your calendar. I've invited Mr. James and Lord and Lady Trowbridge to join us for dinner on Thursday. I should like both you and Reading here."

Eleanor glanced mischievously at Sarah. "We shouldn't miss it for the world."

Sarah wondered if she could find a new flat in Southwark

and move into it before Thursday. She was desperate to see Sam and learn why he'd been in Southwark this morning—was it only this morning? —but she was also slightly terrified of the answer. Not to mention still ashamed of how she'd acted months ago. Yes, a new flat seemed just the escape she—

"Don't even consider it," Lady Chalcroft said firmly, jolting Sarah out of her admittedly far-fetched musings. She tried to pretend she didn't know what Lady Chalcroft was about.

"Consider what, Cousin Elizabeth?"

"You and Eleanor continue to suffer under the delusion that I was not once a young woman who thought she knew everything and who considered her parents to be lack-wits at best."

Sarah gasped. "Cousin Elizabeth, I—"

Lady Chalcroft waved a hand dismissively. "You will *not* make other arrangements for Thursday night. You will be here, nicely dressed—for a dinner in Mayfair, not Southwark, mind you—and you will speak to Mr. James. Extensively."

"But I—"

"Will need to go shopping. You are correct. We should have gone today, but first thing tomorrow morning will suffice. I shall take you myself. That way we will be assured of having something presentable ready in time. You may," she said when Sarah opened her mouth to protest, "See to your duties in Southwark after we've ordered you new clothes."

Sarah knew when she'd been outmaneuvered and meekly said, "Yes, Cousin Elizabeth."

"You may kiss my cheek," Lady Chalcroft said, and Sarah hastened to obey. Lady Chalcroft clung to Sarah's arms unexpectedly and looked her in the eye. "I've said it before, but it bears repeating. I would see you happy, my dear. I have a feeling about you and Mr. James, but if it proves to be incorrect, then at least we will know and we can move on."

Sarah smiled at Lady Chalcroft's use of "we" and impulsively hugged her.

"Thank you, Cousin Elizabeth," she said, and pretended

not to notice when Lady Chalcroft dabbed at her eyes.

"Now run along, dear. I'm sure you shall wish to bathe and change before dinner. There is an...aura of—"

"Onions. Yes, I know. The Bidwells are staying with Mrs. Tilney and she has a penchant for frying everything with onions. Everything in her house bears the distinctive aroma," Sarah explained. "Even when she's not cooking."

Lady Chalcroft shuddered delicately. "Yes, well, I'm sure the, ah, Bidwells are grateful to have a place to stay."

"Indeed they are. If you'll excuse me, Cousin."

Lady Chalcroft nodded regally, but as Sarah continued to her room, she heard the distinguished woman mutter, "Onions!"

Chapter Fourteen

Sam had employed the services of his brother-in-law's valet to ensure that he was immaculately turned out for his dinner at the Chalcrofts. He was grateful his sister Caroline refrained from making any younger-sister-like comments, especially as he had, over the years, repeatedly disdained the idea of having a servant help him dress.

Still, he had to admit the valet did know what he was about and Sam's appearance, from his immaculately close shave to his intricately knotted cravat, did seem to be a notch above how he looked when he saw to such things himself.

The valet peered over his shoulder at Sam's reflection in the full-length mirror.

"Will that do, Mr. James?"

Sam turned and clapped the surprised man on the back. "I doubt my sister will recognize me, you've made me look so dandy."

The poor valet seemed unsure if that was a compliment or not, so Sam clarified, "I've never been turned out so nicely. Thank you, Evers."

At that, the servant bowed correctly and took his leave, while Sam wandered downstairs to await Caroline and Trowbridge, grateful to have a few minutes to himself to prepare for the evening. He wasn't nervous, per se, but it was going to be difficult to talk to Sarah alone this evening and he didn't relish laying his heart out in front of his sister and brother-in-law, much less the Earl and Countess of Chalcroft. He shuddered at the thought. He had little notion of how to go about presenting his idea to Sarah alone, much less with an audience.

His original plan had been to catch Sarah before she left for work two mornings past. He had arrived before dawn because he knew she was an early riser and he had no idea where her kitchen was. He'd had no notion what exactly to say to her; he simply hoped the words would come when he saw her. He'd waited in the coach, feeling bad for the driver as he himself shivered from the cold, but still Sarah did not appear. He glanced up and down the street, making sure of his location, but he knew he was in the right place. The sky had lightened to a dull grey and so it was amazing that Sam had been able to see the smoke against the opaque haze of the clouds. At first he assumed it was coming from a cook fire chimney, though there seemed to be a prodigious amount of it. But then he saw the telltale flicker of orange flames in one of the top windows.

"Fire!" Sam bellowed, though surely even the driver would have had a hard time hearing him. Sam burst out of the carriage and yelled again, then shouted at the coachman, "See if you can find help!"

He bolted across the street and entered the dark hallway of the ground floor, taking the stairs two and three at a time. His first thought was to get Sarah to safety—nothing else mattered to him. Yet as he reached her floor and realized there was no smoke, that the fire hadn't reached this floor, he bolted up the remaining staircase and began pounding on the doors, shouting, "Get up! Get out! There's a fire!"

He reached the door where he thought the fire had started just as it swung open. An elderly man stood backlit by an inferno.

"I don't know—I didn't," he began, but Sam simply grabbed his arm, pulled him into the hallway, and slammed the door shut behind him.

"You must get outside!" Sam shouted.

By this time a few more people had come out of their flats and Sam pushed the old man into their care, racing to make sure everyone else was out before leaping down the stairs to Sarah's floor. The fire was licking at his heels, the smoke billowing around him as he pushed his way through the fleeing residents to pound on Sarah's door. It felt like forever while he waited for her to answer and he ended up kicking it in and pulling her from bed. It was all he could do not to pull her into his arms and hold her, never letting go. Instead, he swung her up into his arms and carried her through the searing heat and choking smoke that surrounded them.

He remembered Sarah had pulled the hem of her voluminous nightgown up and held it over his mouth and nose to try and protect him from the smoke as the stairs seemed to go on forever. Even now that descent felt like a blur of smoke and one jarring step after another. His only thought had been to get Sarah to safety. He felt embers singe his hair and sting his exposed skin, and he'd hunkered protectively over her, willing himself to push on even though he had to feel for each step, so thick was the smoke.

Other than those stairs, Sam didn't remember much else beyond getting her into his carriage and finally pulling her to him. He had an indistinct memory of returning to the burning building at Sarah's concern for the other residents, searching through plumes of smoke for any stragglers, his throat and lungs and eyes burning. What he was sure about was the feeling of Sarah back in his arms, her body draped trustingly along his as the driver took them into the city. It was the most natural and comforting feeling in the world, and any concerns he'd had about returning to England to try and mend things with Sarah melted away.

He cradled her as she dozed, fighting the urge to cough the smoke from his lungs lest he disturb her. Her hair smelled of smoke of course, but beneath that he could detect the warm sweetness that was distinctly her, a scent that had haunted his dreams for the last few months...

Caroline and her husband made their way downstairs, pulling him from his memories. Once in the carriage they made small talk during the short drive and Sam assumed he answered appropriately, though he had no idea what he said as he was playing out different scenarios for the evening in his head. He considered and dismissed half a dozen ways to broach his subject, but they all seemed so contrived. Then, too, he had no idea if he would be able to get Sarah alone, on a balcony, perhaps, or a private salon. He didn't fancy making his grand proposition in front of an audience. Finally, as the coach drew to a stop, he decided to rely on his wits in the moment. His wits and his heart.

Once inside the tastefully lavish drawing room, he looked about for Sarah. Not seeing her, he followed his sister and paid his due respects to Lord and Lady Chalcroft. A sound at the drawing room door had his heart pounding, but it was Sarah's cousin Eleanor and her husband, Lord Reading, or Alex Fitzhugh as the man had instructed him to call him months ago. They were joined by Lord and Lady Worthing, who were friends of Eleanor.

He chatted idly with them, his eyes repeatedly darting to the doorway every few seconds. Finally, when Fitzhugh was engaged in conversation with Trowbridge, Eleanor leaned closer and murmured, "She'll be down soon. The new dress she bought needed more altering than she realized. I believe the maid is sewing her into it.

Sam had an image of using his knife as a seam ripper to carefully pop those stitches, revealing one golden inch of skin after another. He felt a flush heat his body, sweat suddenly beading his brow.

"Mr. James?" Eleanor's voice held a note of concern, but the corners of her mouth belied her amusement at his distraction.

"How has she been?" he blurted out before he could think better of it.

Her smile froze and she studied him intently for several long moments, making Sam wish he'd remained silent.

Finally, however, she spoke. "Sarah is very strong and she's a very private person. I am perhaps her closest friend and confidante and yet even I know almost nothing about whatever falling out you two had. That being said," she paused another moment. "I believe she has missed you greatly. I hope I am not wrong in believing you are in London to mend Sarah's heart as well as yours."

"You are not wrong," he replied quietly.

"Very good," she said with a regal nod of her head. "Ah, here she is."

Sam glanced at the doorway and the breath left his body. Sarah was dressed in a gown of pale green with darker green velvet trimmings. Long white gloves encased her arms and her hair was dressed elaborately in intricate coils and curls. But it was none of these things that had caused his breath to catch and his heart to pound painfully. It was simply her presence. Her silky dark hair, her equally dark eyes, the creamy golden skin of her complexion, the straight slash of her brows and her lush, full lips—god, those lips. It was the tilt of her head which some might consider haughty but which he knew was a defensive gesture, one that hid her unease in formal social settings. It was why he'd jokingly called her Lady Disdain. The delicate swell of breast along the neckline of her gown made his mouth go dry and he unthinkingly lifted his empty glass to drain the last drops.

"You should go to her now, Mr. James," Eleanor said, taking the empty glass from his hand.

"Me? Now?" Surely there was some protocol to this situation that he would be breaching.

Beside him, Eleanor laughed. "You. Now. The whole reason for this dinner is to bring the two of you together. I'd advise you not to let my mother down."

Sam glanced over at Lady Chalcroft and found her staring at him with delicately raised brows.

"Right," he said, and he moved to intercept Sarah who was skirting the edge of the room, carefully avoiding looking in his direction.

"Sarah," he called and then remembering his surroundings, "Miss Draper. Good evening."

"Mr. James," she replied without meeting his gaze directly. "Good evening."

He saw the tiny pulse in her neck beating frantically and realized she was breathing rather quickly too. *She's as nervous as*

I am, he thought. How sad that they should be so unsure in each other's company after having been as close as two people could get.

Striving to put her at ease, he said, "You look beautiful this evening. I trust you suffered no lingering effects from the fire?"

At that, the nervous rigidity began to leave her features. "I am quite well, thanks to you. You surely saved my life as I was uncharacteristically sound asleep until you arrived. Oh, and you look beautiful as well."

"Beautiful?" he said, wrinkling his nose.

She laughed. "Very well, handsome."

"That's better."

"Men can be beautiful too. It's not only a descriptor of women."

"True, but I think it is a quantitative descriptor."

She frowned. "A what?"

"Quantitative. To be beautiful implies a far greater level of attractiveness than merely being handsome. You, Miss Draper, qualify as beautiful. I flatter myself that I may be considered handsome at best."

She stared at him with a small furrow between her brows as if trying to decipher his convoluted sentence. After a moment, she burst out laughing, covering her mouth with a gloved hand as everyone else in the room looked at her.

After a moment she lowered her hand and leaned in as if about to impart a great secret.

"Bollocks," she whispered.

If he'd been in the process of taking a drink, Sam was quite sure he'd have snorted it through his nose. As it was, he choked on nothing more substantial than air.

"I beg your pardon?" he finally managed.

Sarah pretended to study the finger of her glove, but a telltale tug at the corner of her mouth betrayed her amusement at his reaction.

She lifted her gaze to his and her smile won out as she said, "I'm sure that you've been called everything from beautiful to gorgeous to Adonis-like."

He raised his eyebrows. "Adonis-like?"

"Do you deny it?

"Well I can't say that Adonis was the actual god that I—"

He trailed off as she burst into laughter again and he thought suddenly, *It's going to be okay.* Perhaps it was a prayer rather than a conviction, but the notion brought him a sense of peace as well as purpose. He smiled, delighted to have made her laugh. Their gazes caught and the rest of the room fell away. They were lost in that timeless space they had first experienced that night in the pub when all they could see was the other's gaze.

Not wanting to break that connection and yet knowing he needed to tell her why he was here while they were still alone (how was it that they were still alone?) he opened his mouth to speak.

"About the other day—" he began at the same moment she spoke.

"I never asked you—"

They smiled at each other again.

"You go first," Sam said.

"Oh it's—" Sarah began but at that moment the butler entered and announced dinner. She laughed softly and they shared a glance that expressed both relief and frustration.

Sam offered his arm to Sarah. "Shall we?"

She smiled and linked her arm through his. As they made their way to the dining room, Caroline caught his eye and raised her brows expectantly.

He frowned and shook his head slightly, telling her to stop interfering.

Once in the dining room, Sam found himself seated next to Sarah which, while not unusual and for which he was grateful, he found a bit suspicious. He glanced at Lady Chalcroft and found her again looking at him pointedly. Good heavens, was everyone in collusion to see that he carried out his mission? And were they all intent in communicating solely through speaking glances and raised eyebrows?

He wished he could have contrived a way to see Sarah completely alone. Why hadn't he thought to call on her earlier and take her for a walk in the park or a carriage ride? Granted, Lady Chalcroft had made very clear what she had expected to happen, but Sarah was certainly of age and her own woman... *Ah well*, he thought. Nothing to be done about it now. Still, if an opportunity did not present itself to speak privately with Sarah —not simply on the other side of a crowded room—he would at least arrange an outing for the next day.

The dinner guests had just been served the first course when Lady Chalcroft decided he'd had his chance.

"What brings you back to London so soon after your return to America, Mr. James? One would think one ocean crossing a year would be more than enough."

"Ship travel has grown much faster and more comfortable in recent years, my lady, though it does have its inconveniences. Still, Caroline is my only living relative and once I received word of her happy news, I knew I wished to be at hand should she need me."

He wasn't sure of the protocol for mentioning Caroline's pregnancy; the English were rather particular about speaking of any type of bodily function, and indeed, Lady Chalcroft frowned slightly at his words. But then a calculating gleam entered her eyes and she said, "I suppose since we are all family, or very nearly, it is not too gauche to congratulate Lady Trowbridge. But indeed, Mr. James, surely you might have waited a few more months. You'll be cooling your heels for quite a while at this point."

Damn but the countess was ruthless, Sam decided. He cast a glance at her husband whom he'd not talked to beyond a brief introduction. The man seemed amused at his wife's interrogation and Sam wondered uncharitably if he was simply glad Lady Chalcroft was picking on someone other than himself. Turning back to the woman in question, Sam said, "I have some business interests that required I return sooner rather than later."

"Indeed," Lady Chalcroft said and Sam realized with a smile that though the countess might bend protocol to acknowledge an expectant child, she would never lower herself to discuss something so crass as a trade or business at a dinner party.

"Oh yes, I've meetings with printers and distributors in the next weeks. I'll need to talk to any number of delivery boys as well, I'm sure." This last was completely preposterous, but Sam couldn't squelch the immature desire to make her as uncomfortable as she was trying to make him.

Beside him, Sarah choked back a laugh and pretended to be dabbing at her mouth with her serviette. He glanced sideways at her and saw the mirth in her eyes. It was all the encouragement he needed and cast about for another inappropriate topic.

Lady Chalcroft was far too quick for him, however, for she said, "And were your meetings in Southwark, Mr. James? Is that how you came to be outside Miss Draper's home the morning of the fire?"

Sam decided right there and then that if the countess had been in charge of things, Napoleon would never had risen to power, much less returned to it from exile. With a nod to the countess to acknowledge her well-aimed riposte, he replied, "Not at all my lady. I had promised Miss Draper and Lady Reading a donation to their inestimable cause when last I was here and with all the plans necessary to depart England, I quite forgot to deliver it."

"And so you thought to deliver it before sunrise?"

"Elizabeth," Lord Chalcroft said gently, and though he still seemed to be amused at Sam's discomfort, he clearly thought it was time to change the subject.

"I'm simply curious," Lady Chalcroft said. "I don't recall the last time I was up before dawn."

Lord Chalcroft seemed about to say something else, but Sam interjected, "I know Miss Draper goes to the charity kitchen and makes house calls very early. I simply didn't wish to miss her."

"It's true, mother," Eleanor Fitzhugh put in. "I'd never

arisen that early before joining Sarah, but we really needed to get an early start to each day if we wanted to be of any assistance to the people of Southwark. They are a very hard-working lot, despite the unflattering descriptions you read in the papers."

Sam smiled at being defended by the diminutive blond, but it did seem to bring to a close Lady Chalcroft's examination. The formidable countess pressed her lips together as if she wished to say more, but she let the matter drop, nodding to the footmen to serve the second course.

Lords Reading and Trowbridge gamely launched into an animated discussion about horses that led to questions about riding in the American wilderness.

"Don't ask me about Pennsylvania trails," Sam said. "I'm a city boy, myself. Much more comfortable in the streets than the forests."

"Don't listen to him," his sister protested. "He is an adequate horseman and was always willing to accompany me as I rode through the most beautiful territory."

Sam decided to ignore the "adequate" comment as Caroline's animated storytelling style had everyone at the table fully engaged. Under the guise of asking for the salt, Sam murmured to Sarah, "I suspect we shall be duly chaperoned all evening, but there is something I wish to discuss with you. Will you meet with me tomorrow?"

She took a sip of wine and though she didn't meet his gaze, behind the cover of her wineglass, said, "Yes. Where?"

"I can send a carriage for you. Will nine o'clock be convenient?"

"Oh, no. I must visit the kitchen in the morning. But I will have use of Eleanor's carriage tomorrow. May I meet you perhaps closer to eleven?"

"Of course," he said, giving her the address. She frowned, not recognizing it. She'd perhaps been expecting the park or another public place, but she nodded gamely.

"I will see you there," she whispered, then turned to answer a question Lord Trowbridge asked from her other side.

The rest of the meal passed pleasantly enough once Sam decided to avoid the speculative glances from Lady Chalcroft and the questioning ones from his sister. Though he was engaged in the conversation with his brother-in-law and Alex Fitzhugh, he was intensely aware of Sarah beside him. His ears were attuned to the timbre of her voice as she spoke or laughed. He could detect her scent even over the myriad aromas from the meal. Every once in a while, his sleeve would brush her arm and he could have sworn he felt a charge like a static bolt in dry winter rooms from the contact. At one point he knocked his napkin to the floor. Without thinking, he leaned over to fetch it before the footman could. Sarah must have felt his presence closer and turned to see what he was doing. So it was that as he straightened from his awkward bend, he came face-to-face with her bosom. His mouth went dry and he glanced up at her face. Her pupils visibly widened with desire as she stared at him and it was all he could do not to grab her and kiss her right there in front of everyone. In fact, he might have done so even still—he was an uncouth American, after all—but then she frowned slightly and turned her head away.

He murmured an apology and returned his attention to his meal, wondering what the hell was going on in her mind. In the drawing room when they'd been bantering and even flirting a bit, he'd been sure they would be able to reconcile their differences. But suddenly he was questioning that certainty. As a man who rarely questioned his skills of deduction, it was an unsettling feeling.

Snap out of it, man, he told himself. She had agreed to meet him tomorrow. *One step at a time,* he reminded himself. And with forced joviality, he threw himself back into the conversation.

It was just as well he'd made his plans with her at the table for the post dinner activities allowed for no clandestine conversations and it was entirely too cold and rainy to suggest a stroll on the verandah. Then too, the strange unease that had hit him at dinner lingered and he was unsure what he'd have said to her if they had had a moment alone.

Then it was time to leave and as he bent over Sarah's hand, he felt her squeeze his encouragingly. He glanced up and saw her tentative—could it be shy?—smile.

He was a fool, he thought with an internal laugh as he helped his sister into the carriage. Nervous one moment, jubilant the next, despairing right after that. *Ah well,* he thought, better a fool for love than a fool at cards.

Chapter Fifteen

Sarah woke up extra early the next morning. She had to return to Southwark to check on Mrs. Bidwell who was not recovering as she should from the smoke inhalation and she wanted to make sure the kitchen's newest employee showed up. Mr. Thackery, whom she'd last seen holding a knife on his wife and Dr. Kendall, had approached her the day before wanting to make a fresh start to his life. Sarah was dubious, fearing he simply wanted to earn money for his next bottle, but when he said his wife had left him for her sister's house and wouldn't be back until he straightened out, Sara decided to give him a chance. Still, it was best if she made sure he knew he would have to earn her trust as well.

As she was brushing out her long hair, she startled the sleepy maid who came to light the grate for her. The housemaids knew to start with her room first as she generally rose when they did, but Sarah had already lit the fire and was nearly ready to leave when the young woman, Martha, entered the room.

"I'm sorry, miss! I didn't think I was late."

"You're not," Sarah rushed to assure her; the housekeeper did not tolerate tardy service from the maids. "I have a particularly early appointment this morning and I'm used to seeing to my own needs. Would you do me a favor, however, and have a coach brought round?"

"Right away, miss," the maid said and turned to leave.

"The plain one," Sarah called after her, and then turned to finish her toilette.

She was going to have to go directly from Southwark to the address Sam had given her last night, and while none of the new gowns she'd acquired were shabby, she was feeling ridiculously self-conscious this morning and wanted to look her best when she met with Sam. The man was too good looking by half and it was only the roughness around his edges that kept him from being unbearably perfect. She had noticed from time to time that his shave was not always the closest, golden hints of stubble softening his strong jaw. Though his clothes were of the finest quality and well cared for, he always wore them with a haphazard grace that left him slightly rumpled. Deliciously so, she thought with a shiver. And then there was his slightly-too-long mane of hair, full of gold and amber and tawny streaks, always mussed as if a lover's hands had tugged on it.

She lifted cold fingers to her flushed cheeks, trying to cool the heat there. Of course *she* had tugged on his hair. She'd run her fingers ceaselessly through it as she'd cradled his head while he'd kissed her down to her soul.

Shaking her head to clear it of its distracting images, she moved to the dressing table to pin her hair up. Last night, however, Sam had been immaculately turned out, his hair trimmed and pomaded in place, his shave expertly close, his clothes pressed within an inch of their life. When she walked into the drawing room last night and saw him standing there with Eleanor, she'd suddenly been glad she'd allowed Lady Chalcroft's maid to fuss over the fit of her gown and the curl of her hair.

She almost wished she could employ Martha again this morning to dress her stick-straight hair again, but besides it being so early, she didn't want to go into Southwark with an elaborate coiffure. She ruthlessly twisted her hair into a tight knot at her nape. She had to remember her priorities, she scolded herself. For all she knew, Sam really did just intend to deliver his promised donation. To expect anything more would be to set herself up for further heartbreak and it had only been in the last weeks that she'd finally let go of the hurts, the what-ifs, and the whys that had plagued her since she and Sam had their falling out. The last thing she needed was to begin daydreaming again, for such visions inevitably crumbled beneath the weight of reality.

And with that no-nonsense mindset, she rose from the dressing table without a backward glance. She gathered her gloves, hat, and cloak and made her way down to the carriage. She rode in a state of determined concentration, thinking of the tasks she needed to accomplish before her meeting later this morning. Meeting, she thought with a nod of approval. That was how she needed to think of her appointment with Sam. To her disgust, however, just the thought of his name made her fickle heart skip along rapidly.

Once at the kitchen, she asked the driver to return for her in two hours and rushed inside to find her staff had nearly finished preparing the morning's meal for those who needed it. She threaded her way through the busy women, thinking that it was growing harder to remember the days it had been just her trying to feed a hundred people. She made her way to the scullery area where a bleary-eyed Mr. Thackery was scrubbing pots.

"How are you today, Mr. Thackery?" Sarah asked.

The man stifled a yawn as he glanced over his shoulder. "It's a mite earlier than I'm used to getting up, missus, but I'll do. Thank ye."

Sarah sent a questioning glance to Ida and the woman nodded reassurance that so far, Mr. Thackery had fulfilled his duties admirably. Patting Mr. Thackery on the shoulder, Sarah turned to inspect the pantry and make sure there were enough supplies to put another round of boxes together for the displaced residents of her building.

When the Chalcroft carriage returned for her, she was surprised to realize two hours had passed.

"Drat," she said, as her heavy hair slipped from the pins.

"Do ye need some help, miss?" one of the younger women asked.

Sarah pulled out all the pins and began rewinding her hair. "It's grown so long, it won't stay in place. I really must trim it."

"That style won't hold, miss, if ye'll excuse me fer sayin'.

Mam and me sisters say I've a fair hand at hair. I'm happy to help."

"If you can keep it in place, Edith, you're a better woman than I," Sarah said with a laugh.

The girl got to work. Sarah had assumed she would simply put it in a more secure bun, but as she felt her tugging and twisting, she realized the girl had more intricate plans in mind. Hoping she would not regret her acceptance of help—there would be no way of knowing what she looked like as mirrors were a luxury not often found in The Mint—she tried to keep her fingers from creeping up to investigate what was going on.

"There. Ye look a right queen now, don't she?" Sally asked the room at large.

"That suits ye, miss," Ida said. "It's a shame to pull your back like you usually do. Most women would love to have hair as lovely and thick as ye've got."

Feeling reassured, Sarah bade the women goodbye and quickly climbed into the carriage. She pulled out the small watch Eleanor had given her yesterday to replace the one lost in the fire. Allowing Sally to arrange her hair had meant she would be hard pressed to be on time.

"What is going on?" she said to herself fifteen minutes later when the coach stopped. She lowered the window and stuck her head out. They were on the middle of the bridge in a quagmire of carts, carriages, cattle, and people.

The driver was standing up on his perch, craning his neck to see. When he hopped back down, she asked him what was wrong.

"A cart has overturned up there. Maybe two. It shouldn't take too long to clear it."

She nodded her thanks and closed the window, glancing again at her watch. She hoped Sam didn't have other meetings this morning. Despite her determination not to speculate, she wondered again at his reasons for meeting this morning.

When the carriage finally arrived at their destination, Sarah was surprised to find they were just off Fleet Street. Another glance at her watch showed she was forty-five minutes late. She hoped Sam was still here, though she saw no other carriages on the small street.

"Are you sure this is correct?" she asked the driver.

"Yes, miss. I'm sure."

With a nod, she entered the empty building. The first floor had several dark and empty rooms, but the staircase was lit from above so she made her cautions way upstairs. The entire upper floor was one huge open room, and a row of windows provided the brilliant illumination. She thought this floor, too, was empty and was about to climb the stairs again when she spotted Sam standing alone, staring out one of the windows.

He appeared lost in thought and though she felt silly for thinking it, it seemed that his posture held an air of dejection. Could he think she wasn't coming? Would such an idea upset him? She bit her lip to squelch the fanciful notion.

She removed her bonnet and crossed the empty room to him, but he was so lost in thought, he did not notice the rustle of her skirts. She stopped a few paces from him.

"Sam?" she called softly.

He turned immediately and as they'd done so often before, their gazes locked and they seemed frozen in time. Sarah's heart pounded. She wanted to throw herself into his arms at the same time she wanted to run screaming from the room. She was terrified of baring her soul, terrified of having to admit that she'd acted rashly, foolishly, stupidly. She was terrified that she might overcome those fears and lay her heart out in front of him only to have him reject her.

She tried to read his emotions, but all she saw in the multifaceted crystal of his blue eyes was a reflection of her trepidation and she didn't know if it were her own or his. And so she remained where she was, within arm's reach of him and yet as far as if he were across the room.

Finally he spoke. "I'm glad you came. I wasn't sure you were going to."

"I'm sorry I was late. There was a cart on the bridge—or

maybe two, I don't know. But it—or they—had spilled over and apparently the owner had a hard time righting it and people were helping themselves to his wares. Apples, I think. And we got a late start because my hair—well, that's not important. The point is, I'm sorry. I didn't mean to be late." Her rapid-fire speech exhausted, she stood there, feeling exceedingly foolish.

He smiled and said, "It's alright. You made it. And your hair looks nice."

"Does it?" she asked tentatively, touching the plaits wrapped round her head. "Sally did it for me at the kitchen. I've not even seen if it's ridiculous or stylish."

"It's perfect," he replied.

She felt her cheeks flush. "Thank you," she said softly. Then, gesturing to the large empty room, she asked, "What is this place?"

"Well, it's the reason I asked you to meet me here today. You see, I received word from the publisher who had arranged to reprint some of my maps that he was bankrupt. I've always wanted to expand my business, so I'm setting up a print shop here in London and will certainly need to hire many people. I've no idea how to begin advertising my need here, but it occurred to me that you might be able to put me in contact with any number of hard workers in need of employment."

Sarah's eyes widened, even as some small part—oh very, well, a bloody large part—of her was bitterly disappointed that his reason for meeting her was not personal. "Why yes, of course. That would be wonderful. Will you—that is, ah—" she broke off, suddenly shy to ask what she was desperate to know. She cleared her throat and took herself firmly in hand. "What I mean to say is, will you be needing a manager as well since you've your primary business in Philadelphia?"

"No," he replied succinctly and her heart skipped a beat.

"No?" Her voice came out absurdly high.

He smiled. "No. I've hired a manager for my Philadelphia company. I shall be taking up residency here in London."

"Oh?" Another octave higher. "I'm sure your sister is delighted at your decision."

"I'm not doing it for my sister."

Sarah's mouth went dry and she couldn't tell if she were hot or cold as he took a hesitant step toward her.

"I was…highhanded, to put it mildly that last day at your flat. I had no right to spring fully formed plans on you like I did. I had no right to assume you would give up your life here to be with me.

"I hope…that is, I was wondering, if I might see you again." He took a shaky breath and licked his lips and she suddenly realized he was as nervous and uncertain as she was. She felt a warmth flood her veins at the idea and she looked at him expectantly as he continued, "I would like to court you. More formally, that is. Try to do things right this time."

Ten different emotions surged through Sarah's body. Or perhaps it was ten thousand; it was hard to tell. What she was sure of was that for whatever mistakes Sam had made in their whirlwind romance, she had made just as many. More, perhaps, as the hurts and burdens of her past had never left her until the loss of Sam made her realize with brutal clarity just what holding on to them was costing her, even five years later.

Wave after wave of realizations crashed over her, washing away the last vestiges of pain from her experience with Peter Gilbert and the loss of their baby. She suddenly felt scrubbed free and brand new. The cleansing had started months before but it was only now that she realized she was whole again. She knew what she wanted and she knew what she was willing to do to get it.

The fact that Sam had offered to completely upend his life to be near her was simply the final confirmation of what she must do.

"No," she whispered.

His face blanched. "I beg your pardon?"

She shook her head. "No, you don't need to move to London."

"I…see," he said woodenly and she realized all the words

and feelings in her head and heart were jumbled together and not making their way out of her mouth.

"Wait!" she cried as he turned away. "What I mean to say is that you were not the only one who was at fault that day. I—I never forgave Peter Green for what happened all those years ago and perhaps more importantly, I never forgave myself. As a result, I wrapped myself in a…a blanket of misery. Or perhaps it was guilt. Whatever it was, it kept me from being able to move on. Even when I realized how much I loved you—" her words seemed to shoot through him like a bolt. "I could not allow myself to admit it to you. Then when you announced your plans for us—indeed, a bit highhanded," she said with a smile. "That fiercely independent streak that was necessary for me to survive, well, it rebelled. And even though I thought I was the most reserved person I'd ever met, my temper got the better of me." She took a deep breath and said what she knew was in her heart.

"I don't want you to relocate to London." He frowned and was about to say something but she pressed on. "I don't want you to give up your business and the life you've built there because I very much would like to join you in America. If you'll still have me."

They stared at one another, reading each other's souls in their eyes. In two long strides, he snatched her into his arms, burying his face in her hair and holding her tightly to him.

"Of course I'll have you. How could you think otherwise?" he pulled back to cradle her face and stare into her eyes.

"But what of your work? There are hundreds of people in Southwark who rely on you. I know how important that is to you."

She smiled through the tears that blurred her vision. "It turns out, according to Dr. Kendall, that there are just as many people in need in America as there are in England. Philadelphia, in particular, could use another organization to help people get back on their feet, according to what Dr. Kendall hears."

"And your aid society here?"

She laughed and it felt like the sun rising on a new day.

"Eleanor has become a veritable dynamo. She has truly taken my small charity to another level. She's secured so many donations that we've been able to hire staff to help us. They will endure long after my name is forgotten."

"Trust me," he said gruffly. "You are an unforgettable woman."

She touched his cheek gently and he lowered his lips to hers.

It was a hesitant kiss at first, as if their mouths weren't ready to believe the words they had just spoken. But as they nibbled and tasted one another, the heat built. Stealing their breath, even as it made their hearts pound in time. She traced the corner of his mouth with her tongue and the kiss exploded. He wrapped his arms tightly around her and pulled her even more closely to him, tasting her, drinking her in, ravishing her lips, her cheeks, her neck.

"I love you," he said into the skin of her cheek.

"I love you," she replied against his brow.

Their lips came together again, renewed familiarity making the kiss deeper, more intense, more arousing. Sarah felt like her blood was on fire. Without a heater or occupants, the building was chilly, but she felt as if she stood in the midst of an inferno, one that didn't hurt her but instead brought her to life.

She dropped her reticule to the floor and tore off her warm pelisse, somehow peeling her gloves off at the same time without getting tangled. Sam did not have as much luck with his precisely tailored jacket, but she quickly freed him from the fitted sleeves and then set to work on his cravat while he unfastened the long row of buttons down the front of her gown.

Whispered "I love yous" and "I missed yous" accompanied the rustle of displaced clothing. The heat of desire notwithstanding, it was not warm in the building and their impatience to join together was too great. Her gown gaped open, his shirt remained half unbuttoned as he rucked up her skirts and she unfastened his trousers. He caught her by the ribs and lifted her up against him. She wrapped her legs around his waist and as he slid home, they stumbled backwards a few steps until the wall caught them.

Sarah gasped as he sank more deeply in her. They paused, both panting, as their gazes locked and she felt completely at one with him. Except there was no longer a "him" or a "her." There was only a "them."

The bricks at her back were cold and she could feel a tremor in his legs from holding them up and still they remained rapt in each other's eyes. But then she wanted more. She wanted pure, carnal domination of him just as she wanted to be completely owned by him. She clenched her inner muscles as tightly as she could and he gasped. She smiled, feeling like a siren with a mortal at her mercy.

An answering wicked grin curled his lips as he adjusted his grip on her bottom and thrust over and over.

Her breath came in sobs as she clung to his shoulders, riding him to their mutual pleasure.

Despite the coolness of the air, they grew sweaty as they strained to meet even closer. She drew his mouth to hers and kissed him with a wet intimacy that mirrored their physical joining. Her lips pressed open mouthed to his, her breath hitched, and she heard a keening wail escape her as pleasure flooded her senses. Her body spasmed around his in delight and sent him over the edge to the same blissful oblivion.

He buried his face in the crook of her neck and groaned loudly, the erotic sound causing her to shudder again with pleasure.

They remained intimately locked for an eternity after, their breathing labored, their hearts pounding. Finally, Sam lifted his head and kissed her gently on her forehead, her closed eyelids, her cheek, and her lips.

Her eyes fluttered open and she smiled dreamily at him. He gently lowered her to the ground, staggering slightly as he tried to regain his balance.

Her own legs were scarcely able to hold her up and she rested against the wall until they felt strong enough to support her weight.

"I can't feel my feet," he said and suddenly they were both laughing as they held each other up.

Several minutes later, their clothing repaired as much as possible, Sam said, "You said you wished to come to America. You didn't exactly say you wished to marry me. That was part of the original offer." A teasing grin lit his face but she could see uncertainty in his eyes.

"What do you think I wish to do?" she asked.

"What do I think?"

She stepped closer to him, her heart in her eyes. "What do you *know*? Right here," she said, tapping on his chest.

He stared at her for a long moment and then grabbed her to him in another bear hug. When he set her down, she pushed back enough to look into his eyes. "Of course I will marry you, Sam. The sooner the better."

His eyes widened. "Why? Do you think—" He looked at her midriff and she smiled.

"No," she said gently. "Because I can't bear another day apart from you."

He kissed her soundly and she suspected they'd have ended up tearing their clothes off again if there were anything besides the wall or dirty floor to bear them.

"When is the quickest we can be married?" he asked.

"Three weeks," she said morosely. "Unless by chance you have a bishop who owes you a favor?" This said more hopefully.

He laughed and dropped a kiss on her nose, then bent to retrieve his jacket. "Would that I did. I wonder if I could hire a false brigand to threaten a bishop," he said, stroking his chin and trying to look diabolical. "I could then swoop in and save him, thus ensuring his willingness to grant me a special license."

She laughed aloud, realizing that she did so most often while in his company. She thought it was a good sign for the future.

"When will we leave for Philadelphia?" she asked as he escorted her downstairs.

He chuckled and when she paused on the landing and turned to him, she discovered he had a sheepish grin on his face.

"What is it?" she asked.

"Well, the thing is, I really did intend to set up shop here. It wasn't a ploy to convince you to move to America."

"I didn't think it was. I just assumed you were in the beginnings stages of, well, everything and could…" she trailed off. She had no idea what was involved in establishing a print shop.

He smiled and chucked her gently under the chin. "When I go in, I go all in. I've bought out the printer who was going to publish some of my maps. I received word that they had made some bad financial decisions and were on the verge of bankruptcy. It seemed like a sign, so I contacted their agent and I am now the proud owner of two English printing presses and a handful of clients. I'm afraid I'm going to have to stay here for a few months at least to get the business up and running."

"And then Caroline's baby will be due," she reminded him. "You won't want to miss that."

"True," he said with a smile and pulled her into his arms. "Will you be able to stand staying in England until perhaps next summer?"

"Married to you, I don't care if I'm on the Orkney Islands," she said with a kiss. "And that will give me plenty of time to train someone to replace me as I suspect it won't be long before Eleanor will need to limit how much she works."

He laid a gentle hand on her midriff. "You could beat her to the punch," he said, his voice hoarse with emotion.

She felt her cheeks tingle with warmth. She'd not even considered the risk of pregnancy a few minutes ago—further proof that she believed in Sam fully and had finally left her past behind. "I could, though it's not a competition, you know," she teased.

He smiled at that and said, "Let's go inform Lady Chalcroft of our plans and see if it redeems me in her eyes. I don't think I can withstand another inquisition like last night."

Sarah smiled and pulled his watch from the small pocket

of his waistcoat. "Lady Chalcroft won't rise for another hour."

"Excellent! We'll have time to eat before we face the dragon."

Sarah scowled at him playfully. "She's not a dragon. She has simply become very protective of me."

Sam led her outside and helped her into the waiting carriage.

"Nonetheless, I think I shall endeavor to be around when she first makes an appearance this morning. That way I can catch her when she's unaware, let her see what it feels like to be caught off guard."

Sarah laughed but said, "In the first place, I don't think cousin Elizabeth intended to catch you unawares. Surely asking what you were doing in Southwark before dawn was a fair question."

"But the way in which she asked me!" he protested. "It was like she suspected me of being a burglar."

Sarah laughed again—or perhaps she hadn't stopped—and she impetuously kissed him. "In the second place—" she began.

"There's a second place?"

She lifted her eyebrows and ignored the interruption. "In the second place, you should be aware that no one in the history of Cousin Elizabeth's life has ever caught her off guard. I often think if she'd had the keeping of Napoleon, we'd never have had to go to war a second time."

"I thought the exact same thing!" Sam exclaimed, pulling Sarah into the crook of his arm. "Now enough about dragons and cousins. Let's talk about how wonderful you are."

Sarah felt a wide, happy grin curve her lips even as tears of joy filled her eyes. The last ghostly wisps of heartache and grief melted away beneath the warmth of this man's love, and she knew that though the future might bring times of sadness or strife, they would always have this rock solid foundation of love to see them through it.

Epilogue

"Here she is! All cleaned and swaddled," Juliette Wilding said, carrying a tiny bundle into the room.

Sarah winced as she pushed herself up higher against the pillows. As soon as Juliette laid her new daughter in her arms, however, she forgot about all pain and discomfort and stared in wonderment at the tiny being who had worked one arm free and was waving it about as she grunted.

"I think she's hungry," Juliette said.

"I'm not sure—" Sarah began, embarrassed.

"Here, let me help you." Juliette held the baby while Sarah untied her gown and then positioned the squirming bundle against Sarah's breast. "If you tilt it like—oh bother, will you die of mortification if I touch you?"

Sarah laughed. "After six years of working in Southwark, I doubt much in this world will mortify me."

Juliette helped Sarah and the baby get situated and Sarah gasped at the sensation when her daughter latched on. Juliette smiled.

"It is an unusual feeling, isn't it? But then from the moment you're pregnant, it's just one long string of unusuals."

The two women laughed and Sarah offered up thanks that she and Eleanor's friend had become close as well. She'd been on her own for so long, and now to find herself surrounded by friends and family was delightfully overwhelming.

"You make a fine midwife," Sarah said. "Speaking of which, where is the midwife?"

"I believe your husband is plying her with his best brandy and paying her three times her usual fee."

Sarah smiled as she thought of Sam.

"Here," Juliette said. "Switch her to the other side now."

"Thank goodness I have you," Sarah said, laying a hand on Juliette's. She still felt awkward sometimes expressing her emotions, but every day that she was surrounded by love made it easier.

Juliette smiled. "I envy you, having me," she joked. "My only female relative present when Jonah was born was Aunt Constance."

Sarah frowned. "I didn't realize your aunt had had children."

"She hadn't! I had to figure everything out myself once the midwife left!"

Sarah found herself wondering about new mothers in Southwark, if they always had a mentor to teach them how to care for their babies. Her brain clicked into planning mode. When she'd become pregnant so soon after their wedding, Sam declared he did not want to submit her to the trials of sea travel at the same time and while they would eventually depart for America, she suspected she had at least six months to enact some new ideas at the charity. Her plans were interrupted by a surprisingly loud belch.

"Oh very good!" Juliette exclaimed.

"That wasn't me!" Sarah protested.

Juliette laughed. "You must burp a baby after she eats or she'll end up spitting it all up, usually right after you've put on a fresh gown. I didn't realize a baby could burp herself."

"She must get that from her father," Sarah said, and they both burst into giggles.

"You two seem to be having a grand time!" Eleanor said as she brought a pile of fresh linens into the room. She deposited the cloths on a dresser and came to kiss Sarah's brow and coo over the baby.

"What are you going to name her?" Eleanor asked.

"I haven't the faintest idea," Sarah said, then smiled as inspiration struck. "Oh I have it! I shall call her Eleanor Juliette James. Oh wait! It shall have to be Eleanor Juliette Caroline James. I can't forget Sam's sister."

Juliette chuckled and said, "While I am honored to be a namesake, you may want to save a few in case you have another daughter."

"Yes," agreed Eleanor. "Mr. James is out there saying he hopes to have a dozen daughters all as strong and beautiful as their mother."

Sarah winced again as she readjusted her position. "Well he's welcome to have the next one!"

Eleanor smiled and then her eyes widened as she turned and bolted into the adjoining water closet. Sarah and Juliette looked at each other in concern as they heard Eleanor retching. Juliette was the first to realize the implication.

"Congratulations, Eleanor!" she called out over the harsh sounds.

Absorbed as she was in the minute perfections of her daughter, it took Sarah a moment to register what Juliette was saying.

"Eleanor?" she asked when her cousin returned to the room, pale but otherwise recovered.

"I don't know for sure," she said as she sat in the other chair beside the bed.

Sarah and Juliette burst out laughing and Juliette inquired, "Might you decide you're sure in seven or eight months?"

Eleanor smiled wanly. "I don't want to get Alex's hopes up. Or mine, for that matter. It's taken so long," she complained.

"You've scarcely been married two years!" Sarah protested.

"Everything in its own time, dear," Juliette added.

"And I hate to tell you, but if you keep losing your lunch, Reading is going to suspect," Sarah said.

"I think he already does," Eleanor confessed sheepishly.

As Juliette and Eleanor chatted about pregnancy symptoms and expectations, Sarah returned her attention to her sleeping baby. Only the magnetic pull she felt from across the room distracted her. She glanced up and found her gaze captured by the brilliant blue of her husband's eyes.

She should be used to it, she thought abstractly, but after a year of marriage, she still found herself gazing into Sam's eyes, regardless of their surroundings. In the midst of a crowded ballroom, sitting at Cousin Elizabeth's dinner table, while distributing boxes of food in Southwark, she would look up, see Sam, and they would be lost until someone pulled their attention away.

In the depths of his eyes, she saw everything she needed to be happy. She saw passion and heat. She saw strength and support. She saw understanding and humor. But mostly she saw a love that was greater than any she had ever imagined.

Sam froze just inside the bedroom door. His breath left his chest in a whoosh and he felt his fingers tingle.

Sarah was sitting up in bed cradling their hour-old baby and he had never seen anything more beautiful in his life. It seemed like all the light in the room focused in a golden glow on her, as if she were a celestial being.

Then Sarah looked up and air flooded his chest. He was amazed as always at the intense connection he felt when their gazes caught.

With Sarah, he'd found everything he never realized he was looking for. His years of aimless flirtations he now knew had been a quest for a more intimate connection, a soul-deep yearning for his other half. And now that he had found her, his emotional, physical, and spiritual mate, he was so damned happy that it scared him at times, like now. His heart clenched painfully with the realization of what he had to lose.

Sarah must have seen a flicker of distress in his gaze for she gestured for him to draw near. The other two ladies, sensing the pull between the new parents (and how could they not, he wondered in a distant part of his brain...the pull between them was so strong, he rather fancied it was like a pulsating glow) stood and quickly left with murmured congratulations as they passed him.

Finally, it was just the two of them. Well, three, he reminded himself in amazement.

"Hullo," he said, sounding like an idiot to his own ears.

His wife smiled at him, that radiant, bone deep smile she only gave him. She reached her hand out to draw him down next to her.

"I don't want to hurt you," he protested. He'd heard her during the long hours of labor. Though he'd been on the other side of the door (the hired midwife *not* being amenable to husbands in the delivery room), he'd heard every scream and groan like a lash on his heart.

"Shh," she said. "I'm fine. Come meet your daughter."

He stretched out next to her and she lifted up so she could nestle in the crook of his arms. As cozy as he'd ever felt in his life, he stared down at Sarah's shining hair, then transferred his gaze to the small face peeping out of a white blanket in her arms.

For the second time in as many minutes, he felt the breath leave his body. His small daughter grunted and wiggled until she worked one of her fragile arms loose from the blanket. He reached out to touch the tiny hand and felt a jolt when the delicate fingers closed around his forefinger.

"She's perfect," he whispered.

Sarah glanced up at him and he covered her smiling lips with a warm kiss.

"You're perfect," he said.

Sarah laughed. "I'm far from perfect. You're just feeling sorry for me for yelling my head off for an hour."

"An hour? More like three! But I thought you were perfect before that."

She stared into his eyes and though she was exhausted, he could see the happy peacefulness there.

"How about we simply say, this is perfect."

He smiled and snuggled closer to his wife and daughter. "Perfect."

The End

About The Author

Michelle Morrison

Graduating magna cum laude with a degree in technical writing did not guarantee Michelle Morrison an exciting career writing about NASA's latest discoveries. Writing historical fiction proved much more entertaining and she hasn't looked back since. Michelle lives in Albuquerque, New Mexico. She is a homebody with wanderlust: she loves nothing more than snuggling in at home to write…unless it's travelling to another country! Visit her at www.michellemorrisonwrites.com

Books By This Author

Lord Worthing's Wallflower

What do you call a woman with a penchant for scandalous novels, a complete lack of small talk skills, and a quirky sense of humor?

In Juliette Aston's case: a wallflower.

Juliette would like nothing better than to find a husband and start a family (especially when the alternative is serving as her father's housekeeper for the rest of her life). As the best friend of society's reigning debutante, however, Juliette is invisible to the men of London. Compounding her problem is the fact that the only man she wants is courting her best friend!

Jacob Wilding considers himself a good son; at his father's deathbed insistence, he reluctantly agrees to court London's most popular debutante, only to discover he is more interested in an opinionated, headstrong wallflower.

Passion simmers beneath their verbal sparring matches as an all-consuming love blooms between them.

The Lady's Secret

Lady Eleanor Chalcroft is perfect. She has the requisite beauty, bloodlines, and breeding to ensure that she has her pick of England's eligible bachelors. No one need know that written words jump around on the page eluding her understanding, or that the notion of being outside alone sends her into palpitations, or that she isn't remotely interested in England's eligible bachelors.

Alexander Fitzhugh is far from perfect. His paternity has been in question since before he was born and his upbringing around smugglers far from London's ballrooms has left him decidedly on the outskirts of society. He has plans to confront the father who denied him and build a business for himself and those plans certainly don't include falling in love with the most sought-after debutante in London.

Though the attraction is instantaneous and the feelings as intense, their best laid plans for a happily ever after don't take into account the malice of Alex's father, the Earl of Southampton. Eleanor and Alex must forge new lives on their own before they can hope to find a love together.

The Lady Ordinary

Amanda Hayworth's life is the epitome of ordinary. With a dash of average thrown in for good measure. Which makes it all the more inconvenient that she feels a burning desire for more out of life than an indifferent husband and a busy social schedule. But when the rough and dashing Viscount Howard pays her court, Amanda dares to dream big.

The death of Oliver Howard's cousin and heir left him with more than a broken nose. He feels responsible for the death of the man who was closer than a brother and is scarred by the pain the man's wife and children suffered at his loss. He vows to have a marriage based on compatibility but never love. That way, should either of them die, the other will be spared unbearable grief. But the heart is not so logical.

Their passions more than make up for the hesitancy of their

hearts as they struggle to let go of past heartbreaks and give into an extraordinary love.

The Daring Mrs. Kent

She was not always daring...

Josephine Kent risked everything to escape an abusive husband: a perilous sea voyage, a new life in the Caribbean, and the constant worry that Mr. Kent would find her. She settles into a safe new life in her brother's house, content to avoid society and serve as her brother's housekeeper...until her identity is discovered by one of her husband's henchmen.

Hungerford Spooner walks a careful line among the residents of St Kitts' capital. As the son of a wealthy English landowner, he has holdings and a successful shipping business. But he is also the son of a former slave, a combination that puts him on the fringes of Basseterre's high society. When he rescues a young woman fleeing a pursuer, he finds himself drawn to her beauty and spirit. And he recognizes in her a fellow soul carrying a heavy burden.

To save her, he hides her aboard his ship. In such close quarters, their feelings intensify. But just when happiness seems in their grasp, their journey is cut short by a rogue slave ship and now Josephine must overcome her past fears to save the man she loves.

Made in the USA
Middletown, DE
02 December 2023

43883846R00144